Anna had faced
wild animal in I

And yet she'd never been as horrified as she was now, facing Jack and hearing what he had to say to her. This was exactly what she'd been afraid of, what she had known would happen if he found out about Pippa....

He couldn't take Pippa away from her. No. Way.

"Jack. Don't talk like that. You don't take a baby from its mother. You can't." Her hands felt numb and she flexed her fingers.

"I'm not leaving her here. My name is on that birth certificate. I have rights."

"The right to what? Uproot her? Scare her? Take her from the only family she's ever known? You want to take her screaming and kicking, Jack? Is that what your father-daughter bonding experience is going to be about?"

Jack climbed back into the Jeep.

"Let's go," he said.

"I'm not going anywhere until you agree not to do anything crazy."

Dear Reader,

I've always been fascinated by elephants. Such majestic and powerful creatures, yet under an elephant's thick skin is a nurturing, soulful heart and mind that values family, community and love. Yes, love. They're emotional creatures who mourn the loss of loved ones, protect and care for both their own young as well as orphans, and unfortunately, due to brutal poaching, know firsthand that some wounds never heal. And though they march on to the next watering hole, they remember. Behavioral researchers have observed them holding grudges and reacting to the mere scent of someone who has caused them pain in the past.

Memories and experiences shape us, often in good ways, but sometimes they prevent us from embracing life. Fear of abandonment, trust and self-worth are a few of the themes in my debut novel, *The Promise of Rain*. Although both my hero and heroine have marched on with their lives—on opposite sides of the world from each other—neither one realizes just how much they've allowed their past wounds to erode their self-worth and ability to trust in unconditional love.

We all express love differently. Some show…some tell…and others silently ache for love. Sometimes all it takes is one drop to spring a heart to life, so give without expectations, because every living thing has a unique way of reciprocating love.

I hope you enjoy *The Promise of Rain*, the first in a three-book series for the Heartwarming line. I love hearing from readers, so send me a note at rulasinara@gmail.com or pop by my website at www.rulasinara.com or blog at www.awritersrush.blogspot.com.

Wishing you love and acceptance,

Rula Sinara

Rula Sinara

The Promise of Rain

Published in Great Britain 2014
by Mills & Boon, an imprint of Harlequin (UK) Limited,
Eton House, 18-24 Paradise Road, Richmond, Surrey, TW9 1SR

© 2014 Rula Sinara

ISBN: 978 0 263 24483 0

33-0214

Harlequin (UK) Limited's policy is to use papers that are natural, renewable and recyclable products and made from wood grown in sustainable forests. The logging and manufacturing processes conform to the legal environmental regulations of the country of origin.

Printed and bound in Spain
by Blackprint CPI, Barcelona

RULA SINARA

After a childhood enriched with exotic travels and adventures (both in books and real life), Rula Sinara is now settled in rural Virginia with her husband, three boys and crazy but endearing pets. When she's not writing, she's busy attracting wildlife to her yard, watching romantic movies (despite male protests), or researching trees on her garden wish list. According to her kids, she's obsessed with anything that grows, including the seed of a story idea and the love between unlikely characters.

Acknowledgments

I'd like to thank every writer, reader and blogger who, knowingly or unknowingly, taught, encouraged and inspired me. I've made so many dear friends, writers and industry professionals alike, who selflessly helped propel my writing dream forward and have stuck by my side along the way. You know who you are and I thank you from the bottom of my heart for every opportunity you've given me.

Thank you to Mills & Boon and everyone who is a part of their family for being there from the start. The invaluable educational and writing opportunities, community support and guidance for unpublished writers you provide made all the difference.

Also, a heartfelt thanks to animal charities and wildlife organizations who strive to stop both animal cruelty and the endangerment of species.

Dedication

To Stephanie, because sometimes friends know us better than we know ourselves. I'll never forget the day we were having a heart-to-heart while washing dishes, and you turned to me and said that I should write a romance. Here it is, my friend.

To Kaily, whose fated friendship has meant the world to me. Thanks for sharing the writing journey with me, for all your advice and for being my rock along the way. Thank you for everything. There are no words…

To Jeannie, for taking me under her wing. I can't thank you enough for your friendship, advice and constant support. This story would have never come to life if it weren't for your caring nudge and belief in me. You opened the door for this book. I can't thank you enough.

To Victoria, my extraordinary, gifted editor, for seeing something worth nurturing in my writing, from the first manuscript I ever penned, to the story between these covers. Your guidance, advice and faith in me have made this book so much stronger. You've been there from the start and you've made me a better writer. I'm forever grateful.

To my family for encouraging my love of writing since childhood and for believing I always had it in me. And to my guys at home for their support, patience and for taking up the slack when I needed to write. Thank you infinity.

In memory of Anwhar…a kind, patient man and giving soul. Your friendship and advice will never be forgotten.

CHAPTER ONE

"HEY!" DR. ANNA BEKKER shielded her face as she peered up into the sprawling acacia tree that shaded her observation platform, and spotted her primate stalker. One bite of left-over fruit tossed to him in sympathy and four years later the little guy was as much a part of camp as anyone.

"Ambosi, you sadistic fool, fruit pits are not the way to get a girl's attention. Get lost. I'm not playing," Anna said, rubbing the lingering sore spot on the top of her head. He cackled and grinned before scrambling off on his three limbs to a nearby grove of elephant pepper trees for more ammunition. Some guys could not take a hint.

A screech pierced the background symphony of the Serengeti and an elephant rumble thrummed the air as the blood-orange hues of daybreak embraced the left side of Mount Kilimanjaro in the distance. Such a breathtaking balance of power and serenity. A daily affirmation that she'd made the right decision five years ago. Anna downed the last of her coffee.

Time to face her beloved chaos.

Tightening her fingers around the metal handle of her mug, she braced herself on the edge of the wooden platform she'd helped erect, and hopped down. A mushroom of dust billowed around her boots.

Anna looked up at the sky. Solid, morbid blue. They needed rain—badly—and they were still a month away from the start of the next rainy season. The Busara Research camp had tapped into an underground stream, but animals didn't have pump wells or deep roots. Even Busara's well was getting low. If any more riverbeds dried up, the herds would either move beyond Anna's observation area, or die. As if the poaching numbers this year hadn't been bad enough. She sighed and trudged toward the bustle and calls of a camp coming to life. Rounds before research had become her game plan over the past few years. Busara included a small nursery, mainly for baby elephants orphaned

by poaching, but really for any animal Anna
didn't have the heart to turn away.

Even cheeky little monkeys.

She passed the wooden enclosures and
metal-roofed structure that served as her
clinic, and headed for the even more rustic
multipurpose tent that doubled as their kitchen
and mess hall. She needed her morning dose
of sweet, little girl kisses before going on her
rounds, another daily reassurance that she was
doing what was best for everyone. She waved
at two keepers leading their patients out of
the pens for a morning bath, but dropped her
hand at the skin-prickling shriek that came
from the far side of camp.

The children.

Anna's chest tightened and she took off at
a run, dodging another keeper on his way to
their well with a metal bucket. She rushed
into the mess tent, the screen door slamming
behind her.

"*Usijali,* Anna. Don't worry. She's fine. Just
couldn't wait for her *ugali* to cool down," said
Niara, Anna's friend and nanny, as she held a
cup of potable water to Pippa's mouth. Framed
between rampant curls and the rim of the cup,
two green eyes widened.

"Mommy!" Burned tongue forgotten, her little girl pushed the cup away and shimmied off the wooden bench. Anna scooped her up. "I got a boo-boo," Pippa said, pinching the tip of her tongue between two fingers and tugging it as far out of her mouth as she could. Not all the mash had washed down. Lovely.

"I see that," Anna said, her pulse still racing from the scare. "But how many times have I said don't scream like that unless there's danger?"

Crying from pain, Anna could understand. After all, Pippa was only four. But the shrill death call her baby had taken to recently was getting old fast. Anna dreaded what Pippa's next animal imitation would be. She'd already mastered baboons, hyenas, elephants and a number of birds. This piercing alarm of a guinea fowl defending its nest took crying wolf to a whole new level.

"You told me burns are dangewus," Pippa insisted.

Yes, she had. Anna wrinkled her nose. At least her daughter hadn't taken up biting…yet.

"Never mind. Next time, wait until Auntie Niara says the grits are cool."

"I did."

"No, she didn't," Haki said, sitting up a little straighter.

Only one year older than Pippa, Niara's son took his responsibility as the older child to heart—insisting on fairness and the following of rules. Ever since he'd overheard the keepers talk of the tragic fate of a curious Masai child who'd wandered away from her village, he'd chosen to stick to the rules and stay close to his mother...and made sure Pippa did, too. Poor Haki had no clue that he was inadvertently challenging his headstrong playmate. Give her a few years and he wouldn't know what hit him.

He wouldn't know what hit him.

Anna pressed her lips together, steeling herself against the sadness that came in random spurts, like whenever Pippa's determined expression mirrored her father's. A constant reminder of the choice Anna had made. *He's never going to forgive you. No one will. They won't understand.* Anna scratched the back of her neck with both hands. Dwelling on it wouldn't get her anywhere. She pulled the elastic band out of her hair, combed her hair back with her fingers and reset her ponytail.

"How about you finish your breakfast. I

bet it's ready now, and I need to get to work," Anna said.

"Come, Pippa," Niara said, extending her hand. "Let Mama eat something, too."

"I already had coffee."

"Coffee isn't breakfast. You'll start to look like Ambosi if you don't eat more."

The children giggled and Anna couldn't resist smiling. Niara's melodic emphasis on her syllables when she spoke English always added to the warmth of her innocent humor. With Niara, everything came from the heart. A resilient heart, despite the trauma the woman had suffered. After they met, Niara had wasted no time in making sure Anna didn't pity her, or herself.

"No, really. I'll break for lunch early. I need to check on Bakhari's bandages." Anna turned to Haki and Pippa. "Work hard on your books and maybe there'll be time for a ride to see the herds."

"Yay!" Both children clapped, spreading sticky fig nectar and *ugali* on their palms.

"How are we on supplies?" Anna asked, prompted by the food mess. Niara wrinkled her nose and shrugged. Great. So they *were* getting low. She hoped they had enough funds to cover a restocking trip. Especially for water purification.

Approaching the end of her research grant meant the area's watering holes and creeks weren't the only things drying out. Getting her research permit extended a second time wasn't going to happen if funds weren't available. As to whether funds *were* available, Anna still hadn't gotten any email replies.

It didn't help that their power had gone out. She rubbed her temples. Going back to the United States was not an option. Anna wasn't ready to go back. Not now. Not yet. Maybe not ever. Facing the past meant explaining the present…and she couldn't risk losing more than she already had. Her gut turned and she swallowed hard against the coffee's acidity. She was jumping the gun again. Worrying for nothing. She took a deep breath and forced a carefree smile.

"Okay. I need to run an inventory of necessities at the clinic, too. Let me know what we need beyond that and we'll make plans." She rounded the table, kissed Pippa and Haki on top of their heads and left before Niara could read her face.

The funding would come through. It had to.

ANNA DROPPED THE USED syringe in a plastic
container. Her head keeper, Ahron, whisked
it away. All supplies had to be kept outside the
pens, far from trunk reach. She ran her hands
gently around Bakhari's ankle, checking for
any loose wrapping. His bandages were holding nicely. They'd once dealt with a baby elephant who had used his trunk to work off
his dressings during the night. Trunks were
tricky. Anna stood and scratched the soft spot
behind the baby's ear. He flapped it gratefully.
Hopefully, the antibiotics would do their job.
Blasted snares.

They'd been lucky in recent months, but
they lost an orphan often enough, and it tore
her up every time. Painful memories. Bakhari
looked at Anna, then wrapped his trunk
loosely around her arm, as if to say that he
understood she'd been there, too. And maybe
he did. There was something to be said for an
animal's sixth sense. Anna had witnessed the
phenomenon and believed the stories she'd
heard and read about.

"Did he drink any milk?" she asked, as
she unwound herself from Bakhari's hug and
forced herself back into clinical mode.

"Demanding one, he is," Ahron said. "Pulled

my cover off several times to let me know he was hungry."

"That's a good sign. Thanks." Anna left the pen and stopped outside to log notes on Bakhari's treatment and progress, noting the feedings and outdoor exercise schedules.

She looked up at the sound of the camp's battered mobile vet Jeep approaching. A trail of dust lingered in its wake. Kamau must have gone back out in search of Bakhari's mother, after not finding her near the calf yesterday. Elephant cows were highly maternal, and herds stuck together to protect their young, so finding Bakhari alone raised questions. Anna shielded her eyes against the sun and watched them approach. She was so grateful for having another vet on staff. Kamau's dedication to their work at Busara was heart-rending and had made all the difference since he joined them shortly after her research began.

"Anything?" she asked, stepping forward after the Jeep came to a stop.

Kamau jumped down. His team followed suit, unloading the gear and supply boxes that needed cleaning or replenishing. The grim lines on Kamau's face said it all. Anna dropped her hand to her side.

"Oh." She let out a breath and shook her head. "Where?"

"About forty-five kilometers southwest of here. Poachers. No sign of a herd. The herd might have gone back to find the calf, or taken the rest to safety. I already radioed in to the authorities."

"This is bad," Anna said. The crackdown on poaching had made a difference in recent years, but unfortunately, hadn't eradicated it. But this incident… Forty-five kilometers was too close. The camp location had been chosen specifically because of its slight elevation and proximity to the range of one particular herd they'd been studying. If that herd got chased away, or killed… Anna draped her hand across the back of her neck and squeezed at the growing tension. It was more than the research that worried her. The deaths were wrong, and the orphans, well, Busara couldn't afford any more. If she had it her way, Busara would grow into a fully equipped animal rescue center. But that wasn't possible right now.

"Things are worse than you think," Kamau said, walking away.

"Worse? What do you mean?" Nothing was worse than illegal, merciless killing. Anna returned the clipboard to its nail on the post outside the pen and doubled her steps to catch up with Kamau as he trudged toward the mess tent. He stopped a few yards from it and waited for her.

"We finally fixed the generator last night and got the computer running, although the satellite internet connection did give me some trouble at first. We got an email from your Dr. Miller. Apparently, he's sending someone out here to check on our status," he said, lowering his already deep voice so it wouldn't carry through the screens.

Okay. Much, much worse. Why would Dr. Miller do that? Especially with such short notice.

"Like an audit? That's ridiculous. He has reports and photos, and he's never questioned my requests. It's not like we're living an extravagant life here," Anna said, bracing her hands on her hips.

Of course, this grant request involved permit extension fees, an endorsement and lots of paperwork to prove that she'd complete the study and produce a paper out of it. Anna understood that more was on the line this time, but an audit? Overkill, Miller.

Kamau splayed his palms.

"He didn't use the word, but what else do you call sending someone from his board out here to report back on our status? According to him, it's not a big deal. The fellow happens to be in Nairobi giving a lecture and doing some collaborative work. Miller suggested he 'drop by,' as if Busara was in the neighborhood."

Right. Just like some of the locals were convinced that, coming from the States, she had to be best friends with Tom Caine of *Beastly In-Laws*. She had never even seen the show and Miller had clearly not seen a map of western Kenya. Anna shook her head.

"When?" she asked.

"Yesterday."

That figured. Expected yesterday and not yet here. Africa time. Lax schedules were such an accepted part of life here that Anna wasn't sure why she still bothered wearing her watch. She rubbed its dusty face with the pad of her thumb. Given the delay in getting Miller's email, their visitor's tardiness was a relief. She scanned the camp. Everything seemed to be running as smoothly as could be expected. Nothing that would jeopardize

funding other than several more orphans that
Miller wasn't yet aware of, and the threat of
poachers. He'd try to use that on her again,
but Anna had no doubt they were safe. She'd
never have Niara and the children here with
her otherwise. Kamau put a lot of miles on
their Jeep. None of the actual killings had occurred close enough to camp to endanger anyone. Yes, the last killing had been closer than
usual, but the poachers were after tusked elephants. There was nothing of value to them
at camp. Miller didn't understand the difference—just like he didn't comprehend that Busara wasn't "around the block" from Nairobi.
All he worried about was liability and cost
control.

"He's never sent anyone, Anna. This can't
be good," Kamau said.

"You're right. Having someone show up at
the same time as this incident isn't ideal, but
Miller has never denied me funding before,
and he's fully aware of the orphan nursery.
And as far as the Kenyan government is concerned, I'm helping the wildlife. There's no
logical reason for not getting the permits and
funds needed. It'll be fine. Like you said, this
person just happens to be in Kenya for other

reasons. You're worrying for nothing. This is a bunch of red tape. Miller is dotting his *i*'s," Anna said, trying to believe her own words. But she wasn't convinced the nursery's growing needs wouldn't pose a problem.

After all, Miller had been her mentor in vet school. He'd supported her one-year exchange student internship to a Kenyan wildlife reservation after graduation, and had taken on her study suggestion after she told him Kenya had become home and she wasn't ready to leave. She didn't mention that she had a child until the specifics of the arrangements went through. As far as he was concerned, the father was in Kenya. Miller didn't ask and she didn't tell, knowing full well there were things an employer couldn't legally question.

Dr. Miller had included Busara in a university trust he'd formed to support animal rescue work and research. But he had, over the past year, expressed his concern for her. He'd offered to keep the initiative going with a replacement vet so that she could raise her daughter in "civilization." Anna had refused. She hoped this wasn't another attempt of his to replace her. That this person "dropping by" wasn't a prospective vet scoping out his or her future lodgings. Anna couldn't let Miller lose faith in her. This was more than her project. It was her home.

Kamau opened the mess tent's screen door, but turned back to Anna before entering.

"I'm not sure I share your optimism, but let me know when our visitor arrives so that I can smile for them." He gave an exaggerated grin, sarcastic yet beautiful and white against his dark skin. He was quite handsome when he managed to relax. And completely silly-looking with the uncharacteristic expression. Anna laughed.

"Now, how could they refuse that smile anything," she said.

He disappeared into the tent and she watched through the screen as he teased the children, who were doing some activity at a table with Niara. Anna's heart swelled at the sound of Pippa's giggles when Kamau pretended not to know who was hiding under the mop of curls. There was plenty of love here. Plenty of spirit and noble intentions. The truest examples of right and wrong and selflessness.

Nothing like the past.

Anna couldn't think of a more civilized place to raise a child.

JACKSON HARPER HAD always assumed four-wheel drives had shock absorbers—and four wheels. After the last pothole, he wasn't so sure this vehicle had either left. He grabbed the frame of the windshield to keep from getting ejected, and tried to swallow despite all the dust in his mouth. He didn't dare let go long enough to dig for the water bottle in his backpack. As exhausting as his trip had been so far, at least the flight from Nairobi to the small airstrip in the central part of the Amboseli Reserve had been uneventful. But once his driver left the paved road for a more…rustic path toward Busara, things went downhill. And Jack considered himself an outdoorsman. Somehow, camping out by a lake stocked with fish near his parents' home in Pennsylvania didn't come close to getting chased by a female rhino whose calf had ventured too far from the cover of brush. It had been only a matter of yards, but Jack's adrenaline was still pumping strong.

As if knowing that in minutes he'd come face-to-face with Anna Bekker wasn't enough to cause arrhythmia. *Dr.* Bekker. Five years, three days since she'd rejected his proposal. Since she'd refused to even consider his reasoning behind asking his best friend to marry him. A frisson of panic caused Jack to look back through a cloud of dust. What if mama rhino hadn't given up?

"*Usijali.* Don't worry." The driver laughed. Jack turned toward him, annoyed by the implication.

"I wanted to make sure she wasn't following us into Busara," Jack said. *To Anna.*

"Ahh. *We* are the invaders. Not her. Don't worry. She was just showing who is boss."

"Very reassuring," Jack said, wiping his upper lip with the back of his hand.

No doubt Anna would feel he'd invaded her territory, too. As for losing *her* and destroying their friendship, he knew that had already happened years ago. The roar of her silence had carried clear across ocean and land to the corner of his lab. His research on immunology and genetic resistance in wildlife populations had earned him a lot of respect since then, but apparently not hers. And that was fine with him. If it weren't for his collaborative work with a researcher in Nairobi and his department head, Dr. Miller, he wouldn't be here. But Miller had appointed him to oversee trust and grant fund distribution. He'd baited him, too, saying flat out that Dr. Bekker ran Busara and that he needed Jackson to check on Busara's increasing expenses. That the department's projects and expenses needed pruning if they were to adequately fund Jack's latest research initiative.

Jack had been too stupid to resist. Too curious.

The early afternoon sun seemed to crackle against his forearm. The dry heat would have been nice but for the intense equatorial rays. He pulled the brim of his re-purposed fisherman's hat down to shield his eyes. His Oakley sunglasses had disappeared back at the airport in Nairobi, when he'd set them down on top of his luggage while looking through his travel paperwork. Lesson learned, as was the fact that there was no overnight delivery for internet shoppers where he was headed.

They rounded a short hill covered in tall, dry grasses and shrubs, and came to a flat clearing. The driver slowed down considerably, pointing ahead for Jack's benefit.

Busara.

Nothing but wooden, tentlike structures, two with metal roofs, and a number of enclosures to the west side of camp. More like a cross between a tiny village and a campsite. The juxtaposition of cinnamon-colored land dappled with acacia trees against the cool, snowcapped mountain backdrop was a photographer's dream. He hoped his camera was still intact…and not missing. Maybe he'd capture one last picture of Anna to torture himself with.

An elephant blared and a chorus of raucous calls followed. The Jeep veered around the remains of a tree that looked as if it had been beaten down and crushed, then made a straight line for Busara.

The driver came to a stop near the center of camp and climbed out, but Jackson didn't move.

She had stepped out from one of the pens and stood there, beautiful as ever, except for the look of shock—or, more likely, horror— on her face.

She'd changed, though. Still slender, yet more curved. How many times had he imagined seeing her again? How many hours of sleep had he lost to anticipation? He knew they had access to food and supplies as needed, but during his flight he'd dreamed up a ridiculous picture of her as emaciated, waiting for him to rescue her from the wilds of Africa, desperate to return home. Fat chance. She looked about as happy to see him as that mother rhino had been.

Anna shifted her feet and glanced toward one of the screened-in tents, then back at him.

Too late to run and hide, Anna, but don't worry—two days and I'm gone for good.

THE CLOUD OF volcanic dust that had churned up around the Jeep was still settling like smoke in a disappearing act, but he wasn't disappearing.

Jack? No way. Impossible.

Anna stared, unable to move her legs for the life of her. Her thoughts scattered like a startled flock of jacanas. The email from Dr. Miller… She knew he was sending someone to check up on them, but *Jack?* It couldn't be. He didn't work for Miller, at least not that she was aware of, and Miller would have said something. The university's vet school and associated research departments were a relatively small community. Wouldn't her boss have at least mentioned his name? Unless it was in the email and Kamau hadn't thought his name made a difference.

Pippa's laughter carried from the mess tent. Had Dr. Miller suspected all along and sent Jack on purpose? Why now? The lunch Anna had managed to break for less than an hour ago churned in her stomach. She needed to think straight. Control the situation. Prioritize. She needed to get to the mess tent. She needed to tell Niara to keep the kids inside, but she had no way to do that. Not with Jack staring her down.

"This our man?" Kamau asked in a low voice, as he stepped up behind her and waved at Jack. Anna nodded, unable to find her voice.

This wasn't supposed to happen now. She wasn't ready for this. Even though her dream of seeing him again still managed to creep out of hiding every sunrise, Jack standing there in person changed everything. He wasn't here for her. Miller had sent him. That ruined everything.

The driver was busy unloading some cardboard boxes marked "supplies." Apparently Miller had taken some initiative with the last summary she'd sent him regarding what they needed money for this month. Jack grabbed his backpack and what looked like a large metal case, and began closing in on her. Anna braced herself. *Treat this like any other emergency situation. In a calm, cool manner.*

Calm? With Jack, and everything his presence ever did to her heart, here in *her* world? Right. Calm as a wildebeest with its butt in the jaws of a croc.

"Anna," Jack said with a curt nod. He hiked his backpack higher onto his left shoulder, then took off his hat, tucked it under one arm.

"Jack. Um…" She turned to Kamau. *Get it together.* She cleared her throat. "Kamau. This is Jackson Harper. Jack, meet Dr. Kamau Odaba, the other vet here."

Jack shook Kamau's hand.

"*Jambo.* Call me Kamau. I hope your trip was…comfortable," he said. Anna did a double take at Kamau's grin. He'd actually done it! As if a grin could get her out of Hades.

"Absolutely. The scenery is incredible," Jack said. He raked his hair back and his tight, warm brown waves, tamed by his hat, sprang back to life. He'd always hated the curl in his hair and kept it cropped short and neat, almost military style, for as long as Anna could remember. Several days' worth of stubble shaded his jawline, too. So unlike him. And he looked really good in these surroundings, in an Indiana Jones sort of way. *Reality, Anna. Stick to reality.*

"Would you prefer a hug?"

Anna realized belatedly he'd extended his hand and was waiting. She shot her hand out and shook his. No way was he getting a hug, especially not with that daring, smug look on his face.

Get it together, Anna. This is your turf.

She straightened her stiff shoulders and released a steady breath. "Welcome to Busara. It was great of you to bring along some supplies. How long are you staying?" she added, regretting how rude she sounded.

"As long as he likes, of course. Come, I'll show you where you can stay and settle in," Kamau said, putting a hand on Jack's shoulder and guiding him toward the tent adjacent to their mess hall. He looked back, giving Anna a "make nice" frown. She jogged after them. *Niara.* She had to warn Niara. She needed time to figure out how to handle this.

"Wait," she said. "I think you should show him the clinic first. I'm sure you can't wait to see the setup. Right, Jack?"

"I do want to see it, but I'd like to unpack

my lab supplies first. I'm only planning to
be here a couple of days, and I have some
samples to collect." He started walking away,
acting as if she was nothing more than a forgotten acquaintance. Of all the—

"Dr. Bekker." Ahron stuck his head out of
the clinic to their left. "I caught a snake in one
of the pens. I put it in a jar for you."

Jack stopped in his tracks and turned, looking at Anna with raised brows. Ahron noticed
the newcomer and looked at Anna apologetically.

"Don't worry. It's not like it's a black
mamba," he added, for Jack's benefit.

Anna smiled and shrugged. Not a mamba,
maybe, but the area's pythons were deadly, too.
Snakes were fairly shy about venturing through
their camp, but anything could happen, which
was why Niara never left the children alone.
Ever. If she wasn't with them, then Anna or
another responsible person was. Plus, the kids
were kept, for the most part, in screened-in
areas. Jack wouldn't be able to use that against
her. She knew how to run a safe operation.

Jack cranked his neck to the side and ran
a finger along the collar of the short-sleeved
button-down he wore untucked, then wiped

his palm on his jeans. He adjusted his backpack again. He didn't look too comfortable
and she was pretty sure it wasn't the heat.

Perfect. A distraction.

Anna mimicked Kamau's earlier grin.
"Would you like to go see it? It's in a jar,"
she said.

"Mama! Niara said we could see the babies!"

Anna looked past Jack and her heart sank
into the hot dirt. Niara came out of the mess
tent with Pippa perched on her hip and Haki
holding her hand. Jack turned his head to follow her gaze and almost turned back. Almost.
He did a double take, zeroed in on Pippa and
froze. His shoulders tensed visibly. Anna
closed her eyes, but didn't dare imagine what
was going through his head.

"It's okay with you, Anna? We didn't mean
to interrupt," Niara said, glancing shyly at
Jack.

"It's…it's fine." Her voice came out weak,
even to her own ears. She opened her eyes
slowly. "Just stay to the outside of the enclosures, on this side."

Niara passed with the kids, giving Anna a
subtle frown. Jack's gaze stayed trained on

them. Kamau looked at Anna and cocked his head. He couldn't know, but clearly no one had missed the uncanny resemblance—auburn curls, green eyes—between Pippa and Jack. Anna could see suspicion shading their glances. Only suspicion, she reminded herself. She hadn't said or explained or admitted to anything. She still had some control over the situation and she needed to use it to keep Jack from closing himself off to reason. She knew firsthand how single-minded he could be.

Look where it had gotten them.

Jack stared right at Anna and she fought to hold his gaze with equal frost. She couldn't let him win this. He narrowed his eyes and brushed the corner of his mouth against his sleeve. She tucked back a strand of hair that had escaped her ponytail and forced a smile as she set her hands on her hips, challenging him, though she felt as if she'd crawled under the bones in an elephant graveyard and died. She'd never felt so hopeless or as alienated from him as she did right now.

Poached by a single look.

JACK GLANCED AT the kids peering into the wooden pens before turning back to face

Anna. Gone was the innocent, trusting smile he remembered from their college days. Instead, her skin glowed with the same kiss of sun that had lightened her tawny hair, and the expression in her burned-sugar eyes was knowing and determined.

She reached up and scratched her high cheekbone, then pushed the hair back at her temple, a habit she apparently hadn't broken. Nervous? Maybe it was his imagination. But one thing wasn't. The little girl who'd just called her "Mama" didn't look a thing like her.

Jack's head pounded and his throat felt dry. The sun. The heat. Man, he wished he was hallucinating, but no way were the indecipherable emotions ratcheting through him fake. And Anna stood before him as real as he'd ever hoped, and as disappointed as when he'd last seen her.

Disappointment. Apparently that was the one thing they had in common.

Jack shook his head and adjusted his grip on his bags. Anna scratched her elbow, then her neck, and shrugged, as if his standing there was a daily routine and she had no secrets. Nothing to hide. She'd forgotten what an open book her face was to him. She never could put on an act. Not with him.

She gestured toward his load. "I guess it makes sense to put your stuff away first. I could give you a tour after that. Not afraid of snakes, are you?" she asked.

Her attempt at a lighthearted tone was pathetic. He shook his head.

"I'm not the person who looks like they stepped on one," he said, then walked off.

Anna Bekker had it coming.

CHAPTER TWO

JACK SET HIS BELONGINGS on the cot adjacent to where Dr. Odaba said he slept, glad that the doctor had been called off as soon as they'd reached the framed tent. Jack regretted displacing whoever the cot belonged to, but had been told that the keepers usually ended up sleeping with the baby elephants. It improved survival rates. In any case, he needed a minute to digest what had just happened outside. What he'd seen. He sat on the edge of the cot and braced his forearms on his legs, trying to run some calculations. Jet lag and lack of sleep weren't helping. He pinched the bridge of his nose.

That little girl had to be, what, four or five? She spoke better than his three-year-old nephew, was a bit taller, too. He rubbed at the tightness in his chest. No way. The Anna he knew would have said something. The Anna he knew, who'd worn a promise ring through high school *and* veterinary school, who'd always valued family, would have said *something*. Maybe he was jumping to conclusions.

He fished out his bottle and took a swig of warm water, then got up and paced, trying to remember the details of what had happened that day after her graduation, when everything she'd ever believed in had shattered.

And she'd turned to him.

Big mistake.

He'd tried to do the right thing, tried to be there for her. As much as he'd hoped to be, he knew he wasn't good enough for her then, and she'd apparently agreed. Her choice had said it all. Nothing had changed.

Two abrupt taps at the screen door had him looking up. Anna. A mixture of fury and longing for what might have been smacked him in the gut. *No. Never look back.* "We need to talk, Jack," Anna said through the screen. She waited with her hands tucked in her front pockets, eyes on the floor. Couldn't face him, could she?

He got up and took two easy strides to the door. He opened it wide and turned his palm to the room. "*Mi casa es su casa.* How would they say that in Swahili? But wait, I'm guessing you don't need an invitation, since you seem to run things as you see fit."

"Jack, even with the canvas rolled down, voices carry. We need to talk in private. Please."

He stepped closer to her, deliberately breaching her personal space. She looked up at him with doelike innocence. He folded his arms and lowered his voice.

"If you want to talk in private, guess I can assume she's mine."

Anna looked away, but not before he saw her eyes glisten with moisture that she swallowed hard against. He watched the tense movement of her neck and the grinding of her jaw. He remembered how she would grind her teeth while studying for an exam. He used to stay in the library with her, long after the research labs sequestered in the top floors of the vet school were locked up. He'd spend half the time working on his master's thesis and half watching over her. Waiting to make sure she got back to her apartment safely. Didn't seem as if she needed help anymore.

"Well, there's my answer. You think you could spare me a few words to go along with that? You think maybe I deserve at least that?" he asked.

She took a deep breath and Jack didn't miss her jitteriness when she exhaled. "That's why I'm here. I have the Jeep waiting. We won't go far. Just enough for privacy."

He grabbed his hat off the cot and followed her out. Everyone paused midtask and shot them a curious look. She was right. No privacy. Jack got in the Jeep and didn't say a word until they'd parked under the shade of a copse of trees overlooking a dried creek bed. Below Kilimanjaro's taunting, crystalline snowcap, pockets of haze blurred the horizon like ripples of water. A mirage. A lie, like everything else. He pulled off his hat and scanned the distance. Nothingness. She'd been living in the middle of nowhere—with his child. The tension in his neck shot down his back.

"I don't even know her name," he said.

Anna turned off the engine. "Pippa. Not short for anything. She's four. She'll be five on Valentine's Day."

Jack scoffed. Oh, the irony. His daughter's

birthday fell on a day meant for love. Meant for couples. "Where was she born?"

"A hospital in Nairobi. Pippa Rose…Harper."

Jack suddenly felt numb with cold, and then just as abruptly, he broke out in a sweat. He couldn't think. He wiped the back of his neck with his hand and looked at Anna.

"You gave her my name but you didn't bother telling me I'm a father?"

"I—I was going to."

"When? Anna, she's four years old! When were you planning to tell me? After something terrible happened to her out in this… this place? Or maybe you were planning to leave it up to her. Give her a name to go on and let her hunt me down in a decade or so. Nice, Anna. Really nice."

"No! That's not what I was planning."

Jack waited for her alternate explanation, but none came. With palms still pressed against the steering wheel, she stretched her fingers before dropping her hands into her lap.

"She's not in any more danger at camp than a kid living on a farm or some crime-ridden city back home. She's watched, loved, privately preschooled and learning hands-on.

Would you rather she be glued to a television or some handheld electronic device or dropped off at day care every day?"

"That's not the point. At least she'd know who her father was. That she has one." Jack saw Anna's eyes dim. *Unbelievable.* "She doesn't know. Does she?"

Anna shook her head, then dropped it against the steering wheel. Jack got out of the Jeep and paced. He was a father. Had been all those hours he'd spent behind a microscope or sterile hood, studying organisms so small no one cared about them unless they caused illness or death…and all along, there was a tiny life across the world, in the middle of nowhere, learning to speak, walk and… He scrubbed his face with his hands, unable to think of everything he'd missed. Unable to comprehend the magnitude of what had been dropped on him. Taken from him.

A trumpeting filled the air, followed by a throaty burr. From their vantage point he could see a herd of elephants ushering their calves along the edge of the creek bed. Family units.

"She hasn't even asked? Wondered?"

Anna climbed out of the Jeep and walked up to him. A few seconds passed as they both watched the herd.

"I don't think it's occurred to her to ask yet," she finally said.

"All children ask questions. I know." He'd asked many as a child, but most had never been answered. Not in time, at least.

"She's not around a lot of children. Most children's books these days depict varied families. Her playmate, Haki, the little boy you saw, doesn't have a father. His mother, Niara, is my best friend, like a sister to me. She's a teacher and aunt to Pippa. We met in the doctor's waiting room during my first pregnancy checkup. She was there for a follow-up with the cutest little newborn in tow, and I was so…" Anna looked away without finishing. She was rambling.

Was she refusing to admit she'd been scared? Jack recalled his sister's nerves and moods, but she had had her family around. She hadn't been alone, even when her husband was out of the country. Anna had been. But whose fault was that?

"You know, even with elephants, it's usually the mothers who surround and care for the young. The bulls do their thing and they're off," she said.

"Don't you dare project on me, Anna. That's not a fair comparison. I wasn't given the chance."

"I wasn't comparing. I was just trying to answer your question as to why she hasn't asked about you. Making you understand it's not personal."

Wow. Not personal. Jack didn't respond. He couldn't get any words past the pressure building in his throat and ears. *History repeats itself.* Oh, he'd heard the expression, all right. But he'd been determined not to fall into the pattern. He'd vowed never be like his biological parents. They hadn't wanted him in the picture, and he'd sworn to himself long ago that he'd never abandon a child of his.

"Look, Jack. I'm sorry. I am. But I need time to talk to her. I don't want to confuse her, and your being here for a couple of days is not a lot of time. Maybe you could come back and—"

"Hold on a minute." Jack stepped dangerously close to Anna. "Forget a few days. Do you seriously think I'd leave my daughter behind in a place like this?"

Anna had faced just about every dangerous wild animal in Kenya at one point or another, but she'd never been as terrified as now.
Facing Jack and hearing those words. This
was exactly what she'd been afraid of, what
she had known would happen if he found out
about her.

He couldn't take Pippa. *No. Way.*

"Jack. Don't talk like that. You don't take a
baby from its mother. You can't," she said. Her
hands felt numb and she flexed her fingers.

"I'm not leaving her here. My name is on
that birth certificate. I have rights."

"The right to what? Uproot her? Scare her?
Take her from the only family she's ever known?
You want to take her screaming and kicking,
Jack? Is that what your father-daughter bond-
ing experience is going to be about?"

Jack climbed back into the Jeep. "Let's go,"
he said.

"I'm not going anywhere until you agree
not to do anything crazy," Anna said, hands
squeezing her hips. "You don't even have
copies of paperwork to prove she's yours. No
one will let you board a plane with her. Besides, I'd get everyone I know to stop you. The

Masai have great aim," she added, for good measure. Jack lowered his chin and raised a brow.

"Stop with the threats, Anna, and get in. I'm smart enough to do things right," he said. She didn't miss the dig. "We can discuss the best way to go about fixing this, but you can bet I'll be in contact with the American embassy."

Anna swatted an insect away from her cheek. "I, um, never filled out her born-abroad citizenship paperwork. Not yet," she said.

"Why not?"

"It required…"

"My signature, as well." Jack angled himself in the passenger seat so he was facing her. "You surprise me, *Honest Anna*." Jack's reminder of his nickname for her, a twist on Honest Abe, stung.

Anna's radio static picked up, her name barely coming through, but nevertheless saving her from responding to Jack. She pressed a button on the unit hanging from her belt.

"Dr. Bekker here."

"Dr. Bekker. You should come to the clinic. We lost one."

We lost one. No.

"On my way."

She pocketed the radio and bolted into the driver's seat, ignoring Jack. She couldn't handle him right now, and it wasn't as if he could get himself out of Busara without her knowledge.

We lost one. They had several new orphans, Bakhari being one of them. The entire camp mourned when any baby was lost, in spite of their efforts. Jack, having overheard the radio message, had the sense to keep his mouth shut on the way back. She didn't know whether it was out of sympathy or anger. Either way, she was grateful for it.

She pulled up near the clinic within minutes, a tiny part of her relieved to see Bakhari playing gently, given his stitches, with one of the keepers, Niara and the kids. A deeper part knew who she'd lost. The youngest calf, Ito, who hadn't been drinking well. She left Jack behind and made her way to the enclosure where several of her crew had gathered. The keepers stood in silent respect for Ito, who lay motionless. Kamau rose from his crouched position over the little elephant.

"He's gone, Anna. I'm sorry. Too young and refusing to eat." Kamau put a hand on her shoulder as he walked out. She knew he'd tried. He was the best vet around, in her opinion, but sometimes a calf couldn't handle the sadness of not knowing where its mother was, or worse, the trauma of witnessing what had happened to her. Ito had been a witness.

Anna took Kamau's spot near the calf and ran her hand along his side, then down his trunk. She heard everyone leave. They'd learned over the years that she needed a few minutes alone whenever a little one was lost. This time, it seemed even harder. The entire day had been too much to handle. Her emotions were already raw. *You don't take a baby from its mother.* She bent over and laid her cheek against Ito's silent chest and let one, only one, sob escape. She had to harden herself. For facing Jack and for holding tight to Pippa. No way would Anna let her daughter grow up the way she had. No way would she make the mistake her mother had made.

JACK STEPPED AWAY from the pen as quietly as he could when he realized Anna was crying. For all the expanse of nature surrounding them, privacy, he realized, wasn't something she got too much of at camp. And after their argument, he was certain his presence would only make her feel worse. Not that he should care, considering what she'd done to him, but seeing her like that... He couldn't handle it.

He walked back to his tent and found Kamau cleaning his face and neck with a damp cloth.

"What happened?" Jack asked.

The vet hung the cloth on a nail and reached for a dry towel.

"Wouldn't eat. Not uncommon with young orphans, but we've learned a lot from experiences at other orphanages on reserves, so we have a good success rate. Sometimes we find them injured, like the other calf, Bakhari. His ankle was caught in a snare. We were lucky with him. But sometimes they're so despondent over separation or loss of their loved ones. Depression. That one kills. Elephants are more humanlike than most people know. They're very emotional and family-oriented animals. They mourn, protect, play. Ito lost his mother."

Jack simply nodded. There wasn't anything to say. He'd just arrived, and yet the death had

had an impact on him, too. Death, especially the sight of it, gouged him deep. Kamau was right. The image of a dead parent wasn't easily forgotten by a child. Even in adulthood.

"I hate to say it, but around here, it's something one has to get used to," Kamau said. "Especially if you're planning to go out in the field with me."

"I can handle it," Jack said.

He turned and went back outside, hoping to catch the kids still playing, but they were gone. He wanted to see Pippa close up. Needed to. Those eyes and curls. Her adorable nose was Anna's, but everything else resembled the pictures his parents had taken of him shortly after his adoption, even if he'd been older than Pippa at the time. He needed her to know who he was. That he was here and he'd never leave her.

His parents would want to meet her. They'd be overjoyed to find out they had another grandchild. Knowing them, they'd be more forgiving of Anna than he could ever be.

What Kamau had said about the elephants gnawed at him, but this wasn't the same as taking a baby from its mother. Pippa was old enough to understand that her mom could visit. That Mommy was working…that Daddy was, too. Okay. So he still had things to figure out. He couldn't take her to his lab, but he made enough now to be able to afford help. His sister didn't live too far from him, and she had kids. She'd be there for him. That wouldn't be so different than what Anna was doing, except Pippa would have access to great schools, a yard with swing sets, lots of friends her age, cousins and grandparents. And there wouldn't be elephants, lions, rhinos or black mambas roaming through her backyard.

He remembered Anna's plea, but couldn't get over the change in her. The Anna he'd known was crouched in that pen over that baby. The one who had kept his child from him wasn't the same person.

He headed for the tent the kids and Anna's friend had come out of earlier. Kamau had mentioned it was like a mess hall. Maybe they were there. He'd no sooner picked up his stride when something hit him on the head. Hard. He crouched with one hand on the point of pain and the other held up like a shield.

"What the—?"

He looked up in time to see a one-legged monkey swinging away. Screeches and cackles filled the air and sounded much the same as human laughter.

Of all the insane things. The heat really was getting to him.

"Hey, Jack. Come and I'll show you around. Bring any supplies you need," Kamau said, as he headed to the clinic entrance. Guess that meant the coast was clear.

"Be right there," Jack said, more interested in finding Pippa but realizing he was at a disadvantage around here. He'd get further by being reasonable.

Jack went inside, grabbed his case and carried it over. He needed to figure out how he'd get samples on dry ice back to his colleague in Nairobi within a few days, if he was extending his stay. He entered the clinic and set his stuff down on the counter where Kamau indicated a free space.

"You didn't mention it was *Dr.* Harper," Kamau said, filling a syringe. "Dr. Miller just sent another email to see if you'd made it in one piece. It said to advise you to try and remain that way." Kamau chuckled. "Is he talking about the dangerous wildlife or our Dr. Bekker?"

Jack smiled but didn't take the bait. "By the way, it's a PhD, just so you know not to throw any surgery or clinic cases my way," Jack said, changing the subject.

"In what?" Kamau asked.

"Genetics. Specifically, genetic immunity to pathogens in wildlife species. I'm working with a lab collecting genetic samples for a sort of library of endangered species, but also for studies on resistance."

"Ah. With Dr. Alwanga, by any chance? I've read his journal articles."

"The one and only."

"Excellent. Let me know if you need anything. I have to head out on rounds—to make sure I'm not needed in the field and to pick up some of the recording devices we've set out for Anna south of camp. You can come along tomorrow, if you'd like, when you have your things together."

Jack noticed a small room off the one where they stood. It looked as if it contained a lot of recording gadgets and a computer.

"Do you have an inventory of camp needs for me to go through while you're gone?"

"It's with Anna."

Jack glanced out the tiny window toward the pen where Ito had been. Kamau seemed to catch that Jack was wondering if she'd be too upset to work.

"Anna is checking on some recording equipment on the north side of camp. She'll be back soon." He paused, as if calculating his next words. "Our Anna, she's resilient. Stubborn, too, but strong and hardworking. She'll have that list down to bare bones and top it off with more research data than Dr. Miller could dream of."

"And she'll need to work in peace, without anyone invading her space," Anna said, standing in the doorway and looking pointedly at Jack and his supplies on the counter.

Invading her space. Invading her life.

"Anna. Perfect timing. I was just telling Dr. Harper that you'd be able to show him our inventory and requirements," Kamau said, before excusing himself.

"Dr. Harper, is it?" Anna cocked her head. "Five years. I should have realized you'd have finished by now. You hadn't completed your master's yet.... How long have you had your doctorate?"

Jack folded his arms and leaned back against the counter. "About two years."

"So what's your connection to Dr. Miller?"

"Joint grant. Collaboration on a big study."

"Oh." Anna frowned and walked into the room. "But he sent you here to check on us? Your study, I'm sure, has nothing to do with mine."

Jack scratched at his stubble, realizing for the first time that he wasn't looking his best. The disheveled wild man who intended to take her daughter. *His* daughter. Dr. Miller had warned him not to make waves. How was he supposed to tell her that her research funding was in jeopardy?

"Not directly, maybe. Same department, though, and Miller is concerned about the trust money donated specifically to your elephant research running out."

"Running out? Why? We've always had consistent donors."

Jack sighed. He couldn't lie when that was

the very thing she'd done to him. Omission was the same as lying.

"Miller's trying to raise more funds for this new research, and he's reached out to the same people who've donated before. However, many have been splitting their donations between causes."

"You're taking my funding."

Her tone made Jack glance back at the snake in the jar, just to make sure it hadn't escaped. On purpose.

"It wasn't a question, Jack."

"*I'm* not taking your funds. Miller's the department head, not me, and we don't dictate where contributors apply their donations. But it's the way things are panning out, and he simply wants to make sure all his projects are working efficiently."

"Spoken like a politically correct administrator. Are you researching, Jack, or getting sucked into admin? You know as well as I do what that means. If the grant's not enough and Miller wants to put more effort and energy into raising funds for your joint project, he will. He's been planning this awhile now, hasn't he? How could a respected mentor shut down his old student's—and I thought friend's—research project, especially if it would look bad to animal advocates and behaviorists? But if those funds slowly dwindled, or got redirected, the fault wouldn't be directly his. Or better yet, he sends you to—what? Report back on money misuse so I can get scapegoated?"

"Anna, no one is trying to make you a scapegoat. Dr. Miller thinks highly of you, and I've heard him brag about your findings on pachyderm family structure and the impact natural disasters and poaching have had on interherd breeding. Those findings have been important to our understanding of genetic resistance and mutations. But you're not just doing research." Jack waved a hand toward the orphanage area.

Anna's eyes widened. "You can't mean putting a stop to raising orphans. Miller approved that and understood. There aren't that many, and keeping them gives us an opportunity to listen to them up close, get samples and tag, hear them communicating with each other. And when they're old enough to be moved to one of the transitional reservation areas, we let them go, knowing they'll eventually find a new herd. But they need us first."

Like an adoptive family. They were essentially in foster care. Jack wondered if Anna was aware of the analogy, but her attention seemed fully focused on her elephants.

"And how much staff does raising these orphans require?"

"Staff? We're at a minimum, and the keepers don't even have private tents. They sleep on cots next to their assigned calf and rotate daily, so that no baby becomes too attached to one human. It prevents separation anxiety when they leave us, or if one of us isn't around. We're looking at necessity."

"He's looking at numbers, Anna. Expenses are the bottom line, and the number of calves has grown. He just wants to verify the reasons and the cost involved."

"Verify?"

Bad word choice. Jack kept a straight face.

"Am I being accused of lying?" Anna asked. The corners of her full mouth sank a mere fraction of a second after she asked the question. Jack knew she'd realized the absurdity of her question. After all, she'd been lying to him. Defend *that*. He didn't respond.

"Pippa has nothing to do with this. Miller knew I'd have a child with me at camp. And no, he doesn't know you're the father. At least, I've never told him," she added before Jack could ask. "I pay all non-research-related expenses out of pocket. Her care, and Niara and Haki's. Barely, but I do. I can prove it, too. So don't even try to turn this on me, Jack. You're here for one reason only. To make your career better, at the expense of mine. To take away everything that matters to me."

CHAPTER THREE

ANNA MARCHED OUT of the clinic and winced at the stab of bright sunlight. She couldn't look at him anymore. Couldn't digest what he'd just revealed. He had the upper hand. If he wanted revenge for her not telling him about Pippa, all he had to do was pass a negative report on to Miller and whoever else was on the board overseeing funds. Jack could end everything she'd worked so hard to protect and preserve. Everything she'd sacrificed for.

"Wait a minute, Anna," he said, following her out of the clinic tent. She kept walking.

"I'll be back to show you what you came for. I need to go see the kids first."

"I'm coming with you," Jack said. This time Anna did turn around.

"No. You're not." She held up a hand to stop him from arguing. "Jack, I'm not as evil as you think I am. You'll see her. We'll both talk to her. Later. After she's had her nap."

"I think this trumps naptime."

"Have you ever been around a four-year-old who's missed naptime?" she asked.

"No, but—"

"Think rabid monkey," she said, leaving Jack to contemplate how little he knew about parenting, and what he was getting himself into.

BY THE TIME Anna reached the quarters where she, Niara and the kids stayed, Niara had read the last sentence of their favorite book about a dancing hippo and his friends. Pippa and Haki were sound asleep on their cots. Niara set the book down and Anna helped her draw mosquito netting around them. Given the risk of malaria, everyone at camp took preventative meds and sprayed, but screens and netting helped, too. Especially with the kids. It was nothing more than routine for all of them, but it struck her as something that would stand out to Jack. Anna knew travel protocol and was pretty sure Jack had been given a prescription to take, just in case. But he hadn't added it to his list of reasons why Pippa shouldn't be here.

Not yet.

Give him a few hours, and Jack would have a trusty list brimming with more obvious camp dangers. Anna figured she could save some legal agony by making him a counterlist of dangers in the average American suburb, or even in *their* countryside. Getting kidnapped, bullied, or hit by a car, contracting bird flu, and plenty of others she could throw at him. She wouldn't mention drugs, though. She wouldn't stoop that low, but she'd prove how ignorant he was being. Prove Pippa didn't need saving. Prove they'd only end up disrupting his career path, and he wouldn't realize it until it was too late.

She bent down, moved the netting aside, kissed Pippa's marshmallow-soft cheek and put the netting back.

"It's him, isn't it?" Niara asked, keeping her voice to a whisper.

Anna pulled a wooden stool next to hers. "It's him." She sighed.

A moment passed in silence as they watched the children sleep.

"Oh, honey. All these years and you told me Pippa's father didn't care. That doesn't look like a man who doesn't care. What gives? Why have you been hiding?" Niara asked.

"Who says I've been hiding?"

Niara threw her head back in disbelief before squaring her shoulders. "Not hiding? Come on, Anna. You've never once gone back to the States. You haven't even visited your parents, and calling your mother isn't the same. You're not the first person whose parents divorced. To close yourself off for this long? It's crazy. I just don't understand."

"There's nothing *to* understand. This is my work. Everything and everyone that matters to me is here."

Anna hung her head. Niara had been so good to her and they'd shared so much. Niara knew that as a teenager Anna had lost a baby brother, but she didn't know what it had done to her mother…to her family. Some things were too personal to share with anyone.

Niara laid a hand on Anna's back and rubbed gently, like Anna did to Pippa when she needed soothing after a bad dream or a scraped knee. Niara was right, though, and at this point, Anna needed an ally. Someone who loved Pippa and would do anything to protect her.

"My parents didn't just divorce, Niara. They

never married out of love to begin with. The whole time they had been lying. Pretending."

"I don't understand. Where's the lie? Nobody's life is perfect, but no matter what, it's a parent's job—their hope—to guide their children to a better one. All parents use experience to teach their children what they think is best."

"Is it best to not be wanted?"

Niara frowned.

"Niara, my father never gave me the time of day. Always busy with the politics of work. His career came first—at every recital, birthday, parent night at school…even my graduations. Turns out it wasn't just because he was busy. It was because he never wanted me to begin with. I was a burden. In his eyes, the only thing I came first in was being conceived before marriage. All those talks about waiting? My parents didn't wait. My mom got pregnant and my dad married her out of pure obligation. A noble sense of duty that resulted in a bitter marriage, and left me with a bitter dad. Do you have any idea how old it gets, making up answers for 'Where's your dad?' at school functions? Oh, the worst was when I got asked if he was overseas, serving our country, and I had to say no. He didn't even have an honorable reason to be gone. He just didn't want me."

"I'm so sorry, Anna. People do make mistakes. That doesn't mean they didn't love you and truly want your life to be different than theirs."

"My mother loves me. I don't doubt that. But seeing what she went through is why I couldn't tell Jack." *And loving my mom is why I couldn't tell her, either.*

"You made a choice staying in Kenya, but you also chose to keep your child from her father. She has one. You don't know how many nights I wish it was that way with Haki."

Anna reached over and gripped Niara's hand. How could she be so thoughtless? Of course Niara would see her as taking things for granted.

"You don't understand. Jack's just like my dad," Anna said. "So focused on his career, yet at the same time shortsighted about life. They do what they think is right in the moment, their duty, but don't look at what it'll mean later on. They don't see anyone ending up the victim of their regrets."

"Anna, I *chose* not to live my life as a victim, even if I was one. You don't have to think of yourself that way."

"I don't!" she said, glancing at the kids to make sure her voice hadn't woken them. "Okay. I'll admit that I did before I came here. The day my mom told me about the divorce was the same day I graduated from veterinary school. I was due to fly to Kenya shortly after. She'd come down for the ceremony, but my dad didn't make it. Big surprise. That whole day was like being tossed between Mount Kilimanjaro's peak and the Serengeti's heat. Everything I'd ever known had been turned upside down."

Everything. Such as believing, as a young child, that Daddy really did need to work all the time, then noticing, as a teen, that he didn't dote on her mom the way she'd seen her friends' parents act. After her brother's death sucked her mom into deep depression, he'd abandoned them emotionally, and Anna had thought he couldn't cope, either. But what she hadn't known, until graduation day, was that he'd been stuck with her. She'd ruined his life, down to the day her brother died.

"I was devastated. I felt more than sorry for myself, but not anymore. In any case, Jack and

I had been best friends since middle school. I knew I could turn to him."

Niara caught the implication. "So you're saying he's the father for sure?"

"Anyone else would be a physical impossibility. We were both…inexperienced. One time, Niara. My only time. My biggest, most rebellious mistake."

Niara looked at the children but didn't speak.

"Oh," Anna said. "She's not a mistake. And Haki isn't, either. You know how much I love them both. They're the only good, pure thing that has come out of what we've both been through."

"I know that, Anna, but I think your biggest mistake was not telling her father."

"You're wrong, Niara. I've been protecting both of them. Jack from himself and Pippa from growing up the way I did. There's no way I'll let her go through what I went through. And why should I have to endure the life my mom did? Dad never loved her." *Not in sickness or in health.* Anna covered her face with her hands, then pushed her hair back. Niara had always been there for her, and here she was snapping at her. "I'm sorry."

"Don't be."

"No. I am, but you have to understand. Men like my dad and Jack don't know how to love. Career men with a conscience. Guilt and duty...but not love. Jack thinks he wants Pippa, but I know it's only because he's doing what he thinks he has to do." *He tried that on me before.*

"You think he feels obligated?" Niara said.

"Yes. I know he does." *And not for the first time.*

Anna's nose tingled and she rubbed it with the back of her hand, unwilling to break down. The granule of hope that she'd latched on to for five years had dissolved, leaving her feeling deflated, just as when Pippa had been drawn from her belly. Only this time, Jack threatened to take the only person she was left with to cherish and fill the void. Pippa's love was the only love that was real for Anna, and the only love she could trust.

"I don't have time for self-pity anymore. Not as a mother. He wants to meet Pippa later."

"Of course," Niara said.

"He wants to take her, Niara. I can't let that happen."

Niara rubbed her fingertips against her mouth before responding. "No fears, okay? It'll all work out."

"I need to get back," Anna said, standing up and scooting the stool out of the way. She gave Niara a hug. "You're the best, you know that?"

"Always nice to hear." Her friend chuckled. "But you're even better, and stronger than you think. You'll be fine, Anna."

JACK SEALED THE tissue sample and began labeling it as per Dr. Alwanga's protocol. Although it wasn't how he spent most of his research time, Jack had received samples before. Straight to the lab for analysis. Collected by someone else. He hoped that the keeper who'd taken him to the calf had dismissed the sweat on his face as a by-product of heat. Maybe it was in part because he'd witnessed Anna mourning the baby elephant. It wasn't just a calf or a sample to her.

He sensed her the second she walked in, turning just in time to catch her looking wide-eyed at the label before she masked her expression.

"Not wasting time, are you?" she said, walking past him.

"I'm sorry, Anna. I had to. Besides, the sample will let us make sure infection wasn't a factor, and it'll help confirm a genetic connection to poaching victims."

"I know you have a job to do, Jack. No need for apologies. I'm a doctor, remember? I can do autopsies in my sleep. I investigate every death here thoroughly. I don't rely on assumptions."

"I don't doubt that. I just thought that since—"

"Well, don't think," she said. She drew a file from a lower cabinet and plopped it next to him. He flipped open the cover. Their inventory and expenses. "I keep a printed list, just in case. And before you go off on the cost of paper, it's only because power and internet can be unreliable here and the computer is rather old. I do send data and records to Miller, but I don't want to risk losing any of it, so I keep a hard copy, as well."

"How's the generator working?" Dr. Miller had given him the rundown on the camp's setup.

Anna smiled and the memories of when she

used to beam at him hit Jack hard. This one came with a shake of her head.

"Wow. You really are investigating. Guess that's what you're good at. The generator works fine. Most of the time. Again, nothing comes with a one hundred percent guarantee, does it?"

He tore off his sterile gloves and scrubbed at his jaw. "Guess not, Anna."

There certainly hadn't been any guarantee that she'd come back from her postgraduate internship. Only he hadn't realized that at the time. Not until the brief email she'd sent telling him that she'd made plans to stay in Kenya for at least another year or two. A short email. No call. No sound of her voice so he could decipher the true reasons behind her words. To figure out whether he'd permanently destroyed their friendship. A part of him had wondered if she'd met someone else.

She'd always been a romantic. She'd gone on and on in anticipation of her trip to Africa, and how she felt like Elsa Martinelli in *Hatari!*. He'd wondered who, if anyone, had become her John Wayne. Somehow, their roles seemed reversed. Besides, Jack had given up thinking that he'd ever be enough for her.

He knew when to let go. When to stop caring. Until now. Now she had a little girl with her. His little girl. He could forgive Anna for not wanting him; that was her right. But not for this. Not for keeping Pippa from him.

He slapped the folder shut on the papers he was pretending to read.

"So, when do I get to spend time with my daughter?" *My daughter.* The words sounded so foreign to him.

"I was thinking after dinner. Everyone at camp eats the meal together. You'll see her before then, of course, but after that you, Pippa and I can go for a walk or ride…and we can talk to her."

"What time is dinner?"

Anna actually laughed. And he loved it, as much as the mischievous way she looked at him. Boy, was he in trouble.

"It's a small place, Jack. Trust me, you'll know when dinner is. Put an actual time on it and it'll get jinxed into being several hours late."

"Why's that?"

"It's how time works here. Stick around long enough and you'll see what I mean." Anna's face fell as soon as the words left her mouth. He'd stick around long enough, all right.

Long enough to get the necessary paperwork cleared so that he could take Pippa home.

CHAPTER FOUR

ANNA COULDN'T EAT. Not with the way her belly tightened every time Jack glanced at her and Pippa. Pippa wasn't doing any better at finishing her food. Anna tried every trick, conscious of him watching, but Pippa was too busy playing peekaboo with the stranger. She'd duck her face under the table, then slowly peer over the top at him. Every other time, he'd wink and Pippa would giggle. And every giggle would ripple through Anna like a wave that would drag her little girl farther and farther out to sea. Closer and closer to America…and Jack.

Haki watched their interaction intently. "Stop it, Pippa," he said, finally.

"Why should I?"

The little boy came around Anna and whispered into Pippa's ear, then ran back to his spot on the bench. Pippa frowned.

"Haki said I'm talking to stwangers, Mama."

Haki blushed and dropped his head into his hands. So much for secrets. "I'm not. You let him eat with us so he's not a stwanger. Right?"

"He is," Haki mumbled.

"He's not and I didn't say any words." Pippa puffed her cheeks at him, convinced she'd won the argument. Jack raised a brow, waiting for Anna's reply.

"Well, Dr. Harper is a stranger to both of you because you haven't actually met him before, but he's really a friend. He's going to be here a couple of days for work, so don't get in his way, but if he's free, it's okay to talk to him."

Haki dug into his food without a word. Pippa lit up.

"Hi," she said to Jack.

"Hi there." He turned away from a conversation on border patrols that several of the keepers were having with Kamau, and propped his elbows on the table, giving Pippa his full attention. "It doesn't look like you've eaten much there."

She shrugged.

"I bet if you listened to your mom and ate your food, she might let you go for a ride before the sun goes down."

"Is that true, Mama?"

"I suppose so," Anna said. Pippa put a spoonful in her mouth. All mothers loved seeing their kids eat, but the fact that Jack had accomplished, in one sentence, what she'd been trying to do for the past half hour was a bit annoying. "Just finish quickly so you can wash up and get your jammies on before we go." Jammies were nothing but a clean T-shirt and shorts around here.

When Pippa was a colicky baby, Anna used to get one of the men to drive them slowly around camp, close enough for safety during the night. It was the only way she'd fall asleep and it still worked whenever she wasn't feeling well. Anna wasn't sure if their talk with her would rev her up for the night or give her plenty to dream about. Jammies were a safe bet either way, and making her get ready for bed before leaving bought Anna a little more time. If only minutes.

Minutes that made "Africa time" seem like cheetah speed.

After washing up, Niara walked the children out to the Jeep, where Jack waited for Anna and Pippa. Anna needed a few minutes to freshen up. She looked in the small mirror hanging by a nail near her bed, and cringed. Bad enough she looked like someone who'd been hacking through thickets all day, she didn't even want to imagine what she smelled like after working with the elephants. But there wasn't time for a bath and it didn't matter. This wasn't a date. It was the stark opposite. The beginning of the end. She let her hair down, then quickly decided it looked too obvious. She might leave it down for the wedding she'd be attending in a few days, but not for Jack. She pulled it back into a ponytail and started out, only to be intercepted by Haki. For such a composed little boy, he looked as if a dam was about to break.

"Hey, Haki. What's up?" she asked, kneeling down.

"Auntie Anna, is he taking her away forever?"

"What? Oh, Dr. Harper? Gosh, what would make you think that?"

"I heard you and Mama talking during naptime. If he's her father, he'll take her away. Won't he?"

He'd overheard? Anna closed her eyes. Jack wanted to take Pippa away, but not tonight.

Not ever, if Anna could help it. That's all she could give right now.

"No, Haki. We're just going for a ride and I'll be there the whole time. I promise when you wake up you'll find Pippa in her bed. Just like always. Okay?"

Haki swiped away one betraying tear and nodded.

"Walk me out?"

He nodded again and took her hand. Anna held it tightly, her heart breaking for him. For all their battles of wits, Anna knew the two children were close. But this was the first time she realized just how much Pippa's friendship meant to the little boy who was so much like a son to her.

Haki let go of Anna's hand and wrapped his arms around his mom when they got to the Jeep. Niara looked inquisitively at Anna, but Anna shook her head and climbed into the driver's seat. Seeing Jack with Pippa in his lap, his arm wrapped securely around her, was surreal. The three of them. Together. Anna started the ignition. This wasn't a family outing. At least not the way she'd once imagined it.

She drove about a quarter of a mile to a

grove of trees. Thankfully, Pippa monopo-
lized the conversation the entire way there.
She listed all the local animals she could
think of for Jack, even the most dangerous
ones sounding adorable with the way her *r*'s
came out as *w*'s. Even Anna couldn't stop
from smiling when Jack mimicked Pippa
and said, "Zeebwas, huh? I wanna see one of
those!" Jack being silly? She knew his sister
had a kid, but she'd never pictured him as the
shed-the-lab-coat-and-play kind of guy. Anna
turned off the ignition.

"Come here, sweetie," she said, pulling
Pippa into her lap and hugging her tightly. She
looked at Jack before continuing. He stared
back at her expectantly.

This was it.

The moment she'd both longed for and
dreaded. Longed for during moments of insane exhaustion, when sleepless nights with
an infant made her wonder if there *was* something to marrying for the sake of practical-
ity. For having someone to lean on, even if it
wasn't for love. But that's all it was. Insanity.
Because she'd come this far without relying
on him. And she knew he didn't love her. Not

beyond friendship, and probably not even that anymore, after what she'd done.

Anna kissed the top of Pippa's head now, breathing in that indefinable child scent, and steeled herself for what was to come. "Pippa, you know how I told you Dr. Harper is a friend?"

"Uh-huh."

Anna turned Pippa to face her and gently fiddled with a springy curl at her temple.

"He's more than that to you. He's your *baba,* sweetie, although he'll probably want you calling him Daddy," Anna said, realizing Jack wouldn't be accustomed to the local term.

He reached over and tugged on one of Pippa's bouncy curls. "You can call me whatever you like, Pippa. I'm just really happy to be here with you."

Pippa stared at him and sank back into Anna's arms. Her thumb slipped between her teeth. It had taken forever to get her to break that habit. If she regressed…

"My *baba*…like Kahni?" she said, then slipped her thumb back in her mouth.

"Who's Kahni?" Jack asked.

"One of the elephant bulls we observe,"

Anna said, closing her eyes apologetically. She turned to Pippa. "Like Kahni, only Jack's your *baba*. And he walks on two feet," Anna said. As expected, Pippa giggled and relaxed.

"I know an animal with twenty feet," Pippa said. "No, it has twenty hundwed *million* feet and thwee eyes. It's like a monster."

"Wow. And I'd love to hear about all the things you like to do, your favorite games and books and whatever you want to talk about," Jack said, propping his forearms on his knees so they were face-to-face.

"Are you gonna live with us?" Pippa asked, her curls barely masking the wrinkling of her forehead. She looked so much like Jack it hurt.

"Um. No, but we'll figure all that out later," Jack said, glancing at Anna.

"Are you gonna mawee my mama?"

Anna froze. If he so much as implied that it was an option, it would be final proof that he was just like her dad. It'd prove that the last proposal had truly been for all the wrong reasons and that Jack was after only one thing now—and it wasn't her. But if he didn't want marriage… Anna's chest twinged. If he didn't want marriage, it would prove that any inkling of hope she'd ever had about being wrong, about happy-ever-afters really existing, about ever having Jack's forgiveness and friendship again, would be gone for good. And she wasn't sure which response would make her feel worse.

Jack straightened back in his seat and looked at Anna, seconds too long, then back at Pippa. "No, squirt. We won't be getting married."

And there she had it. Closure.

JACK SHIFTED ON HIS COT, adjusting the inflatable neck roll he'd brought along against the curve of his lower spine. His cot backed up against a post, his only support as he sat propped up with the files Anna had relinquished. He reclipped his portable, mini LED light so that it wouldn't wake Kamau. Having never left the States, Jack had only heard of jet lag. He rubbed at his eyes and tried to reassure himself that the mosquito buzzing in frustration near his head couldn't get past the netting. Or maybe it was his brain buzzing at the numbers and lists in front of him.

Anna and Kamau had indeed kept meticulous records. Meticulous to a point. Something didn't add up. Miller had never mentioned that kids lived at the camp. He hadn't specified how many people were allowed to share in the food and essential expenses. Hard to truthfully keep track of how some supplies were used. It wasn't as if Anna could waste time measuring out how much food, ointment, water or bug spray each individual used. She said she paid for Niara and the kids, but it wasn't like they paid rent for the camp's meager lodgings and facilities. He was being a horse's rear and he knew it, but funds were funds. This new research collaboration between Miller, the lab in Nairobi and himself was huge. It would solidify Jack's name and reputation in the scientific community.

Anna's research and her work to provide medical care to the orphaned elephants was significant. He believed that. But in his book, related or not, behavioral studies didn't compare to genetics and immunology. They were the root of everything. The tough stuff. The kind of research that would have his career set and earn him…respect. Respect of his colleagues and of his family. It'd earn him more lecture engagements, and that meant more money.

He shuffled through the stack, taking a cursory note of all the logs he'd flagged in red. He'd have to send Miller an email, if they got service, otherwise it would have to wait until he got home. A satellite call was out of the question, not only because of the time difference, but due to lack of privacy. He didn't need Anna standing by on that one.

Guilt scratched at his chest like a grain of sand in the eye. Miller would possibly shut down funding to Anna's project, forcing her to abandon her work or, at a minimum, merge into one of the more established Kenyan wildlife parks and reserves projects. Jack wasn't well-versed in foreign paperwork, but if she lost her research funds, it could even mean being forced back to the States—a situation that would facilitate getting Pippa back there, as well. Anna would hate him, more than she already did, but at least Pippa would have both parents nearby.

In any case, Jack had more important things to worry about than Anna's work. Priorities were priorities. Ensuring funds for his own project would lead to career success, and career success meant being able to provide his daughter with the kind of life she deserved. He had a responsibility to her. Care and education. A father who'd never abandon her. A father who would make every choice in life, from here on out, based on what was best for his child.

Unlike his selfish biological parents.

As far as he was concerned, and as much as he could see that Anna loved Pippa, Anna was being selfish. Keeping her pregnancy a secret and forcing Pippa to grown up in the wild was selfish. Purely selfish. A kid needed more than just one other child to play with. Pippa needed socialization, even if she wasn't quite school-aged yet. It mattered developmentally, didn't it? For all her observations on elephant family units, shouldn't Anna know that?

It had mattered for Jack. His adoptive family had gone out of their way for him. Given him a life. It was why he'd worked so hard to prove that the scared nine-year-old they'd adopted, after he'd been pulled from the dangerous, drug-infested neighborhood where his parents had overdosed, had been worth all their troubles. All the teen agony they'd put up with.

Jack didn't want Pippa growing up feeling confused or insecure. He didn't want her to suffer the hunger and cold he'd felt because his drug addict parents had twisted priorities, and their neighbors had turned their faces. Not their problem. Well, his daughter was his responsibility. She was going to have him around. He was going to give her the kind of life his real parents, his adoptive parents, had given him.

JACK'S LIDS STARTED to droop down just as a hint of dawn turned the blackness outside his tent into shades of pink and gray. He glanced at his watch out of habit and knocked his head back in defeat, wincing when it hit the beam. Of all the things he'd done to prepare for this trip, he hadn't thought of putting a new battery in his watch. That Murphy guy knew what he was talking about.

Kamau stirred and Jack stacked the files neatly, not wanting him to wake up to all his pen marks. Then Jack rose to use the bathroom, eternally grateful they had running water and soap, along with water purification tablets and filters. That was a must. Not exactly a four-star hotel, but in any case, he planned on beating the line and squeezing in a shave.

JACK TURNED OFF the satellite phone when nothing but static came through, then tried redialing.

"Take five steps to your right." Anna's voice had him turning like a schoolboy caught putting a frog in the teacher's desk. She had Pippa by the hand and Niara followed with Haki.

"Five steps?"

"To your left, now that you're facing me. You'll get better reception. Trust me," she said, continuing on her way. Niara looked from Anna to Jack, then smiled. A tiny one, but he caught it. Halfway around the world and he couldn't escape female gossip. Despite himself, he wondered what Anna had told Niara about him. About *them*.

Trust her? Jack grunted, but then took the recommended five steps. Bingo. He dialed again.

"Dr. Alwanga. Hey. You know the samples I said I'd bring right back?" Jack turned slightly to his right to clear the reception. "No, no. Collecting them isn't the problem. I won't be coming back yet, so I'll need to have someone fly them over. But I have a favor to ask. A couple, actually."

ANNA WASHED HER HANDS after finishing her rounds with the orphans. All things considered, it was a great morning. She'd noticed light coming through the guys' tent on her way out to her acacia tree right before dawn. She figured it was Jack, and took extra care not to let him hear her walk by. The last thing she needed was Jack following her and invading her private time. More than any other morning, she needed it.

Time alone. To think.

None of this was supposed to have happened this way. She'd pictured it every dawn for five years now. He would contact her and declare his love without ever knowing about the pregnancy. Then she'd tell him about Pippa, but only after she knew his feelings were pure. Honest. And he'd be thrilled, not angry. They'd defy her parents' pathetic example of a marriage—of love—and he'd love Pippa the way Anna had missed out on with her dad. With free will.

But it was too late for that. The last email he'd sent, a month after she'd first arrived in Kenya, was signed with plain old "Jack." Not "Love, Jack." Not even "Miss you, Jack." At this point, she'd never, ever be able to trust that anything between them was real, that it wasn't obligatory or misguided. All she needed to focus on now was Pippa, the only person she knew loved her unconditionally.

Anna left the clinic and headed for the Jeep. She needed to check the recording boxes. Hopefully, the herd would be within sight and she'd be able to take notes on how things were going with the big mamas and their children.

She was concerned about one "teen" male in particular. She hadn't seen the bulls nearby in the past week or so, nor had she heard their calls. Teen male elephants were known to get unruly and rebellious without the guidance of older males. Much like human adolescents, they tested boundaries and needed role models, and like humans, they suffered from PTSD. All elephants who'd witnessed poachers in action suffered from post-traumatic stress. It had been documented in studies. The loss of loved ones was hard to recover from.

Anna rubbed her neck. Jack had never recovered, and for all their years of friendship, she wasn't enough to change that. If he'd never been able to truly open his heart to her, how was he supposed to love Pippa beyond any superficial sense of duty?

Anna stepped on the gas and tried to focus on finding the bulls. If she didn't pick up any distant rumbles on the recordings, she'd mention it to Kamau. The Kenyan government took poaching seriously, but despite heavy law enforcement by both Kenya Wildlife Services and the Masai community, it had yet to be eradicated. Far from it. For one thing, the fines weren't high enough. And, unfortunately, southwest Kenya, where most of the elephant herds roamed, bordered on Tanzania, a corridor for poachers and their ivory. Anna bit down on her lower lip. Her bulls had to be okay.

A part of Anna was glad that she didn't often go out in the field for indefinite hours—an arrangement adopted because of the children, especially during the first year, when Pippa was so young and Anna couldn't bear even a few hours of separation. She was thankful to Kamau for acting in a mobile vet capacity, but regretted the gruesome scenes she knew he'd witnessed. She'd seen her fair share during her first summer in Kenya, before she'd discovered her pregnancy.

She pulled up near the first recording location and got out of the Jeep. Three more stops for the day, then she'd need to spend several hours cooped up listening, tracking and analyzing. She never slacked, but with Jack here and Miller breaking the trust she had in him, she couldn't give anyone excuses.

How many times, when she'd encounter a teacher who didn't seem to like her, had her mother told her that success was the best revenge? Anna had listened and studied harder. She'd finished high school at seventeen and her undergrad studies in three years. But being the youngest had had its downfalls.

Come to think of it, her age was probably why do-gooder Jack had taken it upon himself to befriend her and keep an eye on her. She thought of Haki. Were all guys like that? The bottom line was that no one could argue with an A+. Maybe her parents had been right about some things. Right now, success was her best revenge, and defense, against Jack.

JACK HADN'T SEEN Anna at breakfast that morning. Although he got to spend time with Pippa and her friend, Haki, the little boy who kept an amusingly watchful eye on him, Jack couldn't shake the feeling that Anna had skipped breakfast just to avoid him.

He coughed when the Jeep-on-steroids suddenly swerved westward, sending a spray of dust and sand around them. "Sorry about that," Kamau called out over the sound of the engine.

Jack shook his head. "I'm fine."

"The longer the drought, the worse it gets." Kamau pointed toward what looked like a dried-up riverbed, where skeletal remains of some unlucky—and thirsty—animal lay along the bank. "That was a drinking spot just a month ago. We're headed farther out to see if the watering hole is still viable. If so, there'll be herds. All kinds. Watering holes are a source of life, but of danger and death, as well."

Jack nodded, understanding Kamau's point. They weren't hoping for death, but if they did come across it, he could go ahead and get whatever tissue samples he needed. He could also try to get water samples for analysis of organisms, both harmless and pathogenic.

"How much farther?" Jack asked.

"About twenty minutes," Kamau said, a few seconds before taking another sharp turn that had Jack grabbing for anything to keep from taking flight. Then they skidded to a stop. "Forget the twenty."

Jack didn't have to ask why. The stench

of rotting flesh assaulted him seconds before flies, which had undoubtedly landed
and sucked on things he didn't want to think
about, started pelting his arms and face. He
swatted them away and pushed the sunglasses
Kamau had loaned him higher up his nose
to protect his eyes. Ignorance was bliss. Unfortunately, anyone who'd studied pathogenic
bacteriology and virology knew flies were a
vector for river blindness, among other things.
He brought the crook of his elbow up to shield
his nose from the putrid smell, and jumped
down.

Kamau had gone with his men, rifles
loaded, past a clump of dry brush into a small
clearing. Jack followed, catching up just as
all but one of them put their firearms down.
It was important for someone to stand guard
at all times. Jack had questioned the need for
all the guns when they'd left camp, but they'd
explained the necessary precaution. If not for
human danger, then for a wild animal interaction gone bad. Several of the guns were
loaded only with tranquilizers, he was told.
He wished he knew which ones.

A weak squeal full of angst and pain came
from one of the two forms that lay on the

ground. The larger elephant, though it still looked relatively small, lay motionless and bloody, its body a deflated mass of wrinkled skin. Kamau and his men had gone to work on the second elephant. It didn't look any older than the one he'd seen Anna cry over, but this one had two arrows jutting from its body, one piercing its trunk and the other its hind leg

Jack cursed, and on instinct, ran to help hold down the struggling infant as Kamau worked to stabilize him. Jack wrapped his arm around the leg, freeing the team to work on the wounds and secure the heavy calf for transport. Kamau had radioed in for help as soon as they arrived on-scene, but said they couldn't wait. The calf had already lost a lot of blood and they had to do whatever was possible in the field.

"Will he make it?" Jack asked.

"Hard to say. We can only try." The vet jerked his head toward the other victim. "No kill is worth the ivory, but that one was barely old enough to have tusks. All this for the slightest piece of ivory. This baby just got in the way. These two must have strayed, or were somehow lured from the herd on its way toward water."

"Poachers?" Jack asked, adjusting his hold on the rough skin, gritty with dry dirt, at Kamau's direction.

The vet shook his head. "No. Poachers these days are too high-tech. They wouldn't have bothered with arrows. We have a rogue local on our hands. This is a farming region. The proximity to Mount Kilimanjaro has enriched the soil from past volcanic eruptions, and the ice melt usually ensures a good water supply, at least underground and along most riverbeds. But when we get a drought this bad, crops suffer. That means some farmers get desperate enough that they'll deal with poachers. Ivory for money. Money to feed their families and keep their farm running. And so long as need shows its face, greed finds a place."

Jack shook his head, carefully setting down the elephant's limb. The calf had calmed considerably under the drugs Kamau had injected, and the help they'd called on, a large truck, arrived from camp. Jack stepped back to let the team strap the baby for lifting, and moved back in when it came time to shift him. Only when the calf was secured to the truck did Jack notice he was covered in blood.

Someone else took the Jeep's wheel on the way back. Jack sat there in the passenger seat, the calf's cry for help still sounding in his mind. The atrocity he'd witnessed... How could anyone cause suffering or turn their backs on it? The hot sun was nothing compared to the fury burning inside him. His shirt dried from the open-air ride and hot sun, causing it to stick against his chest. He would have ridden with Kamau and the calf, but he'd have been in the way, and there was room only for those who knew how to assist medically. That calf had to live. It had to.

ANNA WAS PREPARED for the arrival of the emergency team, but not for the sight of Jack covered in blood. For a split second, she feared that he'd been injured, but the logical side of her knew, from the focus of the team on the calf, that he hadn't been. He didn't need her— the baby elephant did.

She hesitated, closing her mouth only when he glanced up and caught her staring. Jack looked right at her, his eyes softening, then he mouthed, *"I'm sorry for this."* Sorry for the poor baby elephant or for everything else? Did he now understand why she was so passionate about her work? Why she couldn't leave? That this was one of the many reasons she and Pippa couldn't be a part of his life? Anna cocked her head, let their connection linger for one more wishful and nostalgic moment before turning away to help. Her future with Jack was beyond saving, but she'd do her wholehearted best to save this baby.

Hours later, convinced the new elephant was stable and doing well in Ahron's care, Anna went to change her shirt and check on the kids, who were hard at work coming up with a name. They were always in charge of naming the orphans. It made them feel they were contributing members of the camp, plus it preoccupied them when emergencies came in. Neither Niara nor Anna wanted them to see the gory condition the elephants were often in when they arrived. The children were still too young to witness so much blood.

She walked through camp and toward her acacia tree. She didn't typically head out there in the afternoon, but today she needed to decompress. To gather herself. She hoisted herself onto the platform and spotted Ambosi scrambling above her. Anna smiled and had no sooner settled on the edge when Ambosi's defiant chatter jerked her forward, almost off-balance. Something flew through the air and landed with a puff right in front of Jack.

She hadn't heard him following her. That was scary, given how sharp her hearing was. If she continued to let herself be this distracted, she'd be risking something more dangerous creeping up on her. *More dangerous than Jack?*

He'd shaved his face. She'd noticed, in spite of the mess he'd been earlier. He'd changed his clothes, too. Olive-green camper shorts and a plain white T-shirt. He looked so much like the Jack she remembered, only more filled in. His shoulders looked broader, straighter, but he still stood with his hands in his front pockets and his head cocked. Just like when he used to walk in on her trying to cram for anatomy in one of the classroom labs, and insist that she had to go get something to eat. As good as he looked, she doubted he had the same reasoning now. Whether she'd eaten or not wasn't on his agenda.

"Is that the only one of those around here?" Jack asked, lowering his chin suspiciously toward the primate.

"You mean Ambosi? There are others, but

he's the one who sticks around the most. Sort of has to for survival," Anna said. "Why?"

"No reason, other than I don't think he likes me very much," Jack said.

"He's just overly protective of me. I'm the bearer of food," Anna said, smiling up at her ally. Jack grinned and untucked his hands as he came closer.

"So, if you tell him I'm safe, he'll stop throwing things at my head?"

Anna lifted a brow. "Who says you're safe?" she asked.

"Come on, Anna Banana." He took another step nearer. Ambosi screeched and climbed closer to her.

"He'll attack like a Doberman on command," she warned. Okay, an exaggeration, but Jack deserved it, walking up to her looking all charming and cocky like that. The nerve.

"I bet. Seems everyone here would defend you. You've created quite the kingdom for yourself."

"It's not my kingdom. It's my cause. Don't mock it," she said, snapping back to reality. He wasn't flirting. No. He was still too bitter about her keeping Pippa from him. And calling this her kingdom showed just how little he respected what she was doing. She jumped down and marched past him, but he grabbed her arm, letting go abruptly when some sort of fruit smacked him in the back.

"Hey, stop that!" Jack yelled toward the tree. Anna tugged her arm free. "Not you, Anna. I'm sorry. I didn't mean to upset you. I—I intended the opposite. Just call off your mutant Doberman."

He let go of her arm but didn't break eye contact. Anna wrapped her arms around her waist, staring him down for a few seconds, studying him, before relenting.

"Ambosi, stop. Go play somewhere else," she said. The monkey made a show of his teeth before obeying. "What did you come here for, Jack?"

"To tell you how impressed I am with how you saved what was—"

"Jomo," Anna said. The name the kids had picked out for their newest orphan.

"Jomo. You were amazing, working on his trunk wound and—"

"I had to. Trunks are important," Anna said, interrupting him. But she'd felt the heat creep up her face at "amazing," and had to stop him. She couldn't go there, back to when he'd made her feel as if she mattered. Back to when she'd actually believed he'd felt something for her. Back to when he'd wrapped his warm arms around her and told her everything would be okay. Nothing was okay. Not anymore. And going back was a waste of time. "Without his trunk, he'd never survive reintroduction to a herd when he's old enough. It's their most sensitive body part. They use it for communicating, smelling, eating, manipulating and for sucking up water to drink or mud to bathe in. That's just skimming it. I only hope he doesn't develop bad scar tissue from the wound."

"There you go, avoiding a compliment. Hiding behind facts."

"I wasn't. I thought you'd be interested in the facts."

"I'm interested in a lot of facts, Anna, but right now I simply wanted to tell you I'm impressed with your work, and that I'm sorry for what Jomo has been through."

Anna stared at him, not sure what to say. Taken off-balance by his sincerity, and proximity.

"Thank you."

"Now that wasn't so hard, was it?" Jack said.

She glared at him. "Don't patronize me. I don't care how much power Dr. Miller gave you, don't think you can waltz in here and do that. I know you're up to something."

He ran his fingers back through his hair before setting his palms on her shoulders. Their warmth felt familiar and safe. But he wasn't. She had to keep reminding herself, before her heart cracked open any more. This was a game to get what he wanted. Pippa. Not happening.

"I'm sorry. I'm not trying to patronize anyone. I'm just—look, Anna. Can we just backtrack? Yesterday was a shock to both of us, but we have to figure this out. We have to be able to work together and get along for Pippa's sake."

He was right, of course. Priorities. This was about Pippa. Anna had gotten herself into this whole mess because she wanted what was best for Pippa in the long run. She would give her life for her daughter.

She'd never meant for so much time to pass before telling him, but time and distance had a way of tricking the mind into a false sense of peace. Losing Jack's friendship, his trust, was the price she had to pay, but it was a small one if it meant that Pippa would always know he made room for her in his life because he wanted to. Not because he had to. For that, Anna would make nice, but only as long as he didn't fight her for primary custody.

"Fine," she said. She took a step back, forcing his hands to slip off her shoulders, when what she really longed for was to feel his arms wrapped around her in forgiveness. She paced, trying to focus on Pippa and not Jack. "We can be civilized. Just don't you forget I'm her mother. You want what's best for her? Staying with me is what's best, Jack, and if you don't think short visits are enough time with you, then you can…you can…move here."

CHAPTER FIVE

"MOVING HERE IS out of the question and you know it, Anna."

Her face flinched so briefly that Jack almost missed it. For that fleeting moment, he almost thought she'd come right out and ask him—beg him—to stay. That she'd tell him how much she'd missed him and wanted him in her life. That she had faith in him as a father, if nothing else. That she'd been wrong for saying no. But that card was off the table. He couldn't trust her now. Not after the secret she'd kept. If he knew Anna, he knew she'd do anything to protect what family she had left, not to mention her cause. Even if it meant pretending to think he was good enough for her, even if he never had been. He needed for them to get along, but that didn't mean he had to be stupid about it.

Anna straightened her back, reminding him of how perfectly her petite shoulders fit into his palms and how much he wanted to embrace her. To reassure her. To convince her that he could do this. He'd be a good father. She turned her chin up toward him.

"Of course it is," she said. "I was just making a point."

"And you can make all the points you want, but the fact remains that I'm her father, and now that I know about her, you can't expect me to walk away. Being a rotten parent isn't genetic."

His words sounded as hollow as he felt. His neck muscles tightened around his throat, keeping him from repeating them in affirmation. *Being a rotten parent isn't genetic.* What if it was genetic? What if, for all his good intentions, he ended up sucking at fatherhood? He remembered the self-destructive patterns his biological parents and their friends would fall into. The alcohol. The drugs. The fights. They developed comfortable routines and lost sight of right or wrong or how they hurt those around them. He'd had protective routines, too. Like when he'd lock his bedroom door and hide in his closet whenever his parents had their so-called parties. He'd stay in there for hours, reading a book or studying his

spelling words by flashlight. If he left Pippa
behind with a promise to visit, who was to say
another pattern wouldn't take over? That one
delay wouldn't lead to another? Work would
get in the way, and before he knew it, she'd be
all grown up...without him. If she even survived that long. After what he'd seen in the
field with Kamau, there was no question this
wasn't the place for a little girl.

The heat drained from Anna's cheeks and
she shook her head.

"In all our years of friendship, Jack, when
have I ever treated you like someone I didn't
respect? When have I ever implied that you
were anything but good? In fact, if there's one
thing I never doubted about you, it's that you
always do what's right."

"And the Anna I knew always did what was
right, too, which is why I think you put my
name on that certificate."

She didn't respond.

"Look, Anna. I need—I'm asking—you
to come into Nairobi with me. Just one day,
maybe two, off work."

"Why? I can't—"

"Hear me out. No matter how we...fix this

situation, Pippa needs her papers drawn up. She needs her citizenship, a passport—"

"Wait a minute."

"No, you wait, Anna. She needs them. This isn't about you or me. This is about Pippa's safety and security. What if something happened to you?"

"That's why I put your name on her birth certificate, Jack. I *was* thinking about the future and what-ifs."

"But you didn't follow through."

Anna's cheeks reddened with the slap of his words. She hadn't followed through, just like she hadn't returned to the States. He'd spoken the truth and wasn't going to back down. Jack held his hands up in a peace effort, but pressed on.

"If something did happen, there would be all sorts of delays in paperwork. Is that what you want? Not knowing where she'd be in the interim?" He left it at that. One step at a time. No matter where Pippa ended up living, her legal paperwork was a matter that needed to be addressed. He was being straightforward about that.

ANNA WALKED BACK to the tree and, leaning the side of her head against one leg of her platform, tried to figure out if he was manipulating her. It wasn't in his nature, but tap into anyone's primal instincts and surprising things could happen. She stared out at a herd of zebras grazing unsuspectingly in the distance. In seconds they took off at a fierce run, a cheetah in fierce pursuit. All made it but one. The youngest. Jack winced.

Anna turned, leaning her back against the beam and rubbing her palms down her thighs twice before looking at him.

"It's nature, Jack. Survival of the fittest. The lack of rain is a predator in and of itself. It's a spectacular place, though," she said, looking wistfully back over the dried plains before continuing. "You want me to go into Nairobi with you? Fine. On one condition. You go up there with me," she said, pointing skyward.

She pushed off and strode past him not waiting for a response. He'd cornered her and she hated being cornered, especially when she'd given him a means. Nevertheless, she'd seen plenty of critters who, when they couldn't escape to the left or right, opted for up. Ambosi, for one. And up was a brilliant option. Pure genius, if she could say so herself.

"You want me to climb a thorny tree with you?"

"Oh, for heaven's sake, Jack. Up in the sky. In a helicopter, smart one."

Jack grinned like a hyena at breakfast.

"I know what you meant, *genius*," he said, emphasizing "genius," just as he had back in school, when he'd egg her on until she loosened up and laughed.

She wasn't about to give him the satisfaction, but the memory, and the familiar way he was smiling at her... Anna sucked in her bottom lip and bit down. Hard. A reality bite that hurt a lot less than the pain he'd cause if she fell for his obvious plan. Nostalgia had no effect on her. The past was nothing but lies. She gave him her best *I'm being serious here* look.

"Didn't you bring that camera? The one you never let me borrow?" she asked.

"Of course I did. You're treating me to photo ops? What's that got to do with Nairobi?"

"Nothing at all." Anna started back toward camp and he fell in step. A great sign that she'd turned the tables. She smiled, half show and half satisfaction. "An aerial view is an efficient way to check on herds, movement patterns, which watering holes and riverbeds have dried. You get the idea."

"Checking on poachers?"

"The authorities do that. If we happen to see something suspicious, then of course we'll report it, but this is strictly to check on the elephants."

"If there's a helicopter around here, then why did I have to endure that road trip from Amboseli?"

This time, Anna couldn't suppress her laugh. "Aw, Jack. Was that a little too wild compared to your pristine lab?"

"No. Just wondering," he said, visibly straightening.

"Your supplies might have been too heavy, but either way, we don't have an official landing pad out here. Just a grassy area big enough to set down a chopper in case of emergencies, and for chartering the occasional observatory flight."

"Your expense list didn't say anything about charter flights." The look on Jack's face told Anna that he hadn't intended to say that. She stopped and folded her arms.

"Seriously, Jack? You're unbelievable.

Miller's minion. I happen to know someone who owns a tourist charter flight company. He donates some flight time each month to anyone at a wildlife reserve who needs it. He's already indulged me this month, though, and it wouldn't be fair to ask without offering compensation."

In reality, Mac had been more than kind to her, and she'd been getting the impression that he was interested. The last thing she wanted was to feel beholden to anyone, or to lead anyone on. Taking Jack up would solve several issues at once.

She glanced at him. "You provide the payment—trust me, it's affordable for you—and I'll go to Nairobi with you within the week."

"Affordable, huh? Is this some plan to run my pockets dry and strand me here?" Jack asked, scratching his jaw. She arched her brows and waited. "We do Nairobi tomorrow."

"Can't. I have a wedding to attend tomorrow," she said.

"You've got to be kidding me. Out here?"

"Pretty much, yeah."

"Fine," Jack huffed, as if she was lying to buy time. She really had blown his trust. "We take care of Pippa's paperwork the day after tomorrow."

"Perfect." Anna swung around and resumed walking. Jack always could read her face, and she didn't want him seeing the satisfaction on it. That would only raise his guard.

He was right about needing to sort out Pippa's paperwork. Anna couldn't argue with that. She wanted what was best for their daughter, just as Jack did. He would do what he thought was best, so she had only one option: make him fall in love with Busara, with Kenya. Convince him that being here with her mother was the best thing for Pippa.

And if plan A didn't work, then Anna would have no choice but to go with plan B. A plan she didn't have the money for, but which she'd have to find a way to execute. She'd fight for custody.

MAC THE GQ PILOT was too handsome for anyone's good.

What bugged Jack the most was that he seemed to have it all. The flying skills, the generosity, a passion for wildlife *and* he was local. Everything that fit perfectly into Anna's life. And if Jack had to witness one more round of Mac insisting she sit up front with him in the snug little chopper and Anna blushing in response, he'd suffer a preflight bout of nausea.

How many times in the past few years had she gone up alone with this guy? Or out with him?

"We don't have all day, so why don't I sit up front, since I have the camera," Jack said, patting his camera case.

"Sure, man. No problem," Mac said. He shrugged at Anna and helped her into the back, then got in position.

There was no way Jack was letting on that he'd never been in a helicopter...and had his reservations. The blades began whooping, and revved to a deafening whir. Mac handed them headgear and adjusted his own. By the time Jack realized that having both of Pippa's parents go up in this tin can together might be too much of a risk, they'd lifted off. He made a mental note. *First step as new dad: write a living will.*

Mac veered left, causing Jack's case to slide. He trapped it with his foot, then mustered up the courage to reach down and pull out his camera. The chopper had leveled off.

This was good. He uncapped the lens, tossed it into his case then adjusted his zoom. Man, this camera had seen just about every sunset and sunrise during his gangly, semi-outcast teen years. A birthday gift from the Harpers that he later realized was an attempt to draw him out of his shell. Teach him to trust again. No amount of rain, snow or fog had kept him from taking it to the lake…or to school games. Not that he'd watched them. Every one of those shots had been focused on the warm, accepting, shy face of a girl who, whether she knew it or not, had kept him from looking back. Anna's innocence, optimism and open heart had convinced him that only the future mattered, and all he had to do to shape it was focus ahead and work hard. So he did.

And look where it got him.

Jack leaned cautiously into the windshield and looked down. Incredible. Breathtaking. In spite of every English class he'd aced, he was pretty sure even a thesaurus wouldn't carry a word that adequately described the scene below. The tree-dappled expanse. The veins of blue meandering through endless brown grassland. The flocks of white birds taking flight. It was formidable. He aimed and clicked, lost in the deafening whir of the helicopter's engine and captivating canvas through his lens. From here, there was no smell, no dust, no death. Just...amazing.

They passed over a copse of acacia trees and cleared the camp. Busara looked miniscule against the vast plain. The chopper dipped and Jack instinctively grabbed the side of his seat with one hand. Then, when he noted the corner of Mac's mouth turn up, he pretended he was shifting positions for a better shot. The guy had probably done it on purpose.

Jack adjusted his lens, turned and took a shot of Anna beaming out the window behind Mac. She turned and grinned. *That smile was for me, dude.* Jack clicked. She gave him a thumbs-up and pointed excitedly out the window. He clicked again. She sent him an exasperated look. Within seconds, Jack felt one of her hands grip his shoulder and the other tap the pad on his ear. She, too, wore noise protection, but the movement of her lips suggested that she was talking to Mac, and Jack couldn't hear them. His headset was turned off. Mac reached out and fiddled with a knob, and suddenly, Anna's voice came through Jack's earphones. So did Mac's amusement.

"Look down, Jack. You can't miss this," she yelled, her face close enough for her sweet scent to envelope him. Close enough for a kiss that wasn't going to happen. He ignored Mac's smug look and, obeying Anna, turned toward his window.

"What the…" *No way. Whoa.* Thousands of animals flowed across the plain like a wave of creamed coffee spilling across a maple floor. Beyond them, the unmistakable black-and-white of zebras moving congruously stood out against the neutral backdrop like visitors from another world that didn't belong. Just like him. Jack had seen migrations on those TV nature shows, but in person it was simply phenomenal.

He didn't realize Anna had scooted behind him until he felt her hands on his shoulders. He glanced at her as she peered out his window to gain his vantage point. He could feel her breath on his neck as she spoke through the noise. She pointed.

"Wildebeests. They migrate annually in a large circular pattern in search of water. You saw how dry most of the area is, but that river calls to them. And those zebras? Remember when you'd watch TV with me after school and you'd go on about how zebras had zero camouflage sense?"

Jack nodded. She still remembered that lame joke, his attempt to laugh off his lack of fashion sense back then. He wasn't sure he cared for Mac listening in on this.

"Lions are color-blind. The stripes blend in with the tall grass the zebras hide in. The patterning can also confuse predators who are trying to target a single victim. Just a few benefits to those stripes." She wrinkled her nose and cocked her head playfully at the shared memory.

The chopper dipped again. This time, he didn't even flinch. *Take that, Mac.* Jack looked out and gaped. *Oka-a-ay.* So death was evident, even from up here. And from here, that cheetah had blended into the backdrop so efficiently, she'd taken more than a gazelle by surprise. Jack was amazed.

Anna pressed her fingers against Jack's shoulder to get his attention, though she already had it, and pointed to several different herds of elephants. And then it struck him.

His Anna was in her element.

SOMETHING WAS OFF.

Anna registered every nuance of the camp in one glance, a natural ability that had been enhanced by motherhood. Still, it took a second longer to pinpoint what was odd. She blamed the lag time on the air turbulence caused by Jack walking a step too close behind her. Their proximity in the chopper had been due to the cramped quarters. No other reason. That excuse was null and void now.

Kamau sat with Haki on a couple overturned buckets, playing a game of checkers on a board drawn with black marker on a cardboard box. The pieces were pebbles versus wood chips. Kamau had never sat around playing games with the kids before. Joking around here and there, showing them the animals, or playing a few rounds of catch or tag, sure. But total immersion? She hadn't witnessed it. Plus, this was naptime, and Kamau usually did rounds at this hour. Especially since he was covering for Anna.

Kamau looked up, his lips twisting like a little boy caught playing hooky. Haki looked serious, as usual. A boy definitely cut out for checkers…or chess. He glanced over, but after spotting Jack, quickly propped his cheek

against his little fist and turned his face away,
toward his game.

"He doesn't like me, does he?" Jack asked,
tucking his hands in the front pockets of his
khakis, clearly oblivious to things being out
of sync.

Anna ignored him and instead shot Kamau
an inquisitive look. He responded by nodding
toward her quarters. Okay. So for some reason, Haki and Pippa had to be separated?
They'd argued, but never to that extent.

"Why don't you go hang out with the
guys?" Anna said to Jack. She went to her
tent without giving him an option.

Inside, Pippa lay peacefully on her cot.
Her soft, rhythmic breathing told Anna she'd
been asleep awhile. Niara, however, instead of
reading a novel, as she typically did when the
kids slept, stood staring out the back screen,
arms folded and eyes wet.

"What's happened?"

Her friend turned abruptly, wiping her
cheeks.

"I didn't mean to scare you," Anna whispered. "Didn't you hear me come in?"

"I must have been lost in thought," Niara
said with a dismissive wave.

"What's going on? Why isn't Haki in here?"

"The boy is getting older."

"But he's still young enough to nap, or read with you. He's playing with Kamau, Niara. That's a little different, no?"

Niara smiled wistfully, then smoothed her shirt. "Dr. Odaba is a good male role model," she said.

"A male role—Niara, are you saying that you *like* Kamau? You know…*like?*"

"No! Of course not," she said. But her cheeks said otherwise. "Haki started asking questions about his father. I think this whole thing with your Jack got his mind running. We were outside near the pens and everyone could hear, and he kept going on and on…."

"It's okay," Anna said, pulling her into a hug. She could feel the dampness of Niara's tears on her shoulder. She knew how embarrassed her friend must have been, being taken off guard like that by her own son. Having something so painful, something she'd kept quiet about for so long, come out in front of the keepers. All men. And Anna could see Haki persisting in spite of it all. He was just a kid with questions. Questions, she thought with a pang of guilt, that had surfaced because of her.

Niara straightened, pulling herself together. "I'm okay. It was just unexpected. But Dr. Odaba—"

"Kamau. How many times has he said to call him that? You don't call me Dr. Bekker. It's okay to call him Kamau, Niara," Anna added softly, watching for her friend's reaction.

Niara looked down, barely holding back a smile. Well, it was about time. She had a thing for Kamau! Anna's mind raced and her heart bubbled like a freshly popped can of soda. This was so perfect and so…

Anna took a calming breath. If she pressed, Niara, with her gazellelike grace and beauty, would bolt like prey sensing danger. From what she'd shared years ago, she didn't *know* Haki's father, but she'd never forget his face. Anna sympathized, but there was no way she could understand what it would take for Niara to trust again. Deep down, Anna couldn't blame her, but she wanted to see her friend happy.

"Kamau," Niara continued. "He stepped in, acting like he was in the mood for fun, and he told Haki to save his questions for a full stomach, because they were late for a special game they needed to play, man to man. He had him at 'man.'"

The two women laughed quietly.

"Then he told me I could go put Pippa to sleep and he'd watch Haki. That was it."

"I see," Anna said. Not once had she picked up on any interest in Niara from Kamau. But he was stoic to the nth degree. Good at masking. He had to be, given the stuff he saw on the job. He was also intolerant of cruelty because of all he'd witnessed. Probably why he'd acted so quickly to distract Haki, even if the boy's intentions were innocent.

"Oh, and I'm sorry for keeping him from doing whatever work you had to get done," Niara added.

"It's no problem. I can't believe you're worried about that right now. None of us could function without all you do, Niara. You deserve a break. I'm glad this wedding is tomorrow. You and I are going to take some girl time to get ready for it. And you know what?" Anna said. "When Haki asks again, just say what you're comfortable with. Remember, he's still little and curious, that's all. He's worried about Jack taking Pippa. He told me so. Tell him… Tell him we're his family and we're not going anywhere."

Niara nodded. Anna hugged her then slipped outside. The men were still gathered around their game.

"So, who won?" Anna asked as she approached the guys. Kamau hung his head dramatically in his hands. Jack sat rocking on his heels, rubbing his chin as if he couldn't figure out how it had happened.

"I did! Three times!" Haki said with a laugh. "I bet I can beat you, too, Auntie Anna."

"I bet you could, but I have a job for you. How about you go and wake up Pippa so she can sleep tonight?"

"Okay." Haki's bucket stool scraped the dirt as he jumped up and ran to their quarters. Anna watched to be sure he got to his mom safely, then turned to Kamau and Jack, who stood looking as if all traces of their inner child were gone.

"Beaten by a six-year-old," Anna said, shaking her head as she headed for the clinic. "That's just sad, Kam."

JACK WATCHED AS Anna walked away.

"Do you play?" Kamau asked, gesturing toward the checkers. "I have chess pieces, too."

"I'm too rusty," Jack said, shaking his head. He preferred money-free card games.

"Guess it's back to work, then," the vet said.

"What? Oh, yeah," Jack replied, distracted by how wonderful it was to see Anna acting relaxed. The way she'd been on the helicopter, and just now with Haki, Kamau and himself. It almost felt as if they'd always been together. As if he'd always been a part of the camp and their routines.

"So. You and Anna," Kamau ventured. Jack shoved his hair back. This place was definitely smaller than a small town.

"Me and Anna. And Pippa."

A moment of silent understanding passed as they both stared toward the clinic, arms folded.

"Don't hurt her," Kamau said.

"That's not my intention." *Liar.*

"Why did you ever let her go, then?"

"I didn't. She let me go. Never even told me I was a father."

Jack felt Kamau turn his eyes on him.

"Did you love her, once?"

He did *not* just ask that.

"You don't know me that well," Jack said.

"I know Anna like a little sister. It's my duty to ask."

Jack stared him down. For crying out loud, who was he to argue with that? He liked that someone was looking out for her, and would be after he left. He hadn't expected to be cornered with an interrogation, though. This was like being a teen on a first date.

"That's inconsequential. Anna doesn't believe in love, or marriage," Jack said at last. *At least not anymore.*

"Now *that* I have trouble believing."

"Believe it."

"And I never said anything about marriage," Kamau added.

Jack narrowed his eyes at him. He'd been checkmated.

"I asked once, and she said no."

Kamau cocked his head in silent sympathy, then they both looked back toward the clinic. Another moment passed.

"Look around, Jack. Dust. Desiccation. It's hard to believe that deep beneath the surface, rivers of pure water branch far and wide from Kilimanjaro's ice cap, pulsing like arteries.

In a drought that has lasted this long, even that meltwater becomes hard to reach. But it's there."

"Dig deep enough."

"Ah, see. You catch on quick. You did earn that PhD." Kamau grinned.

"I did. And I'm also smart enough to know when no means no."

Kamau frowned and Jack sensed something more intense in his face.

"All life comes to an end," the vet finally said. "In the Serengeti, it can happen during drought or it can happen during flood. Some have no choice, but you get to pick your path, Jack. With the heart of a woman, or without."

"And are you with or without?"

"Without."

"What a waste. Seriously, man. All that poetic wisdom and no woman to woo it with." Jack shook his head and laughed. He slapped Kamau's shoulder, then headed for the clinic.

"Wait a minute. Are you making fun of me? I don't *woo*. Nobody *woos* anymore," Kamau said, stalking behind him.

"Nobody I know is that poetic, either, Romeo."

Jack chuckled as he entered the clinic.

Both he and Kamau cleared their throats and switched gears at the sight of Anna hunched over her worktable. She had earphones on and was presumably studying her latest recordings. Jack pretended not to notice, and went straight to his lab equipment. He needed to make sure the newer samples were in good shape for dropping off with Dr. Alwanga in Nairobi. A staff member had driven the first ones to the Amboseli airstrip, where they'd been flown out. As for Anna, Kamau was right with his advice...except for one thing. The path to her had long since washed away.

CHAPTER SIX

ANNA SO WANTED to splurge on a two-bucket shower.

She couldn't, though. Not with how low the water pressure had gotten the past few days. The last thing they needed was the well drying up. There were plenty of underground streams, but the cost of digging another well... Wouldn't Jack and Miller have fun with that one.

One-bucket shower it was. Just as soon as she found Niara, so they could play guard for one another. They had a curtained stall in a smaller tent adjacent to theirs reserved for them and the kids. The men had their own, but a girl couldn't be too careful. It was something Niara had insisted on.

As run-down as Anna felt, things were on track. The orphans were doing well. All the keepers were set with instructions on what to do, since Kamau would also be attending the wedding. No vets would be on hand, so she'd decided they'd leave Ahron in charge. He'd been with them the longest and was a trusted member of the team. Jack would be able to use the time to finish up with his "inspection." Maybe he'd even luck out and find some way to shut her down. Or maybe she'd luck out and he'd give up—on everything—and leave.

The look on his face when they were flying… She'd gotten to him. She just knew he was starting to appreciate what a wonderful place this was, and recognize the significance of her work. And besides that, he didn't seem to be going out of his way to spend time with Pippa. Sure, Anna understood work and camp demands, but other than mealtimes, he seemed to be holding himself back. Maybe he was realizing that raising a child wasn't a clean-cut science. That a kid wasn't some simple organism you could inoculate a petri dish with, slip the cover on and watch grow.

She wrapped her arms around herself in spite of the heat, squeezing against the guilt that welled in her gut. Gosh. He did know. That was why he was holding back. He knew firsthand.

She closed her eyes against the memory of his first day at her middle school. The new kid. The one everyone had singled out as different. If there was anything Anna couldn't stand, it was cruelty and snobbery, which was why she began sitting next to him at lunch. Lunch had extended into library period and pretty soon she wasn't doing it deliberately. She'd begun enjoying his company. His kindness and humble nature. Hanging out with him felt natural and easy.

The Jack she'd cared about deserved so much more than this—he deserved to have his child in his life. But there wasn't a way around it. If they lived in the same area—the same country—that would be one thing, but they didn't. And Pippa was staying with her mother. No ifs, ands or buts.

Anna approached the mess tent, but could tell from the angle of light through the screens that no one was there. Where was everyone? Squeals and giggles penetrated the airy space. Anna rounded the back of the tent to a clearing normally used for hang-drying laundry on a plastic cord that ran between a corner of one wooden tent frame and a tree. She peered around a sheet that was clothespinned to the cord. Niara stood laughing in the periphery of the clearing as Jack jumped around with Pippa perched on his shoulders, her tiny hands gripping fistfuls of his hair. He didn't seem to mind.

"Then what did the copter do, Daddy?"

"It dipped like this," Jack said, swooping down, then up again, slow enough not to drop Pippa, but fast enough to give her a thrill. Belly giggles filled the air, followed by hiccups. "And the cheetah did this…." Keeping one hand securely on Pippa's ankle, Jack ran to Haki and scooped him up with his free arm. The three of them swung in a circle. Even Haki laughed. Oh, and the racket Ambosi was making in a nearby elephant pepper tree made his view on the scene loud and clear.

One and a half rotations and Anna was spotted. Jack set the kids down and both ran to Niara, looking back at Jack, who snarled playfully, like a predator.

"That's it, guys," he said, catching his breath. He raked his disheveled hair back. "Any more and I'll be as bald as an elephant's—toenail." He looked right at Anna, then winked and gave her a crooked smile.

That smile.

Heaven help her.

"You did what?" Anna said, digging through her sack of toiletries.

"You heard me," said Niara.

Anna pulled out a stick of clear lip gloss that hadn't been used in over a year, and swiped it across her mouth. She rubbed her lips together and was treated to the taste of strawberries. "I heard you, but I can't believe you did that to me."

"Come on, Anna. You know you can't just leave him here. It's wrong. Even Kamau agrees."

"*Kamau* agrees?" In all these years, Anna was certain she hadn't heard Niara call Kamau by his first name. Even after Anna had encouraged her to stop calling him Dr. Odaba. She'd finally listened. Interesting. "So you discussed this with him?" Anna asked.

"Not exactly a discussion. But I did ask his opinion, and he agreed. So that's that. Dr. Harper is coming with us to the wedding. Besides, you wanted him to see the love and beauty here, where you're raising Pippa. What better place to experience that than a Masai wedding?"

Anna had never seen Niara's face glow or her eyes spark with such excitement. Did this constitute a double date? Oh, for crying out loud. Where had that thought come from? Anna put her gloss back in the sack and gave the drawstring a hard tug.

"Fine," she said, then smirked at Niara. "At least we know he can jump."

JACK HAD BEEN an outsider many, many times, but apart from the day he was adopted, he'd never felt so warmly welcomed. He stood next to Kamau, Niara, Haki and Anna, who carried Pippa on her hip, and watched the wedding, mesmerized by the rhythmic singing—more like calling out in chanting chorus—the colorful orange and red wraps, the long wooden staffs held by the Masai men, the beads woven together like the wide brim of a hat bouncing around the necks of the Masai women as they jumped in place. Everyone jumped. A lot. The sight was nothing short of amazing. So phenomenally different from any church wedding Jack had ever attended. He noticed Niara and Anna bending their knees in rhythm.

"Have you been to one of these before?" he asked Anna.

"A few. Here at this homestead. Most of the Masai here are related to Ahron, so we know them. They've been good friends of the camp and the animals," she said, shifting Pippa to her other hip.

"The jumping?"

"Everyone dances differently," she said. "You should try it. For the men, it's a competition."

"I don't have a staff."

Anna grinned. "The staff is supposed to be a sign of…manliness," she said, shifting Pippa again. Jack reached out and put a hand over their daughter's eyes. Anna laughed. "Virility, Jack. She's young enough to be clueless."

"Here, let me carry her."

Anna hesitated before letting Jack relieve her of Pippa's weight. "Make sure you at least hold her hand if you put her down," she said. "She, um, disappeared in the crowd at the last one we attended. I mean, she was safe and all—one of the girls brought her to me—but I'd rather she didn't disrupt things."

"Got it."

"What's diswupt?" Pippa asked.

"It means I don't want anyone tripping on you. Besides, you get a better view from up here," Anna said, reaching out and wiggling Pippa's button nose in a gentle pinch. In turn, Pippa pinch-wiggled Jack's nose.

"I did that once," Anna added with a frown. "I ran off in a department store. My mom freaked and called Security. Now I know how she felt."

"Got it, Anna. I won't let her go. You can… mingle or whatever, if you want."

Anna nodded and whispered something to Niara. Jack put his hand on Anna's arm and she turned before walking off.

"Let me guess. They found you in the toy aisle. Right?"

Her eyes widened for a fraction of a second, then she looked down at Pippa's dangling foot and fingered the strap on her tiny sandal.

"No," she said, and left without elaborating.

Jack watched her and Niara, both beaming, approach the women, who warmly encouraged them to join their celebration. Anna looked vibrant. Her hair, worn down today instead of pulled back, bounced around her face. Her skin glowed with pure, natural beauty, framed by a peasant-style lavender shirt, a shock of color compared to the mute khaki button-downs she wore daily.

"Stare at her any longer and you might miss the entire wedding," said Kamau.

"I'm not staring," Jack insisted, jumping up and down with Pippa a few times as proof. Kamau grinned.

"You're good with her," Kamau said, nodding toward them. Jack didn't know how to respond. Holding his little girl was starting to feel...normal. He didn't want to be good with her. He wanted to be great with her. "What are you planning to do? About the situation, I mean."

Jack glanced at Kamau, then back at the group of men chanting and jumping with their staffs around one particularly tall fellow, whom he assumed to be the groom. Beyond the group, under the shade of a cluster of trees, an older man stirred a giant pot in what appeared to be an outdoor kitchen of sorts.

The women in the group echoed their chanted responses to the men. Their giant earrings glistened in the sunlight as they moved, but Anna's face stole the show for Jack. She looked carefree. She looked as if she'd let her guard down, even with him present. But he knew that wouldn't last.

"I'm planning to do the right thing," he said to Kamau. "I have responsibilities now."

"You miss the point," the vet said. "You're thinking with your head."

Jack raised a brow at him. "I hear words of wisdom coming. Let me give you some first. Thinking with anything else gets a man in trouble."

Kamau shook his head and laughed. "Man, I'm talking about this." He pointed to his own chest. "Doing what's in here is the only way to ensure you're doing what is right. You're a scientist. Scientists would be failures if they did not listen to their hearts. Their gut instincts. Communication, Jack, is a powerful thing, and it's even more accurate when it happens between the mind and heart. Without it, where would our species be? Any species, for that matter? The heart and mind should not be exclusive of one another."

"So what are *they* saying?" Jack asked, desperate to change the subject.

"Giving thanks, wishing a fruitful life full of energy and keeping enemies away," Kamau said, scoping the crowd. "I wonder where the

groom's brother is? I was going to introduce
you, because he told me not long ago that he
wanted to try and save up to go to college.
He has his sights set on exploring the world.
America, perhaps. I didn't want to discour-
age him, because times are tough, but I figured meeting you would be exciting for him."

"Sure. Let me know if you spot him." Jack
hoisted Pippa onto his shoulders to balance
her weight more evenly. Amazing how a little
thing like her could strain a guy's back with
all the squirming. There were so many people,
so much going on. And as unique an experience as it was, he wanted tomorrow to come.
He needed to accomplish something concrete
toward sorting out the whole mess. Something
solid and secure to calm the waves that kept
rippling through his chest.

Pippa reached down and covered his eyes.

"Hah! Who did that?" he said, grabbing her
hands and peering up at her. More giggles.
This kid didn't run out of them. He straightened, and caught Kamau watching Niara. Jack
wouldn't be surprised if the whole "groom's
brother" thing had been a cover-up so he
could steel glimpses of her and Haki.

"And you're doing what's so obviously in

your heart," Jack said. "Way to practice what you preach."

Kamau went from surprise to sheepishness. "This case is different. Leaving her alone is the right thing. She was the victim of a violent act. A relationship, or trusting a man, isn't possible for her right now. I'm there for anyone who needs me at camp, her and Haki included—even Anna. But beyond that? No. My work is dangerous and demanding. Keeping my distance is the best I can do. She's a great mother. She's all that boy needs."

"Sounds to me like you've put a lot of thought into it. I mean, considering you have no feelings for her or anything like that," Jack said with mock sincerity. "I'm sure this constitutes nothing but scientific analysis."

"I should feed you to the lions," Kamau said.

"No!" Pippa jumped in. His little girl was defending him.

Jack kissed her tiny fist. "He's kidding, honey."

"He's right, Pippa. Instead, we should lock him in a pen with Ambosi and a bucket of pepper tree plums," Kamau said, making a silly face so that she would understand the humor.

Pippa did. She started wriggling and pawing through his hair like a monkey, and before Jack could set her down, she threw herself backward. He hung on to her ankles in a panic and Kamau grabbed her from behind, getting her off Jack's back safely.

"Pippa!" Anna said, running up.

"She's fine," Jack and Kamau said simultaneously.

"She could have fallen on her head," Anna replied.

"I had her the whole time," Jack said. "Really."

"Yes, I could see that." Nonetheless, Anna led Pippa back to where Niara stood. Jack knew he and Kamau looked like idiots standing there, staring after the women.

"They don't need us, do they?" he asked, but it came out like a statement. An affirmation.

Kamau grimaced. That was answer enough.

WITH TOO MANY of them for Mac's charter helicopter, Anna had booked seats to Nairobi on a plane from Amboseli National Park's airstrip. The drive there, piled in an open Jeep, had left them coated in dust that clung to them all the way to Nairobi.

The airport was bustling and the crowds put Anna on guard. She strapped her tote across her chest so that it hung safely in front of her. She shifted Pippa on her hip, unwilling to trust the little girl not to pull free and disappear. Anna grabbed one of Haki's hands, while Niara took the other.

According to Jack, he'd taken care of their accommodations. They had all packed lightly and efficiently for the brief trip. He took their carry-on bags and, surprisingly, led them through the crowd as if he'd lived in Nairobi all his life.

Had he come to Kenya on lectures in the past? Without bothering to hunt her down in Busara? He'd known she was somewhere in Kenya. He could have pressured Miller to tell him where, if he'd actually come through here in the past. Anna thought about the possibility and decided it didn't make sense. Then she saw a tall, dark and well-dressed man waving at them. No wonder Jack seemed on top of things. He had a beacon.

"Over here!" The man shouldered through

the crowd and closed in on them. "*Jambo,* Jack. Back alive, I see." He laughed, shaking his hand and relieving him of one of the bags.

"Did you get the other samples I sent?" Jack asked.

"Yes. Yes. Thank you. They arrived safe and sound."

"Good." Jack put his hand on Anna's back. "Dr. Alwanga, this is Dr. Anna Bekker and my...daughter, Pippa. And this is Niara Juma and her son, Haki."

"*Jambo.* Nice to meet you," Dr. Alwanga said, shaking Anna's hand briefly, then holding on to Niara's a meaningful moment longer.

Well, well. Anna cleared her throat. "We should get out of here," she said.

"Absolutely. I have a car waiting." Dr. Alwanga turned and led the way.

Exhaust fumes ambushed her as she followed the doctor to a white SUV. Anna rubbed her nose against her sleeve. She preferred dust to fumes, although she knew from past trips that she'd adapt to the noise and smells soon enough. Especially if she got a delicious whiff of savory street food. She hadn't had anything but her coffee all morning. She'd been too busy getting Pippa and herself ready for travel. Not that she ever ate breakfast, but since Jack had shown up, snacking had gotten the best of her. Her stomach growled and she quickly pressed her hand against it, hoping no one had heard.

"I figured you must all be starving. We can stop wherever you like before heading to the hotel," Dr. Alwanga said.

Anna blushed. "Actually, it'd be easier if there's something at or near the hotel," Anna answered, climbing into the back with Niara and the kids. The children were getting jumpy. A warning that they were probably hungry and tired, yet excited over the change in scenery—a mix that could inevitably lead to a meltdown.

"No problem," Dr. Alwanga said, maneuvering into traffic. "We can stop at the university after you have a chance to eat and freshen up. I looked into procedure and printed off the forms you asked for when you first got to Busara, Jack. However, the embassy website asks that you send the paperwork electronically in order to book an appointment. I couldn't get that done for you."

Anna caught Jack, who'd sat up front,

glancing at her through the side mirror. She wrinkled her forehead at him. *Planned ahead, did you?* She knew he'd booked a hotel *after* she'd agreed to the trip. But Dr. Alwanga just said Jack had contacted him when he first arrived at Busara. He'd had his doctor friend get the ball rolling before he'd spoken to her. How had he been so sure she'd agree to the trip? What would he have done if she hadn't? Why didn't he just come out and say he'd planned the rest?

It was all moot now. What he'd done partly irked her and partly...felt good. She was relieved that someone was taking care of things. Appointments for legal paperwork didn't happen overnight here. She'd been expecting long delays. But it wasn't all on her shoulders now, as she was accustomed to. She was relieved that the darn legalities, which had nagged at her and worried her for years, might be sorted out.

For an emergency, she kept saying to herself. *For visits.* Just because she was filing forms didn't mean she was going to let Jack take Pippa.

Jack braced one hand on the dashboard as Dr. Alwanga came to an abrupt stop behind a truck making a turn. It chugged and exhaust billowed from its tailpipe before it regained momentum. Anna's head was starting to hurt. Fumes, noise, an empty stomach and nerves over what they needed to get done weren't a good combination.

Jack turned to Dr. Alwanga. "But that could take forever. I thought we'd be able to get in by tomorrow, or by the next day at the latest. Anna has to get back to her work and I only have so much flexibility with my schedule," he said.

That statement caught Anna's attention. When *was* he planning on leaving? Logically, she knew he wouldn't be here forever. But he had said he wasn't leaving Pippa behind, and they hadn't decided what would happen yet. Had he changed his mind already? A mix of relief and disappointment settled in her gut. Her life would get back to normal—with her little angel—all because her view of men like Jack and her father held true. Career first. She'd succeeded in convincing Jack that a child needed its mother. Convinced him that he was doing the right thing once again, and this time, the right thing was leaving them. Exactly what she wanted, she reminded herself. No false pretenses. No false relationship. No one to disappoint her.

"I know, Jack," Dr. Alwanga continued. "I cashed in on a favor. I spoke to a colleague whose sister works with the American Citizen Services, and explained the situation. She said to send the information as soon as possible. She said to go ahead and follow the website instructions, but to call her the minute it's done, and she'll get you in. There's a place I'll take you to get photos, as well. It's on their checklist."

Jack sank back, propped his elbow on the window frame and rubbed his jaw. "Thanks. I owe you," he said.

"You already did me a favor gathering those samples. You saved me the cost of sending a tech out. I figure after eating, we'll head back to the university to drop off the samples you got. You and Anna can use my computer to fill out the forms, and I can preoccupy everyone else with a campus tour. How's that sound?" he said, swiveling around and smiling at Haki, who sat in his mom's lap.

Who was he really looking at? Niara glanced nervously at Anna, but before Anna could crack a reassuring smile, he added, "My younger sister is a student on campus. She loves children and asked if she could join us."

Niara gave a small smile and nodded. Anna noticed the two men share a silent understanding. What had Jack told him about Niara? And why? Wasn't anything private?

Dr. Alwanga turned to face forward just in time to break for a traffic stop. Anna shot her hand out against the back of Jack's seat to keep Pippa safe, and hoped the fact that the kids were strapped against their moms rather than in car seats didn't stand out to Jack. She peered between the front seats to see how much traffic there was. She remembered how odd she'd found the juxtaposition of goats crossing a busy street in front of modern buildings, back when she'd first arrived in Kenya. It seemed normal now, although she guessed by the look on Jack's face it was quite a foreign scene to him.

Maybe he'd decide to stay longer. Go sightseeing. She'd been wanting to tour the historic home of Karen Blixen. Funny how tourists tended to visit more attractions than folks actually living in a place. *Out of Africa* was yet another movie she and Jack had seen together. He might be interested.

Jack glanced at his watch. "Sounds like a plan," he said to Dr. Alwanga. "Let's get this done."

JACK STRUGGLED TO maintain his focus on the computer screen, but the fact that Anna's chair was practically glued to his distracted him no end. Although the lab was pretty average in size, the stacks of books and bulging folders occupying every wall and nook in the adjoining office had shrunk it considerably. And that meant Anna's slender arm inevitably kept brushing his. *Focus.*

He turned to his right just as Anna turned left with the next document in hand. His nose collided with her head and she jerked back in surprise, the file folder she'd brought slipping off her lap onto the floor.

"I'm sorry," Jack said, rubbing the bridge of his nose. Talk about hardheaded. "I'll get that."

"No. Stay put. I'm smaller." She sounded annoyed, but she was right. It was a lot easier to fold her five-and-a-half-foot frame under the desk than it would be for him to do so with his six-foot one. She squeezed down, brusquely handing papers up to him. She *was* annoyed. And he couldn't blame her for being defensive. Clearly, if there had ever been trust and friendship between them, it no longer existed on either end. They had a task at hand and it was their parental responsibility to get it done. That's what he'd told her and that's what he kept reminding himself.

"Do you have her birth certificate?" he asked, flipping through the papers.

"Of course I do," Anna said, settling into her chair once more. She smoothed her hair back and took the stack from him. He did the typing and she located the papers and information. That had been their system for the past hour. An efficient one, too.

"I'm just running down the checklist. I had to ask," he said.

She didn't answer. She didn't even look at him.

"What did you tell Alwanga about Niara?" she finally asked.

"Nothing personal," Jack said, then dropped his hands to his knees. Was this all that was bothering her? "Kamau told me just enough to know she's not that comfortable around guys. I simply warned Alwanga that she was really shy and to chill on the charm he's notorious for. Is that okay with you?"

She shrugged and rubbed her nose against her wrist, leaving her hands free to sift through the stack.

"Anna…"

She looked at him then, and although her cheeks were dry, the rims of her eyes and tip of her nose were tinged with the redness of someone fighting not to lose control. It stung his heart.

"What, Jack? You want me to enjoy this? Smile and joke around as we fill out forms? I know it's necessary, but to be honest, I have warning bells deafening me with every key-stroke. You had Alwanga looking up procedure before I even agreed to come out here. How do I know you haven't already booked her a plane ticket? That you haven't schemed with him to take her back to the U.S.?"

"There's no ticket booked for her, Anna. Be reasonable—"

"Be reasonable?" Her voice hit a pitch he didn't think was possible—except maybe in the wild.

"Just stop. Of course I asked Alwanga to look into it. How were we supposed to get all this paperwork processed in the time frame of my trip? I've already extended my stay, and Miller's already sent me several emails about it. Not happy ones, either. I keep this up and my track to tenure will be irreparable. This isn't easy, Anna. None of it is. But wake up. Busara isn't some place in a movie. There are real dangers there. You want to hide out? Play out some fairy tale with no happy ending? Fine. But you don't have a right to isolate Pippa with you. You may be a heroine to those elephants, but the reality is you're a coward."

Anna flinched and nearly dropped the file again. "I can't believe you just said that. You can't show up out of the blue and act like you have my life figured out. If you try anything—"

"Don't worry. The only ticket to the States that's booked right now is mine, but that doesn't mean this is over." Jack rubbed his eyes. He'd sworn he wouldn't vent—not today. It wasn't constructive. And he didn't want to deal with tears.

Anna stared at him, then sniffed and straightened her back. She reached for her purse and pulled out a travel-size packet of tissues with a picture of a giraffe on the plastic covering.

"You okay?" he asked.

She wiped her nose, then pulled out a container of allergy medication and popped a pill.

"You're taking allergy meds?'

"Dust. Allergies. Put two and two together, Jack."

"Right. Dust." Jack turned back to the screen. *Dust, my foot.* She was used to the dust. Not once had he seen her sneeze, and she hadn't looked like this his entire trip. Dust. Fine.

"Just type, Jack."

He got back to work. "One more form and we can track down Alwanga to make that call. With any luck, we'll get an interview tomorrow."

Anna read the screen, then hung her head in search of the next document on her lap. Jack wished he could tuck her hair behind her ear for her. Tell her it was okay to let go and cry out all the stress, the way he'd done years ago. Make it right. But that wasn't possible, because time changed things. It changed people. There was no happy solution. Two different people. Two different sides of the world. One child caught in the middle.

He accepted the paper from her and finished up the online application.

"Anna, wait," he said, as she gathered her purse. He reached into his back pocket and handed her an envelope with the vouchers he'd printed while Dr. Alwanga showed the group his department.

"I had reward miles," Jack admitted, realizing a second too late how stupid that sounded. He couldn't help being a little nervous. This had to work. "These vouchers are enough for two tickets. I meant it when I said that I hadn't bought Pippa a ticket out of here yet. These are for both of you. Round trip."

Granted, round trip tickets were more economical, but it was also the only way Anna would give him a chance to prove life with him would be better for Pippa. Maybe they could do this without a fight.

"You know I don't want to leave her here, but I don't have much choice," he added. "Miller wants me back and there's no way her passport and documents will be ready before I leave. It'll probably be a few weeks, even if they're expedited, but I want you to bring her to Pennsylvania. I'm *asking* you to bring her. Alwanga said he could get temporary help from the university's vet program to cover for you with Kamau."

"Is this some sort of sick joke? Use your charm to lure me this far, then get me to put her right in your hands, knowing power will be on your side once she's in the States?"

"No! Anna, if the situation was any different, you wouldn't hesitate to let her visit her grandparents and cousins. I realize you've found the perfect spot to hide out, pretend your life never happened, but you can't do that to her. She's not a secret anymore. Keep doing this to her and you're the one she'll grow up resenting. Pippa has a right to meet her relatives. My family has a right to meet her, as much as your parents do."

"My parents? You have no right to tell me how to handle my parents."

"No more right than you had to keep my daughter from me."

Anna glared up at him, her face mere inches from his. Then she turned abruptly and left. And Jack knew in spite of the deep-seated feelings he still had for her, they could never be a family with Pippa. Building a family required trust and forgiveness, an ability Anna had lost...and Jack had never had.

ANNA TOOK A DEEP BREATH and did a slow mental count as she released it. She and Jack sat patiently in two chairs flanking a desk at the American Citizens Services, waiting for the woman behind it to check the paperwork. She pushed another sheet toward Anna.

"I'll need your signatures on this one, too, please."

Anna let Pippa climb off her lap and onto Jack's, then leaned forward and signed, holding extra tight to the pen to keep her hand from shaking. She passed the sheet to Jack, who had no problem reaching over Pippa's head and scrawling his name.

"Let's see," the woman said. "I believe I have all I need. I'll try to expedite this, but I can't promise anything."

"We appreciate it," Jack said.

She placed her hands on her desk and smiled. "They do unique and beautiful ethnic ceremonies in many of the lodges near where you live, Dr. Bekker. Are you two planning to get married there?"

"No," Jack and Anna said simultaneously.

Anna hoped the woman would assume they just meant not specifically there. She was in no mood for judgment or an awkward social situation.

"I'm sorry. I shouldn't have assumed. The three of you paint such a pretty family picture."

Yep. And pictures only show the surface. Not the reality.

"And you, my dear—" she tilted her chin down at Pippa "—are adorable. Has anyone told you how pretty you are?"

"Yes," Pippa said honestly.

The woman got up and Anna and Jack followed suit.

"Thank you so much," Anna said, extending her hand.

She was dying to get out of there. Needed to exit the building and let her body breathe. It was done. Over. Five years of worrying, imagining this moment and letting anticipation anxiety plague her dreams...and it was over. Her energy fizzled into the sidewalk as she waited for Jack to call Dr. Alwanga and let him know they were ready.

They were scheduled to meet up with the others and get some more shopping done before the end of the day. Maybe they'd catch a few sights. Anna needed a distraction. Something to clear her mind.

It would give Jack a chance to share more experiences with Pippa, because no matter what he'd said or how right he might have been, Anna knew she wasn't going to use those tickets. Going back was asking too much.

CHAPTER SEVEN

HE WAS GONE.

No sightseeing. No hanging out. No pretending, for just a day, that they were carefree.

Anna latched the hotel room door behind Niara, the kids and Dr. Alwanga's sister, who'd come to pick them up for a trip to the open market before dinner. Niara wanted to shop at Nakumatt, a Walmart-like chain. She seemed happy. As if she'd rediscovered her inner girl. The fact that Jack had warned Alwanga off—like a big brother—had made Anna's heart ache with gratitude…and something deeper she wouldn't let herself explore. He'd done the right thing, as Jack always did.

Dr. Alwanga was waiting for them downstairs, but Anna needed to be alone. After collecting Jack, Pippa and her from their appointment at the embassy, he'd driven straight to the airport. It wasn't until the runways were in sight that Anna had realized what was going on.

Jack hadn't told her specifically when he was leaving. Somehow, she'd assumed he'd be returning to Busara with them before doing so. Instead, she'd found herself breathing in taxi exhaust as Jack hugged Pippa tight. The only betrayal of emotion was the flush of his face as he buried it in the crook of her little neck, whispering promises of seeing her soon.

He was counting on Anna using those tickets. She'd stayed silent. Then there'd been the awkward moment, when he and Anna just stood there. Families around them hugged and kissed their goodbyes. Real families, or so they seemed. One never knew. He'd finally pulled her into a brief hug and kissed her forehead tenderly. And then he'd disappeared into the terminal.

Just like that.

He was gone.

It was over.

Anna leaned her back against the hotel room door and slid down it to crouch on her heels. She could still feel the warmth of his lips on her skin. She pressed her palms against her forehead and sucked in a sudden gasp of

air. She held her breath against the next gasp
until her head pounded and blood rushed in
her ears. Her breath forced its way out with a
sob and she gripped fistfuls of hair in a futile
attempt at control.

She didn't know what she wanted. She
wanted Pippa. She wanted her life's work at
Busara. She wanted the family she used to
dream of. She wanted… Another gasp escaped, this time followed rapidly by more.
Then the tears poured uncontrollably, like the
rain she'd prayed so hard for, only with each
drop her life drained away.

TWO WEEKS OF HEARING Pippa ask incessantly
about her daddy was wreaking havoc on Anna's patience and peace. Not that she had any
peace of heart or mind to mess with. Anna
hadn't heard from Jack. Dr. Miller, on the
other hand, had emailed her more in the past
week than he had in three months. He needed
to meet with her—undoubtedly a vein of pressure Jack had tapped into. It didn't bode well
for her or Busara. If Miller really wanted to
meet, he could come to Kenya or she could
go into Nairobi and find somewhere to talk

on Skype with him. Modern technology. She didn't have to go to the States.

She replaced the recording device and got back in the Jeep. The herds were thinning. Moving farther from camp, probably closer to the river she'd pointed out to Jack from Mac's chopper. The ebb and flow of animals in search of water happened annually, but this year was worse than before. This drought was threatening everything, including her research. They couldn't afford to move camp, which meant if the herds wandered far enough, she wouldn't get good data. And without productivity, she couldn't justify her expenses to Miller, or her presence to the Kenyan immigration officials.

She stepped on the gas pedal and adjusted gears. Another orphan had joined them two days ago and she needed to do rounds. They would run out of enclosures soon, not to mention adequate staff and food for the ravenous beasty babies. Research aside, she couldn't abandon those calves. She needed to be able to take care of them. She wanted Busara to expand. She wanted to do so much more. And what killed her the most was that it wasn't the drought that had taken their mothers. The increase in orphans meant an increase in poaching, and Busara wasn't the only facility taking elephants in. The numbers were disheartening.

She rounded a copse of trees and flattened a trail through the tall, brown savannah grass. Spotting the camp not far ahead, she slowed to a safer pace. At this hour, the kids would be out playing, or tossing fruit to Ambosi.

She parked the Jeep and lugged her equipment to the clinic. Kamau stood at the counter stocking his repurposed toolbox with emergency meds and tranquilizer darts for the road.

"Hey," Anna said, walking through to set her stuff in the back room.

"Hey." He kept on stocking. Anna came back out and took the patient log off the wall hook. "Another email came from Miller," Kamau said.

"What's new?" He'd been bombarding her with them. All or none. Either drought or monsoon.

"Look, Anna." Kamau put a vial down with a tad too much force and turned. "Just go. Deal with the man, but this...this not knowing? It's affecting more than just you. We need to know what's happening to this place. Are we losing funding or not? If we must close down, then when? We have animals to relocate. People, Anna, people who need to figure out their next step."

Like himself? Was he saying he was out? She couldn't have him leave and have the staff fall apart before Busara had a chance. She needed him to make Busara work.

"I'm not trying to mess up everyone's lives. I don't control the rain or the wind or the sun, Kam." She dropped the clipboard onto the counter with a clank. "Did I ask for any of this?"

"You had to have known it would happen at some point."

"I'm talking about funding. The tie to Jack was a coincidence."

"Was it? Do you seriously believe Miller didn't orchestrate this? How naive can you be, Anna? He knew exactly what he was doing, sending Jack here. When I first told you about Miller sending someone, I had no idea it would be someone from your past. Someone important to you. Ah," Kamau said holding his palm up when she started to protest.

"I've seen the way you look at each other. I bet Miller was counting on that."

Anna shook her head in denial, but inside, the truth resonated. Of course Miller had to have known, and as much as she'd chosen to believe he was always on her side, he wasn't. Not anymore. People did whatever worked to their advantage. The story of her life.

"You call Niara your best friend," Kamau said, softening his tone. "Have you for one minute thought about what she's feeling? If you have to move back to the States with Pippa, where does that leave her? Alone. Nowhere to go. You're all she has. She can't follow you, Anna. You need to decide what you're going to do, so the rest of us can plan our lives."

You call Niara your best friend.

His words opened a dark door. Did he really think she would turn her back on Niara without a second thought? Anna pressed her palms against her brow then raked her hair back with her fingers. He was assuming she was capable of letting down friends because she'd abandoned Jack and kept his daughter a secret. Kam was her friend, too, but he didn't know all about Anna's history. Even if he did, Kamau was a man. He was probably identifying with Jack more than Anna. He was judging her like everyone else would, her parents included. He didn't understand that Anna would never turn her back on Niara. He didn't know about the guilt she'd lived with all these years, staying so far away from her mother, though she knew she was doing what was best for Pippa when she kept her pregnancy from Jack.

"I'm not going anywhere, so everything you're saying is a nonissue. We'll find our own funding if we have to. I'm not abandoning these animals or our home, and research or not, I'll find a way to stay in Kenya. It's where I belong."

Anna grabbed the clipboard and started flipping sheets. Niara and Haki. Ahron, Kamau and everyone else. Kamau was right. What would happen to them? This wasn't just about her and Pippa. How could she be so selfish? If there was anyone she owed loyalty to it was Niara. Which was exactly why Anna needed to figure out how to help her friend and save their home. She sighed and let her arms fall to her sides, the clipboard papers falling upside down.

"I'll fix this, Kamau. I'll fix it. But don't underestimate Niara. She's stronger than all of us put together." *And I'm going to help her. I'm going to help both of you.*

Kamau resumed stocking his supplies, his back to her. "Maybe so," he said.

"Oh, I know so. You should have seen her in Nairobi. Smiling, full of energy. She had a great time going shopping with Dr. Alwanga and his sister. Good-looking, educated family, I might add. Niara loves children and is a natural teacher. If she ever wanted to go get a degree, I'm sure he—"

"Do you have a point?" Kamau said, glaring at her over his shoulder. That was the very reaction Anna had hoped for.

"Yes. And I believe you just made it."

ANNA RAN HER HAND soothingly up and down the new baby's trunk. The little elephant flapped her ears once, then curled her trunk loosely on Anna's arm. She hadn't been named yet. First, there had been the trip to the city, then the kids had been preoccupied with all the new workbooks and storybooks Niara had picked up. They said they might find a name in one of the books.

Anna held on to the bottle of formula the calf had been refusing to take from the keeper, hoping she would take an interest in eating if she wasn't forced. "Hey, girl. It's going to be okay. You just have to drink this. For me, sweetie. Just a taste. Please," Anna crooned. It wasn't working.

Anna heard Bakhari shuffling on the other side of the pen. The elephants were socialized in a larger enclosure, but only if they had healed from any surgeries and there was no danger of bandages or stitches coming loose. Bakhari had recently spent time with other orphans, but this one hadn't been introduced yet. She was too young and weak. Anna looked at Ahron, who stood back, waiting to see if she'd have better luck.

"Ahron, let's take this side down, make this pen big enough for two."

He jumped into action, understanding her intention without explanation. Good help was hard to find. Staff who could read your mind? Priceless. Anna kept coddling and crooning to the calf, though she knew nothing she did could replace her mother's love. Or maybe… Maybe she was wrong. Anna thought about Jack and how his adoptive parents had given him more love than anyone he'd known before them. She thought of the elephant orphans being taken in by adoptive mothers from their own or different herds. She thought of rambunctious Ambosi. It didn't matter where love came from, as long as it was there.

Kamau was right about Niara. Anna loved everyone here like family, but had she been holding them back? She'd taken for granted that they were all here for each other on a daily basis. Niara had always said she was happy, but what if she was silently refusing to move on with her life, live anywhere else, because she felt Anna needed her? Anna had never thought of herself as being needy. No. She was a hard worker. Tough, because she had to be, for everyone here. For Pippa and Haki, too. That proved she wasn't needy. Didn't it? But what if Niara *did* want more?

All this time and not once had her shy friend let on that she liked Kamau—until Anna had caught on to the signs a few weeks ago. Even then, when asked, Niara had denied the attraction, though Anna knew better. And after Kam's reaction to that mention of Dr. Alwanga, he apparently liked Niara, too. How could Anna have been so blind? Just because she no longer believed in her own happily-ever-after, that didn't mean it wasn't possible for someone else. Two deserving people like Kamau and Niara who, despite living in a tiny camp, never spent time really getting to know each other because of Anna. Because of the kids. Maybe if Anna wasn't around for just a little while… Maybe if she got on with her own life…

She rested her head gently on the calf's forehead and closed her eyes. "Come on, baby," she whispered.

Ahron led Bakhari next to the calf and offered him a bottle. Bakhari went at it in noisy gluttony. The calf watched with dull, tired eyes. Anna moved to the side, letting the baby reach out to smell Bakhari with her trunk. She touched the bottom of his bottle. Ahron glanced at Anna and she cocked her head at the two.

Please. Please. Please.

She held the bottle within easy reach. The calf moved closer to Bakhari, feeling, smelling her way. Then Anna's pulse kicked up.

Yes. Yes. Yes.

The tiny elephant reached for the bottle she held out, hesitating once before beginning to suckle. Anna looked at Ahron, wide-eyed, but afraid to utter a sound until the bottle was finished. Bakhari drained his first, of course, then went about welcoming his new friend. Something about the two made her think of Haki and Pippa.

Friendships. Families.

Anna had lost both in the past. Losing them again was not an option.

The question was, which ones to save, and which to let go?

"WHEN IS DADDY coming back?"

Pippa sat on her heels in front of Anna. Anna looked left and right on the cot. She'd put an elastic down somewhere. Where did it go?

"Sweetie, I don't know." She craned her neck and found it behind her, then picked it up and wrapped it around the end of the French braid she'd woven into her daughter's hair. A third attempt.

"But I miss him. Do Bakhari and Jomo miss dehr daddies?" Pippa asked, reaching back to feel the end of the braid. Anna noticed she hadn't asked if they missed their mommies. Pippa didn't identify with that. She'd always had Anna around.

"I'm sure they do."

"Will dey ever see 'em again?"

Anna's heart broke in half. How could she answer that without taking away part of Pippa's innocence? She was too young to deal with harsh realities. Anna thought of how she and Jack weren't parenting together. Maybe Pippa was already dealing with more than she was ready for. She was trying to figure out if she'd ever see her daddy again.

"I don't know for sure. Perhaps they'll find them after they're older and released to the wild." That was the best Anna could do.

Curls started springing out from the braid. A record minute. Anna gave up and took out the elastic, then pulled the curls gently apart. She grabbed the large-tooth comb, the only thing that wouldn't snag Pippa's tangles too badly, and got to work. Wild hair. How appropriate.

"Daddy promised he'd see me again and play chopper."

"He did, did he?" Anna pulled Pippa up onto the bed and picked up a book from the table next to it. A story would get her mind off things.

"Yes. And a promise is a promise. You said dat."

Anna closed the book. Perhaps a story wasn't enough. Pippa needed to get away. Expand her horizons. She was too curious and high-energy not to. And Anna needed her to stop dwelling on Jack.

"Let's go find Auntie Niara. I have an idea."

"ARE YOU ABSOLUTELY SURE? I could cancel," Anna said, zipping her bag shut and triple-checking that she had everything required within easy reach. She hadn't left camp for this long in a while, and not for a non-work-related purpose. There were a few years when the rainy season had been so bad she'd taken Niara and the kids to stay in Nairobi, but they'd been together. Not like this mother-daughter trip to get away and give Niara some space with Kamau. If this was all wrong, Anna would never forgive herself.

"We'll be fine. You'll be fine," Niara said.

"But—"

"No buts." She gave Anna a big hug, then held her at arm's length. "Listen to me. I trust him. Okay? I know you do, too. This place is in good hands with Kamau. You need to concentrate on what you need to do. And don't be afraid to enjoy yourself a little."

"I don't know about enjoy, but I promise we'll be back in just a week." The longest week of her life.

"Haki made a calendar. He said he'll be marking it off daily."

"Oh, poor thing," Anna said, looking out the screen to where the kids were already near the Jeep, where everyone had gathered to see them off. "Tell him I'll be bringing back a present. I'll think of something good."

"Just be safe."

They hugged once more and headed outside. One by one, the keepers shook her hand, out of respect. Kamau extended his, but Anna closed the gap and gave him a hug.

"Take care of them," she whispered. She looked back at Niara and Haki, and grinned when she caught Pippa giving Haki the most heartwarming hug.

"Okay, Pippa, sweetie. Time to go."

Everyone backed away from the Jeep to

172 THE PROMISE OF RAIN

make way for them. Anna smiled at her personal escort in the driver's seat.

"Ready for an adventure?" he said.

"As ready as I'll ever be, Mac."

CHAPTER EIGHT

JACK TOOK THE RESULTS of their latest radioim-
munoassay from his new lab tech and flipped
through them blindly. *Focus.* His ability to
concentrate, since he'd gotten back from
Kenya, had been about as reliable as his last
lab technician. The one who'd quit—after
ruining a batch of samples—while Jack was
in Kenya. How was this place running any
more efficiently than Anna's? He raked his
hair back, then plopped the papers onto his
desk and scooted his chair back. The clock in
the corner of the lab read 3:02 p.m. There was
no way he was getting anything done today.
He felt like a guy in a room with nothing but
cactus plants to sit on.

His tech looked at him expectantly.

"Thanks, I'll go through these this afternoon," Jack said. "Run the next sample. I'll be
in the EM room." No one was using the elec-
tron microscope right now. It would be quiet.

"Okay." The tech pulled a rack of tubes out of the freezer and set them down next to the centrifuge to thaw.

"And don't forget to go get your badge read today," Jack added, relieved he wasn't too distracted to remember important obligations. Anyone working in a lab that used radioactive isotopes had to wear a badge that kept track of exposure. Jack took safety seriously, unlike some. How anyone could eat lunch in a no-food-zone lab that housed tissue samples, viral DNA and radioactive material beat the crap out of him. That's what protocol was for. To keep people from letting their guard down once they became too comfortable with their surroundings.

Like Anna in Africa.

The lab's phone rang just as Jack opened the door to leave. His tech started removing one glove to answer it, a small act that Jack found extremely reassuring. His ex-tech had never fully grasped the concept that sterile gloves were not sterile once used, and touching the phone with one would contaminate it. Good help was really hard to find, but things were looking promising.

"It's okay, I got it," Jack said, letting the lab

door shut. He picked up, regretting it when he heard his sister's greeting. So much for avoidance.

"Zoe? Why are you calling the lab?"

"You haven't answered your cell or my messages all day."

Jack heard kids yakking in the background. Probably rummaging for after-school snacks, he figured, glancing again at his watch. She was right about his phone, only he hadn't answered it for a very good reason.

"I'm making dinner tonight," she said. *That* reason.

"You don't have to, seriously. Pick a different night. Any other night this week and I'll bring dessert," he said, hoping she'd listen to reason.

"I already started it. Dessert, too. If I waited for you to answer my calls, everyone would end up eating frozen food."

"Everyone? Ben's not back, is he?" Her husband, Ben, was deployed overseas and had been gone a month since his last leave ended. His deployments were usually much longer than that.

"No. I wish. But Mom and Dad are coming over. Mom said she'd skip her book club."

Oh, man. Dinner with the entire family? Tonight? He winced. Too much, too fast. And Mom never skipped book club. Jack sighed and tapped the receiver against his forehead.

"Stop that," Zoe said. "You have a hard head. It's louder than my kids. Look, Jack. You're at work. It's not like you'll have time to cook. And we've hardly seen you since you returned."

Jack didn't answer for a good six seconds. He watched the clock tick away. There was no getting out of this. Zoe didn't say a word, but he could hear Maddie arguing with Chad in the background over his double-dipping of a carrot stick. Didn't even have Jack's genes and she was anti double-dipping. Smart kid. She'd make a great babysitter for Pippa.

"Okay. I give up. See you around seven-thirty." He was going to regret this. He was doomed from hello.

"Yes! And, Jack, ignore my last voice message. I was a bit annoyed, but you're totally forgiven now and I love you."

"Right." Jack hung up and left the lab. The EM room was at the end of the hall, just past five labs that comprised Dr. Miller's domain, when he wasn't in the admin wing. They'd tactfully avoided each other since Jack's return. Jack had left his report regarding Busara on Miller's desk, but hadn't heard from him.

Jack wasn't sure if he was angry or grateful to the guy. Either way, he didn't feel like dealing with an awkward conversation. There wasn't a way to discuss what had happened without getting personal, and Jack didn't need his personal business colonizing the department like strep in a petri dish.

"Jack."

Great. So much for that. He might as well be wearing a shirt that said Bug Me today. Jack stopped, tucked his hands into his lab coat pockets and turned as casually as possible.

Miller sat behind his desk in a small office next door to his main lab. "Have a second?" he asked.

Not really. Jack walked into the office, willing himself not to lose it. He checked his watch, taking an extra long second to do so. "I'm actually running a tight schedule today," he said, not bothering to sit in the chair in front of Dr. Miller's desk.

"Yes, yes. However, I wanted to touch base

with you about Dr. Bekker and Busara. I read your notes."

"And that's all I have to say about it. Don't involve me in this anymore."

"But you are involved. I sent you with a purpose," Miller said, impatience seeping through the subtext of his words. Oh, he'd sent him with a purpose, all right.

A burning heat rose up Jack's chest and through his face. He shut the office door, and leaned forward, bracing his hands on Miller's desk. His colleague relaxed back in his chair, trying to look casual, but effectively putting distance between Jack and himself. Probably wise.

"And which purpose was that?" Jack asked.

"The report, of course. The funds for our project. You can't climb the ranks without expecting to deal with logistics."

"The report? Logistics? You knew, didn't you? You sent me to Kenya knowing I had a daughter there. How long, Bob? How long did you know and not tell me? A year? Two? The entire time?"

"Now, wait a minute. I didn't know she was yours. Not for sure. I knew Dr. Bekker had a child. She was up front with me about that.

Had to be, given the accommodations, visas, divulging who stayed at the camp…. It wasn't my business to ask who the father was."

"You didn't *want* to. There's a difference."

"You know, an employer can get in trouble for asking the wrong questions."

"Give me a break. This department isn't that big. She was more than an average employee. She spoke about you like a father figure."

Miller sighed and pushed his chair away from the desk.

"Look. It wasn't any secret around campus that you two were old friends. Faculty and staff talk. We're not a stupid bunch here," Miller said, waving a hand at their surroundings. "Out of the blue, you two stopped talking, or even asking about each other. The timing was suspicious. I didn't really know you personally back then, but I knew Anna. I tried talking her into coming back, even to visit, but with no luck. I figured if there really was anything to be sorted out between you, it would be. Technically, it wasn't any of my business. But then you and I started this project together, and…and…a couple of months ago, my daughter had a baby. My first grandchild. The father asked her to marry him in the hospital room."

"Congratulations. But that has nothing to do with me discovering I have a daughter," Jack said. The weasel's justifications weren't going to cut it.

"But it does. I realized in that moment, seeing the look in my son-in-law's eyes, that every parent has a right at a chance. If they screw it up, so be it. But they have a right to try. You had a right to know. You were going to Kenya for that lecture, and there was no harm in sending you to Busara. If Anna's child turned out to be yours, then I did the right thing. If not, no harm done."

"No harm done? Five years. Five. Years. I don't see how acting now absolves you of keeping my daughter a secret all that time. Of trying to use me against Anna. Did it just happen to make financial sense now? What if my child had gotten sick there? What if she'd gotten malaria? Or bitten…or worse? Then what? Would you have kept your suspicions to yourself forever, so that you wouldn't be held liable for having allowed a child to live at one of the research facilities? You could have told me Anna had a child from the beginning."

"I didn't know she was—"

"You knew enough." Jack slammed his hands on the table, then turned and left. He didn't stop at the EM lab, or the elevator. He needed air. Space. He descended five flights of stairs, exited the building and didn't stop until he'd reached his car. He needed to drive, to think, to put things in perspective. He reached for his keys and realized he was still wearing his lab coat.

Seriously? He'd scheduled a day off tomorrow and needed to leave a to-do list for his tech. And he never left campus with his lab coat on. If this day was foreshadowing how the evening would go, he was in trouble. *Chill. You're stressed and probably blew any chance at tenure through a black hole, but you're not Miller's puppet. You can make this right.*

Jack walked back at a deliberate, controlled pace. A humid breeze cleansed his face. He took a deep breath of fall air and gave a silent, obligatory wave to a group of sophomore vet students who'd called out to him. The same group of young women who'd made a habit of sitting at whatever table was next to his in the cafeteria, whenever he went there. The past couple of weeks he'd started packing lunch and eating outside for that reason. Anna wasn't his, but having anyone else show the slightest interest made him feel like a traitor. As if he wasn't one already.

He cut across the lawn, where several students sat on blankets with their noses in textbooks. The bright sun reminded him of Kenya, but the lush, verdant lawn was so different from the desiccated soil and grasslands surrounding Busara. The tall, erect evergreens gracing the university grounds...so different from the sprawling, horizontal branches of the acacia trees. He pictured Anna perched on that platform of hers, under her precious shade. He should have taken a picture of her sitting there. His memory would have to do. Once the research project he and Miller had presented in their last abstract started, he wouldn't have time to go back and visit.

He took care of lab business and was back at his car within fifteen minutes. He looked at the clock on the dash. He still had a couple hours to kill, if they didn't kill him first.

He took a left off campus and headed toward the same toy store he and his sister had practically lived in after his adoption. He needed to get Pippa something. Zoe had loved dolls back then, the kind that ate, peed and pooped like real babies. Only disease-proof.

Pippa would probably think it was cool, but a fake baby as a gift? Something told him Anna wouldn't find that funny at all.

ANNA FELT LIKE a foreigner. Like a crippled gazelle stuck in a stampede of kin escaping a predator. She clutched Pippa's hand tighter and lugged their carry-ons to the edge of the crowd exiting the international arrival area.

What am I doing here?

Proving you're not selfish. That Pippa comes first. And making sure Mom will be okay.

The words had been running through her head ever since they'd landed. Exhaustion? Nerves? It didn't matter. She'd made a choice and there was no turning back. No hiding. At least, not with the mega-high-tech airport security she'd just survived.

She looked at Pippa for reassurance. Her daughter had slept on the last leg of the flight, limp and drained from all the excitement. Clearly, the nap had done its job. She bounced up and down now, her sleep-ravaged curls following suit. *You're doing this for her. One week and you'll be back home.*

"Mama, I need to go pee."

"Now?" Anna asked rhetorically. Of course she meant *now*—the worst time possible. And why did kids jump when they had to pee? Didn't that make it worse? Anna had tried taking her before landing, but the line on the plane had been too long. She scanned the area and spotted a women's restroom.

"Okay, let's hurry."

JACK SWORE UNDER HIS BREATH. He should have known she'd change her mind at the last minute. He'd put the power in her hands, so to speak, giving her those tickets. What more could he do to get through to her? To get her guard down long enough for one visit?

He'd move the universe to keep his daughter in the States, but he knew now that wasn't going to happen by butting heads with Anna. He needed—wanted—to see both of them, but he also wanted Anna to see Pippa in his home, around her cousins. Alienating herself was one thing. Alienating her daughter was entirely different. If she could just see how comfortable Pippa would be, then maybe Anna would come to the right conclusion on her own. Work with him to do what was best for their daughter.

But that wasn't going to happen.

She hadn't come.

Jack dodged the crowds around the luggage carousels and went to check the flight arrivals one last time. The plane had arrived, and yes, he was at the right baggage claim.

Anna and Pippa simply weren't here.

The anticipation that had buzzed in his chest now twisted in his throat. Not coming proved that she didn't care about him, about his feelings as a father…and that she didn't trust him. He turned away from the reunited families laughing and embracing and catching up while waiting for the last of the luggage to make its way around the belt. Jack headed for the glass doors, the skin on his face numb to the cool, early-evening air.

"Jack!"

"Anna?" He turned. Relief washed over him at the sight of them. They were here!

She'd scooped Pippa up by the waist like a rag doll and was running toward him, almost stumbling over her wheeled carry-on when she tried to avoid a man and his load. "Jack! Wait!"

He ran toward them and grabbed Pippa, pulling her into a squeeze.

"Hey, little monkey," he said, burying his face in her hair to mask the second he needed to gather himself. "I missed you."

"I missed *you,* Daddy," Pippa said, placing her palms against his cheeks and patting them. "I know where cotton comes from."

"You do?" Jack looked at Anna. She stood there, biting her lip, frazzled and oh, so beautiful. She'd come. They were here. The reality of it was just sinking in.

"Hey, you," he said. "Thank you for coming."

He hesitated, then leaned forward and kissed her on the cheek. Friends did that all the time. It didn't mean anything and certainly wasn't enough to spook her. He hoped. Pulling Anna into his arms the way his instincts screamed for him to do certainly would have.

She blushed and a tiny, tired smile relaxed her face. "Hey," she said, then cocked her head toward Pippa. "Clouds."

"Clouds? Oh, *clouds.*" Jack laughed and felt the tension leave his body.

"Cotton comes from up dehr," Pippa said, pointing up.

"Does it, now?" He grinned. "Let's get your luggage and head out. There are very special people waiting to meet you."

"People?" Anna said. "Jack, it's after midnight for us. We're exhausted. I'm tired and... gross." She motioned toward her body.

There was nothing gross about her. As far as Jack was concerned, she'd look wonderful even if she'd taken a mud bath with an elephant.

"Anna, I tried getting them to wait, but my sister, her kids and my parents are dying to meet Pippa and see you, too. We'll stop by my place first and you can freshen up. I'll make a pot of coffee, and we'll leave her house early. Promise. Besides, pushing through it is the best way to get over jet lag. Trust me."

"I thought I asked you to book a hotel room," she said, pointing to a green suitcase with brown straps coming around the carousel.

"You did," he said over his shoulder as he grabbed it, followed by another she pointed to.

"That's all of them," she said. They headed out. "Can we just stop at the hotel first?"

"I didn't book one. Anna, there's plenty of room at my place. It's a two-bedroom apartment, and I've already fixed one room up for Pippa. You can have the other, or stay with her if you prefer, and I'll take the couch. There's no point in paying for a hotel. I want to spend every last minute with her, and that includes waffle breakfasts," he said, directing the last words at Pippa.

"What's a waffle?" she asked.

"What's a waffle? That's criminal," he said, looking pointedly at Anna. She shrugged. He hoisted Pippa into the spare car seat his sister had loaned him and helped him secure in his car earlier in the week. "Well, it's as sweet and delicious as you are, and you'll get to try one tomorrow morning."

He opened the front passenger door for Anna.

"Okay. First stop, home."

FIRST STOP, HOME?

Anna slipped the seat belt over her shoulder and snapped it in. *Home?* Pennsylvania would never be home again. Home was somewhere a person felt safe and loved. This place held nothing but disappointment in others and in herself. She was here to do what was right— to let Pippa have a relationship with her father and relatives. That was it. *Home?* They'd be back *home* in a week.

She twisted around to check on Pippa, who swung her legs as they dangled from the car seat and stared out the window with her mouth gaping. He'd brought a car seat. Anna closed her eyes briefly. Oh, no. He probably thought she was a terrible mother for taking Pippa around without one in Kenya. He'd hold it against her. Anna rubbed her face and smoothed her hair back. This…this…paranoia. She had to stop. It had to be fatigue. She'd barely been able to sleep during the flight.

"Thanks for bringing a car seat," she said, focusing on the street signs they passed, rather than looking at Jack, no matter how much she wanted to. Some of the landmarks had changed since she'd last been here. It took a second to register that an entire block of trees was missing, replaced with a shopping center. But even the things that hadn't changed brought her an uncomfortable sense of déjà vu, rather than comforting familiarity or nostalgia. And she'd forgotten how fall was her favorite season. Colors had yet to peak, but the change had begun. Still, the grass and pines were so…green. It almost seemed unfair, given how badly they needed rain back home.

"No problem. Zoe helped with that."

Anna remembered Zoe. She'd always been kind. A sweet mom. Peppy.

"How is she?"

"Zoe's great. I don't know how she manages with Ben overseas, but she does. A downright Wonder Woman. She has two kids now. You probably remember Maddie? She's really grown. Eight years old. Chad is three. Pippa will have a blast with them."

Anna nodded and stayed quiet as Jack spoke excitedly to Pippa about everything she was seeing and everything they'd be doing.

Anna wouldn't have a blast tonight. Jack's entire family probably hated her for keeping Pippa from them…from Jack. Going to dinner would be like walking into the lions' den. With her baby. *This is stupid. They'll try to keep her.* No. She had to pull herself together. He'd left her with tickets. She had to keep reminding herself of that fact. He didn't stay in Kenya long enough to leave with his daughter. He hadn't fought her, but had trusted her to bring Pippa to see him. That had to count for something.

Anna could see her alma mater in the distance, but Jack took a left into a gated apartment community. This wasn't anything like the student housing near campus he'd used to live in. The units here were brick-faced with white-trimmed balconies, many of which were decorated with hanging baskets of ferns and ivy. Rows of holly bushes with pansies in front of them grounded the building foundations. The sidewalks leading up to each cluster of apartments were separated by well-manicured—and fertilized—lawns. Anna had no doubt a place like this had a swimming pool tucked away for the residents. The monthly rent had to be steep.

Jack's unit was halfway into the complex. Anna waited for him to lead the way. His apartment was masculine. Quite sparse, actually, save for floor-to-ceiling wooden bookshelves and a telescope on a stand near the balcony. A dark red afghan carpet anchored a leather sofa, an armchair with matching ottoman and a mission-style coffee table.

Anna wasn't one for frills, so she didn't mind at all. In fact, the couch looked so inviting she was tempted to take it over a bed.

She did want privacy, though. It wasn't until she'd reached the center of the room that she noticed the fireplace. On the mantel was a line of carved wooden elephants, arranged according to size. She'd seen similar carvings in shops in Nairobi. He'd bought the elephants there. Something pinched in her chest and she took a deep breath to gather herself. The table by the sofa had a framed picture on it. Anna stepped closer. It was of her carrying Pippa while reaching out to pet Bakhari's trunk. They were all smiling. Even Bakhari. Anna had no idea Jack had taken that photo.

Pippa ran and jumped onto the sofa, distracting Anna. "No jumping, Pippa," she said. She never had to worry about her breaking things at Busara. Everything was so meticulous here, she half expected Jack to say something about house rules. But instead, she turned and caught him standing in the doorway, staring at her.

He didn't bother masking the fact that he was watching her. For a moment, Anna could have sworn she saw longing in his eyes, a tenderness she wanted to believe in. But that was nothing but the old her—the once misguidedly romantic her—surfacing for a last breath. He didn't want her. He wanted her co-operation with Pippa, wanted to make things right. Nothing more. Which was just fine with Anna, because she no longer believed in more.

She motioned toward a pair of running shoes parked neatly by the door.

"You've taken up running?"

"And swimming. I'm not a total lab rat," he said, quirking the corner of his mouth in a small, self-deprecating smile. "Pippa's room is the first down the hall to the right," he added. He shut the door and motioned for them to go ahead. Pippa beat them both. Jack carried their bags through a door at the end of the hall. Anna followed Pippa into her room.

Her pink room.

Very pink. Jack must have thought it was a required girl color, and that Pippa had been deprived.

Except for the gray stuffed elephants covering her bed, the walls were decorated with framed photographs he'd taken at Busara. Some were aerial views. Anna's eyes stung. Pippa jumped onto the bed and started hugging the animals.

"Look, Mama! Can I name them?"

"Of course you can," Jack said, coming up behind Anna.

"Of course," she repeated, then cleared her throat. "You must like elephants," she said to Jack, trying to laugh off her shock.

"They're special to a certain someone I know, which makes them special to me," he said softly, his breath touching her cheek. She could have stepped farther into the room, away from him, but she didn't. They both watched silently as Pippa named each elephant. He was referring to Pippa, Anna kept telling herself. Pippa was the certain someone.

"There's a bathroom in the other bedroom. I put your bags there so you can freshen up. Don't worry about Pippa. I'll fix her a snack or something and we'll get her ready when you're done."

"Okay," Anna said. She started for the other room. After that long flight, she needed a shower like the Serengeti needed rain.

"Anna," Jack said. She looked back. "Take your time. It's okay to relax."

Okay for you, maybe. I have to face your family.

Anna closed the bedroom door and let out

a long breath. The mere knowledge that she could have a real shower beating down on her stiff neck and muscles—not a bucket shower—felt like the ultimate luxury. She peeled off her stale travel clothes and turned on the bathroom light.

Have mercy a million times over.

A bathtub, and what looked like a brand-new canister of lavender bath salts. She was 100 percent certain lavender salts weren't Jack's style.

They were going to be very, very late to dinner.

SOMEONE REALLY LOVED GARDENING. The sun, slung low in the sky, gave a warm glow to the burgundy, orange and yellow mums in the garden beds that bordered the walkway leading to Jack's sister's house. The tart smell of fresh-burned leaf mulch filled the air. This place looked like a newer build, not the starter home Anna remembered them living in. So storybook perfect. So unlike Busara. It hit Anna what Jack's first impressions of Busara must have been after being accustomed to this. The perfect place his sister was raising her kids. No wonder he'd freaked out about her raising Pippa there. But Anna knew from experience things could look perfect from the outside, and not be on the inside. Manicured lawns did not a happy family make.

She held her breath for the few seconds it took for Zoe to answer the door. Anna felt so much better after the bath, and the buildup of nerves was counteracting any time-difference issues. Still, she couldn't help the apprehension.

How could Jack have agreed to this? As punishment? Some sort of modern-day scarlet letter hanging? She should have feigned travel sickness and stayed back, but then Pippa would have been on her own with so many new faces. Strangers. And Anna wouldn't have known what the Harpers were saying about her. Plotting custody…

Anna's heart hit a record pulse and her palms itched with sweat. She needed to stop before she had an all-out panic attack and appeared crazy. Then they'd really have a case. *Breathe. Just breathe.*

The front door opened.

Zoe was just as pretty as Anna remembered, only instead of loose, she wore her dark, wavy hair up in a practical clip. A little boy clung to her jeans and an older version of the Maddie Anna had met a few times stood behind her, eyeing Pippa.

Zoe held her arms out. "Anna! It's so good to see you. You look great. And this must be Pippa," she said, giving Anna a surprisingly solid hug before kneeling down to greet her niece. "Hi, Pippa. I'm your aunt Zoe and these are your cousins, Chad and Maddie."

Pippa slipped her thumb in her mouth and scooted behind Anna's leg. So not the headstrong four-year-old who gave Haki a hard time. Good thing Anna hadn't chickened out of coming. Pippa needed her.

"I'm sorry," Anna said. "She's really excited about being here, but I think she's a bit tired and overwhelmed." *Ditto for me.*

"Totally understandable," Zoe said, waving her hand dismissively.

"Are you letting us in, sis?" Jack said, with a twisted smile and a twinkle in his eye.

"Oh, my gosh, yes! Come in. I'm so happy you're here, I've forgotten my manners. Out of the way, kids," Zoe said, standing up and scooting her kids aside to make way. "Mom and Dad are in the living room. *They* had enough sense not to crowd the doorway."

Much to Anna's relief, Jack picked Pippa up, unlatching her fingers from Anna's slacks. He seemed to catch on that Pippa would need a buffer to slow the well-intended barrage of hugs and kisses. He was definitely a protective parent, something she could appreciate and understand. Somehow, she wasn't feeling so alone anymore. She wasn't there by herself with Pippa, facing a firing squad. She was there with Jack.

"Mom, Dad, you remember Anna. And this here is Pippa. Give her a minute and you won't be able to get her back in her shell," Jack said, ruffling Pippa's hair. Thumb still in her mouth, Pippa hid her face in his neck. Anna resisted the urge to take her from him and be her shield.

"Mr. and Mrs. Harper," Anna said, extending her hand. Jack had taken their last name as a teenager, a decision that had helped him get over his past. He'd told her about the legal name change their senior year in high school, while they sat in the bleachers long after the game was over and all the other students had gone off to celebrate.

His parents shook her hand, their greetings infinitely more reserved than Zoe's. In all honesty, Anna couldn't blame them. They were his parents, and undoubtedly worried about the situation and their son. Just as Anna was worried for Pippa.

"It's been a long time," Mrs. Harper said. *Well, come right out with the elephant in the room.*

"Yes, it has," Anna said directly. "And you still look wonderful."

"Oh, thank you. I hope you don't mind—I got Pippa a welcome gift."

Mrs. Harper went to a shopping bag in the corner of the room and pulled out a wrapped box. Pink paper. Anna had a clue as to where Jack had gotten his decorating advice.

"Pippa, dear. This is for you," Mrs. Harper said.

"Don't let her take all the credit, now. It's from me, too," Mr. Harper said. "I'll make you a deal. Call me Gramps and you can have the box."

Pippa lifted her head and looked at the present.

"It's a bit heavy, so you might need two hands to carry it," Mrs. Harper said.

Pippa slipped her thumb out of her mouth

and reached for the gift. Jack put her down, then let her take it.

"What do you say first, Pippa?" Anna said.

"Tank you."

"Why don't you go sit on the carpet by the coffee table and open it with Chad and Maddie," Jack said.

"Kids, don't take over. Let her open her own gift," Zoe warned. "Chad loves paper," she explained to Anna.

"Can't blame him. It crumples, rips and makes noise. What's not to love?" Anna smiled, hoping she didn't sound as awkward as she felt. Small talk was her parents' forte, not hers. "I'm so sorry that I didn't bring anything. We should have stopped on the way here for flowers or dessert," she said to Jack.

"Absolutely not," Zoe and Mrs. Harper said simultaneously. This family was so together they even answered in unison.

"We're thankful you made it at all tonight," Jack's mom added. "You must be tired and hungry after your long trip."

"I made lasagna and everything is ready, so why don't we let the kids play, and get started on dinner? They're probably too distracted to join us just yet…and I would *love* to eat in the company of grown-ups," Zoe said.

"Guess I'll go play with the kids then." Jack smirked.

"Very funny," Zoe deadpanned. "Although, perhaps you should. Grown-ups know how to answer their cell phones."

Anna was completely and utterly entertained. Sure, she'd visited the Harpers' a few times, usually brief in-and-outs after school, but she hadn't really seen this side of Jack. The Jack she'd known had been more serious, analyzing his past and planning his future. She hadn't seen this part of him until, well, until he'd met Pippa. Anna tried to mesh the memory of him playing helicopter with her at Busara with the scene now, but it only made her homesick.

"The food smells wonderful," Anna said. Just a few hours. She'd get through this, if she managed to stay awake.

"Zoe's a great cook," Mr. Harper offered. He'd been rather quiet, which Anna took as disapproval. She was used to fatherly disapproval. She was a doctor and researcher. She knew when she was being studied…analyzed.

It made her hyperaware of every word she spoke and every action she took.

They entered the dining room. The table was already set, and everything but the main course was in its place. Anna hoped with every cell of her body that Jack hadn't called and told them they were running late because she was taking her time soaking in a tub. She could hear their reactions. The lazy, self-indulgent mom. No comparison to Zoe.

Mrs. Harper motioned Anna to a chair on the far end of the table, but Mr. Harper stopped her.

"Anna," he said. "Why don't you take that chair, next to Jack."

DINNER WAS EXCELLENT, but there was nothing like pasta to boost sleepiness. That and the fact that everyone was making her feel… comfortable. No one had bitten her head off, or interrogated her about why she'd kept Pippa a secret. They were being careful. No doubt, at Jack's request.

Anna watched from the kitchen doorway as Jack and his dad sat on the floor with the kids, playing with toys that had multiplied since she'd arrived. The kids had taken a break to eat, but were more interested in playing. Pippa fit right in and seemed to know she was the star of the evening. A young Shirley Temple. She'd come out of her shell, no question.

A kiddie computer that taught reading skills sat on a chair. It was an expensive gift, especially with the added cartridges the Harpers had bought, but Pippa had gravitated toward some of Chad's older toys, like wooden puzzles and blocks.

"I hope she likes it," Mrs. Harper said from behind Anna. "It's supposed to make kids more interested in reading. They like anything that talks out loud."

"It's wonderful. Pippa already loves reading and I'm sure this will add a lot of fun to stories for her," Anna said. She was trying to be tactful, but a part of her went on the defensive. She didn't want anyone thinking Pippa was a babe raised by wolves just because she lived in the Serengeti. Anna was a good parent, as was Niara, and with a one-to-one ratio on the homeschooling front, both Pippa and Haki had been early readers. Each child was reading at a grade level above expected.

"Really? She's four, right?" Zoe asked.

"An early reader. She's schooled privately.

Loves books, which is why she'll love that computer. Thanks so much," Anna said.

"I'm impressed," Mrs. Harper said, setting the dish she'd dried in a cabinet. Zoe had sink duty and both had insisted that Anna take it easy, though she'd in turn insisted on at least helping to clear the table. In all honesty, she was ready to leave, but wasn't sure how to get through to Jack without being obvious.

"So, Jack said you work with elephants." Zoe turned off the water and dried her hands.

"Yes. Hopefully, work that will help preserve different subspecies and raise awareness." *Please don't ask how much longer my research will take.*

"Maddie absolutely loves animals, and when she heard Jack telling us about how beautiful the area you live in is, she got all excited. She's been begging him to take her on a visit. She wants to go on an African safari," Zoe said.

Anna was speechless. Jack had told them Busara was beautiful? Had he told them he was returning for a visit, or was that Maddie's suggestion? Because that would change everything she'd assumed about his intentions with Pippa. Or maybe he'd told them he planned on keeping Pippa here, but would bring her to Busara to visit her mom, and take Maddie along. Anna was confused.

"I mean, only if it wasn't an imposition. It wouldn't be for a long time, anyway. School and all. Plus, her dad would have to approve. She wants to be a vet, too, you know," Zoe said.

Anna realized Zoe had mistaken her silence for not wanting visitors at camp. Was Zoe suggesting she mentor Maddie? Mentoring Jack's niece? This was all too weird. They were supposed to hate her. Or was it all part of a big scheme to get her guard down? To make her feel letting Pippa grow up here, with such a wonderful, warm family, would be best?

"Of course it wouldn't be an imposition," Anna quickly said, deciding to leave out any warnings about roughing it. "It'd be a great experience for an aspiring vet." If they didn't get shut down by then. Even so, Anna knew many reserves with summer volunteer programs she could recommend.

"Jack said your friends there were very nice," Mrs. Harper said. *Fishing.*

"They're wonderful."

Mrs. Harper put away the last dish, then

folded her arms and leaned back against the granite counter.

"Anna, I know it's not my business exactly—"

"Mom, can you pull the dessert out of the fridge, please? Let's get it on the table."

"In a minute, Zoe," Mrs. Harper said. She turned to Anna.

"Mom, not now," Jack's sister said. *Bless you, Zoe.* Anna knew what was coming. The inevitable.

"No, I have to say my piece. She's only here a week," Mrs. Harper insisted.

The mix of fatigue, adrenaline, nerves, food and now questions were starting to do a number on Anna's stomach. *Hello, lasagna.*

"Like I said, Anna, I respect privacy, but I'm a mother, and I know you can appreciate how protective we can be. We care about you, too, Anna. Don't think we don't remember how kind and special you were to Jack growing up. You have a good heart. I've seen it. I've also seen how special the two of you were to each other. So I don't understand any of this. I don't understand why you disappeared on him. Why you shut him out. You must know how deep that type of pain goes with him."

That was it. Anna felt her face go hot and the rim of her eyes burn with moisture. Zoe closed her eyes and shook her head.

"Mom." Jack's voice startled Anna. "I hate to interrupt, but we have to get going. If wooden blocks going airborne are a sign, I think Pippa and Chad are getting tired," he said. His timing was almost too perfect. Had he been listening in from the living room?

Anna grabbed for his lifeline. "Yes, airborne blocks are a definite sign. Thank you so much for dinner, Zoe," she said. "It was so nice to see all of you."

Jack's mom had the decency to blush and give Anna a hug. Zoe rushed up and hugged both Anna and her brother. Anna didn't miss the knowing look that passed between them. A big sister buffer.

"Let me pack some cheesecake for you to take with you," Zoe said.

She had the dessert in a plastic container within moments and ushered them out of the kitchen. Many hugs later, Jack, Anna and Pippa were in the car.

Anna turned her face toward the passenger window and closed her eyes.

"You okay?" Jack asked.

She didn't answer. No, she wasn't okay. Far from it. But letting Jack think she'd fallen asleep was easier than facing the facts. Jack had a family and a support system. Anna was the bad guy who'd hurt one of their own. And as far as they were concerned, Pippa was family. Anna was nothing but incidental to them.

Just as she and her mom had been to her dad.

CHAPTER NINE

NO MATTER HOW MUCH she willed it to move, Anna's body didn't want to cooperate. A stream of sunlight came through a gap in the curtain and hit her eyelid. She winced and rolled over onto what felt like clouds. Yes, they were flying through them. She was way too comfortable. Grogginess consumed her.

Wait a minute. She was supposed to be at her tree before sunrise. She needed to drink her last sip of coffee as it broke the horizon. Her ritual. Something was wrong.

She opened her eyes and jolted upright. It took a second for her surroundings to register. Jack's room. She let out a breath of relief and flipped the covers off. Pippa would be up. If she'd woken up already, as disoriented as Anna… She needed to check on her.

Anna walked barefoot down the short hallway. She'd grown so used to slipping sandals on in Busara. She never walked barefoot there. This felt intoxicating.

Pippa's room was empty, but the faint smell of pancakes and coffee lingered in the air. It was too quiet. No sound of cooking utensils clinking. No voices. Anna's chest squeezed and blood rushed. She crossed the empty living room to the kitchen. No one. *No. No. No.*

"Pippa!" she called, knowing there wouldn't be an answer, but hoping she was wrong.

The front door swung open and her hand flew to her chest as she spun around. Jack stood there in jeans and a white T-shirt that said I'm Not Just a Y Chromosome." He held Pippa's hand and a crumpled red-and-white bag.

"Hi. We were wondering if you'd be up yet," he said.

"Pippa, come here, sweetie," Anna said, getting down on her knees and holding her arms out. She needed a hug more than ever. Pippa ran into her arms and planted a wet kiss on her cheek. The sight of Pippa… Gosh, she'd really let her mind go wild.

"You look pale," Jack said. "Are you getting sick?"

Anna slackened her hold on Pippa and

glanced up at him. He had the oddest expression on his face.

"You didn't think…" He shifted his weight and frowned, then looked out the front door, still ajar, and back at her. "You didn't seriously think I'd tricked you and taken—"

"No, I did *not* think that," Anna said, putting her hands over little ears and standing up. Okay. So the thought had sort of crossed her mind, but only for a few seconds.

"The look on your face when we walked in said otherwise," he said, shutting the door and setting the paper bag on the kitchen counter. He ripped a note off the fridge and handed it to her. Anna stared at his perfect, block letters stating that they'd be back soon.

"You walked in before I saw that. I just got up." She let the rest of her excuse die. Jet lag and paranoia.

"We had fun, Mama," Pippa said. "I got a balloon but it popped so we went to a p'aygwound and Daddy had to climb up to get me because I was stuck."

It was Jack's turn to grow pale.

"Uh, she wasn't really stuck. It was no big deal. Just one of those fast-food playgrounds. She got a little panicked up in one of the tunnels. Can't blame her. I felt a little claustro-phobic up there myself."

Anna pictured Jack lugging his big body through kid-sized tunnels…tunnels plastered with the prints of a zillion germy, boogery hands, to save Pippa. Now that was heroic, given how he felt about germs. She had no doubt he'd be changing his clothes.

"Fast food?" she asked.

"Yeah. We had pancakes for breakfast and watched some cartoons. You were still zonked out and I figured you needed some rest, so we went for a walk. By then it was lunchtime so we stopped to eat—"

"Lunch? What time is it?" No way she'd slept that long. Anna felt her wrist, but her watch was in the bedroom. She looked around. No clock. There'd be one on the microwave. She started for the kitchen. Man. She better not have missed the meeting.

"It's one-ten. What's the big deal?"

"I'm supposed to meet with Dr. Miller at three. I made the appointment before getting here."

"Mama, I have a tummy headache," Pippa said, leaning into Anna's leg and rubbing her face against it. Anna picked her up and felt her head. No fever.

"A tummy headache?" Jack asked.

"Anything that hurts is a headache, according to Pippa. Did she eat too much? She's not used to junk food, Jack. Maybe if you go potty, sweetie, you'll feel better."

"She said everything tasted good, and what do you mean, you're meeting with Dr. Miller?" Jack looked downright angry.

"I can't come here and not touch base with him. And I need to make sure everything is going to be okay with Busara's funding. I'm taking her to the bathroom and then I need to get ready. If you don't mind giving us a ride, that is. I could rent a car while we're here—"

"I'll give you a ride."

"Thank you."

"Mama-a-a," Pippa whimpered.

"Okay, to the bathr—"

"Whoa!" Jack jumped back.

Anna glared at him, puke drenching the front of her T-shirt and dripping onto the carpet. Pippa started bawling. Jack covered his mouth and nose with his palm, then ran his hand over his face. Boy, she sure hoped he

had the stomach to handle the smell of sec-
ondhand fast food.

"Um, I'll get paper towels. Don't move,"
he said.

"Afraid we'll dirty more carpet?" Anna
called out. And he thought he could handle
having a kid? She rubbed Pippa's back. "It's
okay. We'll get you washed up in a sec."

Jack came back armed with rubber gloves,
several plastic bags and paper towels. From
the way his face twisted, Anna bet he was
holding his breath. Then again, he'd helped
Kamau at that poaching site. Anna knew from
experience the smell of decaying flesh was far
worse. But there was something about puke…

"Here. Let's get her clothes off and put
them in this. I can run the washer while you
wash her off. You can put your shirt in here,
too," Jack said.

Anna raised her brows at him. "I am *not*
taking my shirt off here."

His eyes widened with the realization of
what he'd just said. "Of course not. Why don't
you wipe as much off as you can."

Anna knew he was focused on cleaning up
and not spreading the mess…or the germs.
She was pretty angry that he'd stuffed Pippa

like one of those dolls on her bed, but at the same time, seeing him experience a parenting low was kind of funny. Just weeks ago, he'd been under some misguided impression that he could leave Kenya with his daughter and just take up parenting where Anna left off. *Right.* Anna knew many people didn't have the choice, but she was still Pippa's main parent and Jack wasn't going to change that.

AN HOUR LATER, Jack sat in his armchair, his head cradled in his hands. He'd really screwed up. His good intentions had backfired. As skittish as Anna had been acting since her arrival, he wouldn't be surprised if she came out of the room ready to head back to Kenya.

A breeze rattled the standard-issue vertical blinds on his sliding balcony door. He hadn't been in the apartment long enough to deal with getting curtains, or better blinds. The breeze was doing its job to air out the smell of disinfectant and cleaner he'd used while Anna and Pippa were in the bathroom. He preferred plain soap and water in most cases—none of that antimicrobial stuff that messed with immune systems—but he did keep disinfectant on hand for emergencies. And those products smelled a lot better than the pungent vinegar that filled the air. He'd called Zoe to see what she did with colored laundry when her kids got sick, and she'd suggested adding vinegar. Who knew?

Despite the odors wafting around the room and the churning of his washer in the hall closet, he knew when Anna walked in. He sensed her presence even before the scents of fresh soap and shampoo reached him. He looked up and gave her a sheepish smile, and was about to apologize, when she curled up at the end of the sofa closest to him. She was in a pair of sweatpants. Not escape clothes or packed bags.

"You're not going to meet with Dr. Miller?"

"Not today. I borrowed the phone in your room and called the department secretary to reschedule. He's apparently leaving for a three-day conference in D.C. and won't be able to meet until he gets back. Pippa comes first, though."

"I could watch her," Jack said, knowing how stupid he sounded after what had happened.

"You'd have to give me a ride, and I don't want to wake her," Anna said.

"You could take my keys."

"Uninsured with an expired license? Don't worry about it. It's a done deal."

Anna tucked her hands under her legs. They gazed at each other in silence, until Jack couldn't help himself.

"You look beautiful, you know that?" he said.

Anna glanced at her lap, clearly uncomfortable with his compliment.

"Kissing up?" she asked, then squeezed her eyes shut.

She didn't need to be embarrassed. The memory of the tender kisses they'd once shared were burned in Jack's mind. Kisses he'd hoped had conveyed to Anna that she was his world. His universe. But they hadn't. And he was pretty sure she'd locked the memory safely in the past along with everything else. Or maybe she'd deleted it along with the Anna he'd known. The Anna who wanted a career, but also cherished the idea of a family of her own.

"No. I mean it. You're beautiful. How's Pippa?" he added, stepping to safer ground.

"She fell asleep while I was telling her a story. She's fine, though."

"I'm sorry, Anna. I was trying to help. I thought I was doing you a favor," Jack said, leaning back in his armchair.

"I know."

"You do?" He scooted to the edge of the chair and faced her.

The corner of her mouth turned up. "Yeah, I do. Jack…" She let out a quiet laugh and shook her head. "I haven't had my coffee yet. That's my excuse and I'm sticking to it."

He handed her the fresh mug he'd poured for himself. She sighed and took a sip. "Mmm. Thanks." Another sip. "Jack, I know you've always aimed to do the right thing. You wouldn't intentionally hurt anyone, but the right thing is relative."

He held on to the words *aimed* and *intentionally.* He'd read a *but* between the lines before she'd said it.

Jack knew hearing about her parents' divorce had been the only reason she'd turned to him that night. The catalyst for everything that had been messed up about their lives since she'd graduated. And he knew from experience that trust was the hardest thing to rebuild. Maybe impossible. Anna was right to be afraid, because he was far from perfect, regardless of intent. And forcing him to make a choice between her and his daughter was just as impossible.

"Back in Busara, I said some things…." Jack paused, running the apology through his head to avoid another screwup.

Anna placed a hand on his knee. "Not anything I didn't deserve. I'm sorry for how things turned out…for the choices I made. I truly am." She took back her hand, and the breeze stripped the warmth from his knee. "We need to talk about what we're going to do here on out, for Pippa's sake. We're always going to be a part of each other's lives, Jack, because we share that little angel. We need to be able to move on without hurting her."

He didn't like how final that sounded. Jack scratched his head and got up to close the sliding door. Then he paced the room a couple times before sitting again. Options. There were always options. When he'd told her he wasn't leaving Pippa with her in Kenya, he'd been hurt. In shock. He hadn't trusted Anna then, but she was here now.

She'd used the tickets. She'd gone along with visiting his family last night, and as she'd watched his dad playing with the kids, Jack had caught fleeting moments of the dreamy look he used to see in her eyes. He was certain it wasn't sleepiness.

Maybe there was hope. An option she hadn't considered.

Jack's pulse kicked up. The last time he'd asked, she hadn't been pregnant, hadn't had Pippa. What if she *wanted* him to ask again? What if that's why she'd used the tickets?

His cell phone vibrated on the kitchen table. He ignored it. No lab emergency was going to interrupt this conversation. If that tech botched an assay, they'd simply have to redo it. This was *Jack's* redo and there wouldn't be any more after this. One shot, because he understood what it meant to not be wanted, and he wasn't about to live through the pain of his childhood and that of the past five years again.

He braced his elbows on his knees and linked his hands. "Anna, they didn't find you in the toy aisle. Back when you disappeared in a department store and scared your mom. They found you in the bridal department, weaving your way in and out of the satin dresses as you watched ladies trying on gowns."

"Because I thought that was what fairies and princesses wore," Anna admitted softly. "How did you—"

"You told me. It was one of the things you shared back when we'd sit on the top bleacher after school and just hang out…or when we'd go fishing on a Saturday morning. When I asked you if they'd found you in the toy section back in Busara, I just wanted to see your reaction. To see if you remembered us. We shared a lot of things, Anna. We were friends."

It was her turn to pace. She looked upset and had her arms folded in front of her.

"We were best friends. And we still can be," she said.

No way. You are not giving me an "I like you like a friend" line.

"We have a child together, Anna. We're more than friends."

She put her hands on her ears and squeezed her eyes shut. "Don't say it. Please don't say it," she begged. Her face flushed and her chest heaved as if she was going to hyperventilate. Or throw up. He repulsed her that much?

"I don't get it," Jack said. "Is that why you ran away? I ruined our friendship by proposing, and the thought of being married to me was that disgusting to you?"

"What?" Anna stopped in her tracks and finally looked at him. "How could you possibly think that? Jack, I'd just confided in you about my parents. A bombshell had been dropped and I told you how everything I'd ever believed in had changed. Then you go and propose? Out of the blue? It was the last thing I needed to hear in that moment."

"Is it the last thing you need to hear now?"

The color drained from her face and she reached for the TV cabinet. Jack rushed over and grabbed her arm. She shrugged free and slowly walked back to the sofa, slumping onto the end farthest from his chair.

"Yes, Jack. It is," she whispered.

"I don't get that. It's not out of the blue. We have a history...a child. It's the perfect option."

Anna smiled sadly and turned her face away from him. She followed the line of the ceiling toward the far wall with purpose. Jack knew by the glide of her neck muscles that she was trying to compose herself. If he was lucky, she was actually considering his suggestion. They'd be a family.

"An *option*," she said. Her tone made his heart sink. "I…care about you, Jack. The last thing I'd ever do to either you or Pippa is put you through that. I'm sorry, but I don't want to be an option. Our lives are separated by over seven thousand miles. Don't set us all up for disappointment. I think you and I have both suffered our fair share of it already."

Anna got up and disappeared into his bedroom, leaving him dumbfounded. She'd admitted she cared about him. She never would have turned to him that day, never could have given up all she'd believed in, if she hadn't had deep feelings for him.

He hadn't misread the signs. And all these years he'd felt so guilty for giving in, for not staying strong for her when she'd fallen apart and begged him to be with her. He still did, but that day, he'd believed they were going to be together forever anyway. He'd planned for it. Envisioned it. It had all made sense…until she'd said no and left him as dumbfounded and lost as he'd felt the night he'd found his parents dead, and child services had taken him away.

He'd been lucky. The Harpers had been there for him. He wanted to be there for both

Anna and Pippa—he really did. But if Anna didn't want him, and two rounds of "no" were enough to get through to him, then his hands were tied. He'd need to concentrate on raising Pippa, and cope with the hollow ache that would invade him every time he saw her mother or heard her voice.

He just didn't know how.

CHAPTER TEN

MORTIFIED DIDN'T BEGIN to describe how Anna felt. She splashed cold water on her face for the third time, then drank a sip from her cupped hands. It did nothing to soothe the tightness in her throat.

Jack had confirmed everything she'd feared. He was just like her father. That bit of psychology about girls gravitating toward men who reminded them of their dads and guys liking girls who were like their mothers was true, after all. She'd almost said the word *love.* She'd almost admitted that she'd loved him. The humiliation would have killed her. Just like the last time he'd proposed. She'd have given him the word *love* and gotten the word *option* in return. How like her father. How logical and scientific of Jack. Better yet, he should have come up with a *hypothesis* on how they should manage parenting Pippa.

Anna wiped her face and hung up the towel.

Jack had always been her best friend. She used to dream about the day when he'd get past his hang-ups and let her into his heart. Really let her in. But then she'd changed. And it turned out she'd been right in rejecting him back then, because it wasn't just his timing that was off—his motive had been, too. Dutiful, like her dad. He'd felt responsible for her taking off her promise ring, so he'd proposed. He'd seen it as an *option* to fix things...no different than he did now. And he'd just proved that her fears of him insisting on marriage if he'd known she was pregnant weren't unfounded. She'd essentially saved all of them from heartache, even if it had been replaced with a different kind of hurt.

Anna straightened the bedcovers she'd neglected earlier, unable to face him again. She'd wait for Pippa to wake up. With her around, Anna and Jack wouldn't have to focus on one another.

The doorbell rang and she could hear the weight of Jack's footsteps on the floor, followed by voices. She sighed and plopped a pillow into place. She picked up the hair band she'd left on the dresser and pulled her hair into a ponytail. She really wasn't in the mood to socialize with Jack's parents or his sister, but it wasn't as if she had a choice. And if Jack's mom decided to continue where she'd left off last night… Anna wasn't sure she could take it right now.

There was a tap on the bedroom door. "Anna?" Jack said.

So much for hiding.

"I'm coming." She sighed and took one last look in the mirror before opening the door. Jack stood with one hand on the door frame, blocking her exit. He brought his face close to her ear and kept his voice low.

"If you just called your mom, she must have broken the sound barrier getting here," he said.

"*My* mom?" Oh, no. Anna hadn't spoken to her mother yet. Hadn't explained about Pippa. How could she know? "What's she doing here? How'd she know I'm here?" Anna could barely hear her own voice.

"She wants to see her granddaughter. Don't look at me like that. I'm innocent, and I could use you out there. She isn't too happy, and greeted me with a few choice words. They were probably deserved, given the circumstances."

Anna dug her nails into her scalp. This was not good. Damage control.

"She was supposed to hear it from me. I needed to explain in person so I could tell if she was okay."

"Now would be a good time."

Jack left Anna standing in the bedroom doorway. The explanation she'd carefully planned during the flight over became muddled in her head. All these years of not telling her mom…of protecting her…and now this.

Anna could hear Jack offering coffee or tea, and her mother declining. Choice words or not, she was probably putting up a front for Jack. She sounded meek, nothing like the energized woman Anna had spoken to six months ago, after she'd emailed about a new job. New jobs were becoming an annual event, but she'd seemed enthusiastic this time.

Gosh. Five years. Anna fought the lump in her throat and walked down the hall. She'd faced far worse in Kenya. She'd endured a pregnancy and child-rearing on her own. But this. Seeing the pain in her mother's face and knowing she'd caused it…again.

Pippa's door was still closed. Thank goodness. Anna passed it and entered the living

room. Her mom stood by the fireplace, ex-
amining the elephant carvings with her arms
folded protectively. She'd cut off her hair and
had this shorter version tucked behind her
ears. The gray streaking through it screamed
of how long it had been since Anna had seen
her in person.

"Anna!" Tears began falling freely, smear-
ing mascara down her mother's cheeks, and
something unhitched in Anna.

"Mom," she said, falling into her embrace.

"I missed you, Anna," Sue exclaimed, holding her tight.

"I missed you, too!" Anna sniffed back her
own salty tears. For a minute it felt like old
times, when she'd come home, upset over a
grade, and her mom would hug her and say
it didn't matter, that she loved her anyway.

It felt so good to let go and let herself trust.
To believe that maybe she'd been wrong all
this time. Staying safely away.

Then Anna remembered. She could not let
go. She needed to stay in control and make
sure Mom didn't fall apart and lose the fragile stability she'd managed to tightrope in recent years.

Jack cleared his throat. "I need to pick up a

few things at the grocery store. Do you need anything in particular for Pippa, Anna?" he asked, grabbing his cell phone and keys. Privacy was so much easier around here than at Busara.

She shook her head.

"I'll be back soon, then. Call me if you think of something."

He stopped at the door and looked at Anna over the back of her mom's head. Sue didn't turn to say goodbye. Anna cocked her head slightly to indicate she'd be okay. He nodded and left.

"Can I get you anything, Mom?"

"You could bring me my granddaughter," she said, relaxing her shoulders after the front door closed. She looked from the armchair to the couch, as if judging the lesser of two evils, and chose the couch.

"Can we give her a few minutes and see if she gets up on her own? She'll be cranky otherwise."

Anna cringed inside, her own words hitting home. The memory of that morning when her baby brother didn't wake up had never stopped haunting her, but now, with her mother waiting to see Pippa after her nap, and the whole situation, it was like reliving it all over. No doubt the impact was even greater on her mom.

"Especially with a stranger, I'm sure," her mother said. *Touché*. Sue pulled a crumpled tissue from her pocket and wiped her nose.

"Mom, I'm sorry I didn't tell you." Anna took a seat next to her.

"I'm your mother, Anna. After all I've lost, after a marriage like mine, I at least deserve to have a grandchild to love."

Anna pressed her knuckles against her mouth to stop her lips from trembling. The last thing she'd intended was to deprive her mom of love. It was all she wanted for her. But to tease her with it…let her cling to it and then rip it away? That would have been cruel, and Anna knew her mother couldn't have handled the pain.

Nothing Anna tried to do could make up for the pain she'd caused. Even loving her mom wasn't enough to balance the loss of her baby brother. And now she'd done it again. She could see the signs. The sunken corners of her mother's lips. The hollow of her cheeks and her ancient, oversize sweater—the one she hid in when things weren't going well.

The same faded blue knit Anna would find her curled up in on the couch, asleep, when she came home from school. It had happened every December. Like clockwork.

Anna fingered the end of her mother's sleeve. "Mom, you deserve all the love in the world, mine included. And I know Pippa will adore you. I'm so sorry I didn't tell you. I—I wanted to bring her to you in person. A surprise."

"A surprise? You couldn't surprise me over the phone or in one of your emails? You didn't trust me, just like your father. You blame me."

"No. No. Mom, of course I trust you. I didn't want to…" Anna couldn't say the words without sounding insulting or distrustful, but her mother needed a reason as much as Jack had needed one.

"Anna, I'm not stupid. It's so obvious you kept her a secret because of your brother. Did you really think I couldn't handle loving another baby?"

Loving. Yes. Maybe too much. To the point of paranoia.

"I don't live here. I didn't want you worrying or missing her too much. Dad had just asked for a divorce and I wasn't here to be with you through that. I didn't want to add to all you were going through."

"Or what? I've never been suicidal. I've spent thousands on therapists who'll vouch for that. This whole depression thing is nothing but a diagnosis code for insurance purposes. Gives people an excuse. You should have told me." Sue got up and paced.

Anna stayed seated. When fired up with a goal in her sights, her mother could spin circles around anyone. She was an expert at justifying or convincing, skills that had helped make her husband both a business and political success. And for what? He had it made. He'd married his marketing specialist because he'd gotten her pregnant, used her talents and dropped her when she'd needed more from him than a roof.

There was a time when Sue had been a stronger, more persistent woman, but misplaced persistence had its pitfalls, and she sank into them unpredictably. Insisting she was fine was one of the exasperating ways she'd justify getting off meds or self-adjusting her dose.

Anna pulled a sofa pillow into her lap and hugged it. Good thing she'd canceled seeing Miller today.

"Maybe I should have told you." Anna flicked at the corner of the pillow with her thumb. If she turned the tables on her mother, perhaps she could convince her to talk to her therapist about her surprise grandchild. Knowing her mom had a therapist at all gave Anna peace of mind. "You know, since I messed this all up, it might be a good idea to have a family visit, Pippa included, with Dr. Seth while I'm in town."

Sue went to the balcony, drew aside the sheers and looked left, then right, without answering.

"Tell me you're still seeing her," Anna said, slapping the pillow aside and getting up.

"I don't need to see her anymore. I'm fine. Why can't anyone understand that what I went through was situational depression, not the real thing? Anyone who loses a child or goes through a divorce can't be expected to spring around, laughing and joking, for goodness' sake. It's been four years since I signed the papers for your father. I'm over it. Why should I spend hundreds a session on therapy—or per month on medication—that I don't need anymore?"

"Maybe you were fine *because* of the sessions and meds," Anna said, gritting her teeth to keep her voice down. "Please tell me you didn't quit the antidepressant on your own again, too."

Her mom shrugged and tipped her chin up. "They made me gain weight. For nothing."

"Oh, for crying out loud, Mom." Anna raked her hair back and squeezed her eyes shut before exhaling long and slow. This. *This* was why she worried about burdening her mom. Taking care of animals was so much easier for her. The countless talks to get through to her mom about her health only proved that. Despite language barriers, animals respected and listened to her far more than people ever did.

"I. Am. Fine," her mom declared. Her puffy eyes said otherwise.

Anna may have earned a DVM—doctor of veterinary medicine—rather than an MD degree, but the basics of medication and hazards of noncompliance were the same.

"Okay. I get it. You're fine. It was all situational. So now work is good, life is good and if you can meet your granddaughter, all will be fixed."

"Yes, and speaking of work, it's a good

thing I left that useless place last month. Now I can spend quality time with her."

"Wait a minute. You were fired again?"

"This time it was more of a mutual consent thing."

"Mom. How many days did you miss?"

Sue pursed her lips and scowled. Anna had crossed the line, but knew better than to believe her mom hadn't been fired. It wouldn't be the first job she lost because the days she couldn't drag herself out of bed had added up.

"I had sick leave and didn't even use it all. That wasn't the reason. I have found that one should live life in a way that makes one happy. I was being proactive. Quitting made me feel relieved. Besides, I have plenty of savings from the settlement and from stopping therapy, so it's all working out. It was meant to be."

Anna nodded in defeat. She stood and got two glasses of water, drinking and refilling hers before returning to the living room and handing her mom the other one.

"How'd you find out?" she asked.

Her mom took a sip. "Jack's mother tweeted this morning about a wonderful dinner with her son and his daughter who'd been born in

Africa. I put two and two together and called her."

Tweeted? Geez. Now the world knew. Anna must have scrunched her face without realizing it.

"What?" her mom said. "I've tweeted before. Once. Mostly I lurk for entertainment. I've searched your name, but it never comes up.

"Uh, yeah. Social media. No, thanks."

"Well, I hadn't spoken to her since your graduation, but when I called, she congratulated me for joining grandmotherhood. She didn't realize she was confirming my suspicions."

"I'm so sorry, Mom. I'd planned to see you first, but we ended up there last night and—"

"What I want to know is how in the world you could have done this? How could you have thrown away all I taught you? What happened to waiting? To not letting a man steal your life? You turned to this…this man." She waved at the apartment door. "And then hid from everyone. Hid my grandchild from me."

"I have not been hiding. I have a life. A career."

Her mother recoiled and looked away. Anna

knew from the twitch in her frown lines that her mother was considering, calculating. She reached over and took Anna's hands in hers.

"Never mind the past. We all make mistakes. I want you and my granddaughter in my life. I want you to come home. You could stay with me. There's plenty of room."

"Mom, I work in Kenya. I live there," Anna said.

"But you could change that."

"No, I can't. I need to be there." Anna had no energy left. Moving her Mom to Kenya wasn't an option, either. She'd suggested it once, out of desperation, but Sue had never left town, let alone been on a plane. And planes, especially with all the threats and tragedies in the news, scared her.

But even with a bottle of antianxiety drugs, ripping her away from a society and lifestyle she understood and was comfortable with wasn't wise. It could backfire. Anna couldn't even begin to picture her mom roughing it at Busara. If she ever saw the camp in person, she'd drag Anna and Pippa back to the States and make sure National Security never let them leave again.

"A camp surrounded by hyenas and lions is hardly the right place for a little girl."

"The right place for a little girl is with her mother. Pippa is well-adjusted, loves books, can stand up to anyone and has an appreciation for all living things. She's a happy kid."

Anna's mom sat back down and set her glass on the coffee table. "I just want to make sure you don't make the mistakes I made. I didn't have a choice, of course. Times were different. I was starry-eyed. He wasn't. Your dad did the right thing marrying me. His only mistake was regretting it. I'm not sure where I went wrong. Who I was wasn't good enough for him, I guess. You're stronger than I was. Smarter. Make sure Jack pays child support, but that's it. If he fights you for custody, I'll help pay for a lawyer. In fact, you should see one while you're here, for advice. You know, just in case."

Anna raised her brows. Her mom was seriously antimarriage. Where had that attitude been when she'd raised her? Before the tragedy? She'd filled Anna's room with books, from Cinderella stories to modern-day clean romances to every volume on animals Anna wanted. Unless she'd done it because, all along, she thought books were the only place Anna would ever witness true love.

Jack certainly wasn't romantic. However, Anna had seen into the man's heart. It existed. It certainly was pure—especially since everything that came out of it went through a logic filter. He just didn't love her. Not that way, at least. And perhaps, Anna realized, he'd never be able to love anyone that way.

She was certainly a skeptic now, but hearing her mother's attitude made Anna's hair curl. She wanted to argue and defend marriage, love, romance and all that she'd grown up believing. Even if she knew it had all been a fantasy. Even if she'd been her parents' last straw.

Maybe if little Ricky had woken up under Anna's watch, their marriage would have survived. Maybe if she'd checked on him one more time, she'd have discovered he'd rolled over onto his belly. Instead, she'd fallen asleep halfway through studying for her history midterm. Technically, no one was to blame, but she blamed herself.

"Jack did try stepping up to the plate, but I'm not marrying anyone. We'll work things out regarding Pippa, but that's between us."

The sound of a door creaking let Anna know that Pippa had woken up.

"Mom, give me a minute and I'll bring her out."

She hurried to sleepy-eyed Pippa and re-directed her to the bathroom for a potty break. Anna needed a quick break, too. She needed to process what her mom had said. Mrs. Harper had always been sweet. What was going on with her? Couldn't she have at least asked Anna last night before tweeting to the world?

She lifted Pippa up to the sink and let her wash her hands, then wiped the dried drool from the corner of her daughter's mouth before walking her out. Anna didn't miss the way her mom had wrung her hands pink, stopping only when the two of them appeared.

"Pippa, this is your grandma Sue."

Pippa rubbed her eyes and frowned. "What happened to Gwandma Nina? You look scary."

Grandma Sue's eyes widened, which only emphasized the whole mascara-gone-wild look.

"Makeup," Anna said, trailing her finger down her own cheek to explain. Her mom mouthed an *oh* and smiled. "Nina is your other grandma. Your dad's mom," Anna added. "Grandma Sue is my mom."

Pippa thought for a minute, rubbing her puffy face against Anna's shirt, then peering sideways at her grandma. "Did you get me a p'esent, too?" she finally said.

Anna winced. Spoiled in one night. Her mom had always taught her never to ask for gifts, and what's the first thing Pippa did? Insult her, then ask for a present. Great. It did nothing to prove Anna could raise a child properly.

Sue actually slipped off the couch and onto her knees in front of Pippa. New tears freshened up the already smeared mascara tracks. Anna didn't recall her ever being so emotional, at least not before that graduation day, when she'd vented like a steam engine over her divorce.

"Pippa, we don't ask for presents," Anna said softly. In her defense, she hadn't had that many opportunities to reinforce certain social rules. Stuff like this didn't come up much at Busara. Maybe Pippa did need more exposure.

"Nonsense. I didn't bring a present because

I thought it'd be more fun to go to the toy store and let you pick."

Pippa looked up at Anna. "She's not a stwanger anymore, right? I can go?"

"We'll go when your dad gets here. He has the car seat. But you don't have to do that, Mom." Savings or not, without a job, Grandma didn't need to be spending on toys.

"I want to," she said, standing up. "And don't you stop me from filling the cart. Now, I'm going to borrow your bathroom to freshen up, if that's okay. Grandmas shouldn't look like ghouls," she said, poking Pippa playfully in the belly.

Pippa squealed. The tummy troubles were gone for sure.

"Do I have another gwandpa, too?" she asked her grandma.

Sue's eye's brimmed. "Yes, you do," she said, without elaborating, and in that moment, Anna realized she'd hurt her mom as much as her father had.

THE TOY STORE visit was pure insanity. Total child indulgence. Trying to get her mom to understand that they could not take half the stuff she'd bought to Busara was futile. Jack squeezed a doll house into the last remaining space in his trunk, while Anna got Pippa buckled in. Sue sat next to her, opening a box with miniature dolls meant for the house. The situation was getting out of control. And to top things off, after the "surprise" way her mom had heard about Pippa, Anna had to make sure her father heard about his granddaughter firsthand. So while everyone else was browsing toys, she'd gone off to a quiet corner and tried calling his office. Just like old times, almost sensing he wouldn't be available. Only this time wasn't quite the same. His secretary informed her that her father had been admitted to the hospital and that as far as she knew, Sue hadn't been told. Needing to see her dad, Anna had confided in Jack.

She shut the passenger door, leaving her mom and Pippa occupied in the back seat, and headed around the car.

"Hey, don't worry about it," Jack said, clicking the trunk shut. "It all fits in her room at my place. I'm sure everyone will tone down the gifts soon. They're just excited."

"But this isn't good for her. And what happens when she goes home—to Busara—and has her shared tent and basic toys? You don't mind filling her room here, creating a wonderland, because it's all a competition, isn't it? Where do you think she'll want to stay? It's not rocket science. This is brainwashing. It's like one divorced parent buying a puppy when the other can't."

"You have elephants. That's kind of hard to compete with."

"You're missing the point."

"I see. Forget 'not good for her.' What you're really saying is that it's not good for *you.*"

Anna glared at him. "That's not fair," she hissed.

"What's not fair is assuming I conspired with your mother to manipulate my daughter with toys. Stop for one minute, Anna, put your insecurities aside and see how ridiculous that is."

"I am not insecure and I didn't mean to imply that you were conspiring." *But Pippa is the only person in this world who'll ever love me unconditionally, and I can't lose her to any of you. I need to keep her close, safe and loved.*

"Then what has you on edge? The hospital?"

"Would you lower your voice?" Anna glanced at the car's rear window just to be sure her mom was still preoccupied.

"If you don't want to stop there, then don't, but I think you should. He's your father. You don't want to leave with any regrets."

The double entendre gouged her like an arrow in the gut. She had so many regrets already. Like not checking on her brother one last time. Like breaking a vow she'd made to herself to wait for her one true love. Like not telling Jack. She had regrets, and no, she didn't want any more. She was tired. So tired.

"I don't need your warnings, Jack. I'm a big girl and I can deal with my father. We'll drop my mom at her car, stop at the hospital, and after that I need to borrow your computer or get ahold of a satellite phone at the lab. I want to see how things are at camp." *I need to feel in control again. Back in my world.*

"Not a problem. But just so you know, Anna, no amount of toys will ever replace you. Novelties are like puppy love. They don't last. They're not the real thing. In spite of everything that has happened, I know you're a great mom. The values you've instilled in her, no matter what detours she takes, they're what she'll always fall back on. We all come full circle…you included."

He's right. All you had with Jack was one-way puppy love, and it didn't last. It wasn't real, any more than what your parents had was, or the fairy tales you put stock in, once upon a time. And now here you are again.

JACK GAVE A QUICK WAVE as Mrs. Bekker drove off, then told Anna he'd be right back. He ran up to his apartment and grabbed three water bottles and his laptop. Anna wasn't going to relax until she made sure everyone was okay back home. She could do that from the car. No point in waiting if it brought her stress levels down.

He felt his phone vibrate in his pocket and pulled it out. His mom. Boy, she had some explaining to do.

"Hi, Mom."

"Jack, is Anna there?"

"She's waiting in the car. I think it's a little late to check with her before calling Mrs. Bekker."

"Oh, I'm sorry. I was afraid Sue had already come over by now. That's why I need to apologize to Anna. You didn't tell me she hadn't told her parents she'd be here. I assumed they knew, and Sue called earlier, so I congratulated her on becoming a grandparent. You can guess the rest. I tried calling you right away, but you didn't pick up. You never pick up, Jack. What's the point in having a cell phone?"

He remembered his phone vibrating on the table, but he'd been so caught up with Anna he'd ignored it. Then her mother had showed up and he'd forgotten to check his missed calls.

"It's been a hectic day, Mom. In any case, what's done is done. We're headed over to the hospital so she can see her dad."

"Sue didn't mention him being ill. Is he all right?"

"She didn't know. Apparently, they haven't spoken much since the divorce. Anna called his office and found out from his secretary that he had a minor heart attack earlier this week. He's being monitored, but he'll get released soon. Listen, I've gotta go. They're waiting in the car."

"Can you all come over for dinner tonight?"

Jack paused. Anna would hate him if he said yes. He needed an evening to recover as much as she did. Well, maybe not quite as much, but he did.

"Let's pick another night, Mom. We already have plans."

"Okay, I understand. But Jack…please…be careful. Open your eyes."

ANNA BLINKED AT the woman holding her father's hand as he lay propped up in his hospital bed. The new Mrs. Bekker. Anna had a stepmother. *A stepmother.* The shock of their email announcement almost a year ago didn't compare to seeing her standing by her father's side, where her mother should have been and would have been if he'd given her the chance. If he'd made the slightest effort to heal her heart rather than leaving that to a teenage girl. Anna wondered how much news of his remarriage had impacted her mother's decision to quit therapy. Had she been trying to prove she was just as strong and together as his new wife?

Anna looked down at the bank papers he'd handed her. Funds designated for his granddaughter's expenses. Her father who, except for his wedding announcement, had rarely taken the time to return her messages or calls.

He'd washed his hands clean of his past life with them and had probably gotten sick of Anna asking him to check on her mom. He didn't want the responsibility of them anymore. He couldn't take the time to contact her, but now he expected her to take his money? Was everything about money and business with him?

How ironic that he had someone to stand by his side. Of course Anna wanted him cared for, but the child in her could still hear the dial tone after begging him to come home on time, because although she'd tried fixing dinner, she couldn't get her mom out of the deserted baby's room, where she sat staring at the wall. He always had work excuses and never came.

Of course, Anna was now old enough to understand that everyone mourned in their own way, but he still should have helped his wife through, not to mention his remaining child. She remembered the helpless, desperate and guilty feelings that had left her crumpled in the corner of her bed after her brother died. She'd needed her dad to be her pillar. To hug her and tell her he still loved her. To help her with her mom. But he'd closed himself off—probably blamed the two of them for his loss.

Now Anna didn't need to rely on anyone. If her father had done anything, he'd made her stronger and had taught her that time did not heal everything. Money didn't, either, but it seemed to be the only way he knew how to give.

Hearing her dad had had a heart attack had scared her. She cared. She wished he could see that and care back.

"I can't accept this," Anna said, holding the papers up. He sure hadn't wasted any time in calling his accountant and having them drawn up and faxed over.

"We want you to. Please," her father's wife said.

Anna's back prickled at her use of the word *we*. This Mrs. Bekker dressed so disconcertingly similar to how Sue used to. Simple, yet smart and businesslike. Down to the plain beige slacks she'd paired with short pumps, and the small gold hoops in her ears.

Anna racked her mind for her stepmother's first name and drew a blank. She'd introduced herself, but the momentary shock of seeing her in person had rendered Anna's ears useless, and she couldn't recall the wedding announcement. Was it Missy or Mindy? Anna was too embarrassed to ask. Jack would remember. She'd ask him later.

"I really can't," she said.

Jack, his jaw popping rhythmically, stood by the hospital bed with Pippa on his hip so that she could see everyone. Her grandpa reached out with his free hand, the one without an IV taped to it, to hold on to Pippa's. He looked pale, his face drawn.

"Anna," he said. "It may seem like a lot to you, but it's nothing compared to what I would have spent on my granddaughter had I known she existed. We'll start a college fund for her, and add to it every year."

Anna wanted to argue, but the beeping of his heart monitor and all the tubes and gadgets he was hooked up to held her back. This wasn't the place or time. He needed to get better, not worse. As much as his absence had hurt her mom, he was still her father, and it was wrong in so many ways to see him weak and bedridden. Anna didn't want to cause him harm. She didn't want to cause anyone pain, but to him, money meant power—having the power to dictate how things were going to be. Giving money was a brush-off. He didn't truly want to be a part of his granddaughter's life.

Anna glanced at Jack, who seemed to understand how tortured and tongue-tied she felt.

"Sir, that's generous of you, but I intend to cover my daughter's expenses," he interjected.

Jack looked pointedly at Anna. They hadn't discussed child support. Anna hadn't questioned that he'd step up to the plate, given his nature and how badly he wanted Pippa to live with him. Still, hearing it was odd. It was right and good, of course, but a tiny part of Anna felt it was one more step in her losing full control of Pippa's life.

Anna's father gave him a dirty look, one of doubt and disapproval. "Trust me, there'll be plenty of expenses for you to cover," he said dismissively.

Men. Anna had been managing fine on her own, yet here they were, locking horns over supporting Pippa.

"It's really not necessary, Dad."

"It is because I say it is," he stated firmly. His mental faculties, tone and voice hadn't weakened at all, apparently. "It's my money to do with as I please, and I want to give it to my granddaughter. I could die tomorrow. I'm adjusting my estate planning in a way that will benefit everyone and not burden anyone, and this is part of it. End. Of. Discussion."

Anna flinched at his raised voice. The man still had the power to put her in her place. From the corner of her eye, she saw Jack distracting Pippa with his cell phone, pressing buttons for her, in spite of the stark look on his face and hard set of his jaw.

Her father's wife showed no reaction until he coughed and started to raise himself on the flat hospital pillows. She immediately reached back to fluff and adjust them for him. Anna stared. Watching him with another woman was surreal.

"Thank you, Mary."

Mary. How could she forget such a simple name?

"Gwandma used money and got me dis," Pippa said, holding out her arm to show off her dress-up bracelet.

Richard craned his neck. "Is that so?"

"We saw Mom earlier," Anna explained. "I'm thinking she doesn't know you're here.

She didn't mention it, but I can let her know. I'm sure she'll—"

"No. Don't tell her. I don't need her showing up."

Anna was taken aback by his sharpness. The papers she still held were getting crumpled by her grip, and the corners of her eyes stung. She felt like a little girl again, being yelled at for begging him to come to her play, or track meet, or home.

"Oh, okay. I realize she's no longer your wife, but I just figured—"

"Leave it alone, Anna. When you get older, you'll see that life is too short for misery. You can't force yourself to love someone, and you can't force someone to love you. I've moved on."

You can't force someone to love you.

He'd moved on long ago.

Anna scratched her cheek and cleared her throat. *Don't let it get to you. He's just grumpy and not well.*

"If you want, I'll make sure you can stay in touch with Pippa." Anna watched his expression to see if the words sank in. *If you want.*

The pulse on her father's monitor began beeping rapidly and Anna leaped out of the

chair at the same time as Mary, who pushed a
red button on the side of his bed. Jack stepped
away with Pippa, letting a nurse who rushed
into the room check his status on the mon-
itors. They all waited as the nurse injected
something into his IV and the beeping began
to slow down.

"I'm so sorry, Dad." Anna felt terrible. Men-
tioning her mom had upset him that much? Or
was it Anna showing up with Pippa? Meeting
his grandchild should have made him happy.

Anna looked over at Jack for some indication that she wasn't crazy. His forehead was
beaded with sweat and he was staring blankly
at the heart monitor, hugging Pippa tighter
than necessary.

"There are too many visitors in here. I'm
afraid I'm going to have to ask you to leave,
and come in no more than two at a time," the
nurse said. "Mr. Bekker, no more excitement.
If you can't talk about the weather or something happy, like that cutie pie, then don't
talk." She smiled at Pippa, then left.

"I'll take Pippa down to the car and wait.
Let you have some privacy," Jack finally said,
twisting his neck to the side.

"Yes, thank you. A little privacy would be

nice," Richard said, completely unaware that Jack looked paler than he did. "First let me kiss my granddaughter. Pippa, be good and don't be a stranger."

So he did want to see her?

"I'm not a stwanger," Pippa said. Her dad and Mary chuckled, but not Jack. He carried her out swiftly and Anna told her dad she'd be right back. She caught up with them down the hall.

"Jack, you don't have to go to the car. You could just wait out here," Anna said. "I can go get you a cold soda or something."

"Do you have any idea how resistant the strains of hospital microbes are? Pippa shouldn't be here. She's used to fresh air," he said, but Anna knew it wasn't the real reason he wanted to wait outside.

Her parents had never liked him. But a parent was a parent. And Jack had seen his die from needles up their arms. How could Anna not have thought of that when he'd agreed to come along with her for moral support?

She put her hand on his arm. "Are you sure you're okay?"

"I'm good." He pushed the elevator button impatiently. "Pippa and I just need some fresh air. We'll meet you downstairs." He was in the elevator before the doors fully opened.

"Okay. I won't be long," she said.

She walked in on Mary kissing her dad's cheek and holding his hand to her chest. Both looked up at the sound of her footsteps.

"Um, I just wanted to say bye. I'll be in touch to see how you're doing."

"Thank you. Take care of my granddaughter," he added. Anna couldn't help but read into his words, *Take care of your brother.* She blinked twice. No. She was not taking after her mom. She wasn't going to get paranoid about everything. "I always do, Dad. And just so you know, Jack is an intelligent man who is well-respected in his field. If and when you want to see Pippa during her visits here, he'll be the one who'll be bringing her to see you. So please, be nice."

Her dad grumbled. "We'll see," he said.

She hesitated before going over and kissing him on the cheek. "Get well."

"It was nice to meet you," Mary said.

Anna smiled briefly and turned away, as eager as Jack had been to get out of there, and in knots from her efforts to reach out. Her dad just didn't care. He was clueless, oblivious to what he'd done to his first wife.

"Anna. Please wait." Mary had followed her out of the room. Anna dried the tears from her eyes before turning around.

"Yes?"

"I was hoping I could talk to you for just a minute. I know how difficult this must be, meeting me like this," Mary said.

"Yes," Anna murmured. She couldn't lie. Besides, the tension was obvious.

Mary wrung her hands and glanced downward, as if trying to find words. "I think you should know that nothing happened before the divorce. Out of respect for another woman, I made sure of that."

Anna wrapped her arms around her waist and frowned. So they'd met while her parents were married? They'd connected on an emotional level, betraying Anna and her mom long before the divorce was announced and Anna became pregnant. Mary had no idea how much worse that made accepting her as her dad's wife. Anna looked up at the fluorescent panels overhead and waited a few seconds for her tears to slip unnoticed down the back of her throat.

"I'm trying to clear the air, because I'd love for us to be comfortable with one another," Mary said.

Anna nodded and swallowed hard, trying to keep her composure. She sniffed and wished she hadn't run out of tissues in her purse.

"I appreciate that, but I can't do this right now," she said.

"Right. I should let you go. Jack and Pippa are waiting for you."

Anna nodded and started to leave.

"Mary? Take care of him…and good luck."

JACK SAT ON A BENCH in the front lawn of the hospital and unwrapped a granola bar he'd bought, along with a carton of milk, in the hospital lobby, and handed it to Pippa. He was sipping on an ice-cold can of ginger ale. Jack didn't do hospitals unless he didn't have a choice. Same with needles. If anyone knew that he, Dr. Jack Harper—grown man, accomplished scientist—hyperventilated every time he had so much as a flu shot, they'd drown in tears of laughter. Getting vaccinated for that trip to Kenya had given him nightmares. And being in that hospital room…the chemical smells, the IV…the moment of panic when he'd thought Anna's dad was having another heart attack. One that could have killed him right then and there. In front of him. In front of Pippa. *That* did him in. He'd wanted to be there for Anna. He'd wanted to support her, and he didn't last.

He took another long swig of ginger ale and watched Pippa play under the overhanging oak tree. A cool breeze fluttered the branches and soothed his senses. Pippa had taken to collecting acorns. They were currently at a pile of twenty and counting.

"Look, Daddy! Dis one is bigger. I want to take dem back for Ambosi. Dis one is for Ambosi and dis one is for Haki." Pippa picked the two largest and set them apart.

Jack glanced up automatically, half expecting a monkey to chuck an acorn at him. A squirrel chittered, obviously annoyed that someone was raiding its tree, and scampered off. Jack was safe.

That Ambosi had a way of sticking in one's mind. Jack realized Pippa was homesick.

"I don't think they'll let you take those on the plane."

"Uncle Mac lets me take things on his chopper." Pippa pouted. No doubt those adorable chipmunk cheeks had Mac caving to her pleas a time or two.

Uncle Mac. Jack didn't know much about Mac and Anna's history. The man was clearly fond of her. What if he was the one for her? Her John Wayne? They lived in the same place and worked for common goals. Maybe they were in love and Jack showing up had thrown a wrench in their plans. For as much as he hated Jack, Mr. Bekker was right. If Anna's heart was in Kenya, there wasn't any point in trying to convince her to marry him. She'd said no twice already. The thing was, he didn't want another man raising Pippa. He'd be forever grateful that his adoptive parents had saved him from the life he'd been born into, but Jack was here, and able. He wanted to be a father. A great one. And the look on his parents' faces when he'd brought them Pippa said it all. He'd made them happy. He'd given back to them. Finally.

Anna joined them on the bench, the acorn pile separating them. Pippa took a sip of milk, then ran for more acorns.

"You okay?" Jack asked.

"Yeah. I'm good. I will be, anyhow," Anna

said. She smiled at the collection of nuts. "What about you?"

He shrugged.

"I'm sorry, Jack. I wasn't thinking. Why didn't you just say you don't like hospitals? It didn't occur to me that it would still bother you, after all the lab stuff you do."

"Guess I thought I could handle it."

Anna sighed and eyed his soda. "Do you think you can handle dinner?"

"If you're hungry enough. I can handle anything. Just not that," Jack said, thumbing over his shoulder toward the hospital building.

They watched Pippa in silence, except for the exuberant praise they gave when she reached thirty acorns, counting aloud. And she'd skipped only one number. Maybe there was a little scientist in her.

He looked at Anna. She seemed deep in thought. He'd told her about his mom's call when they were headed to the hospital, and that he'd left the evening free.

"Do you want to go to a restaurant or eat in? We could stop and pick up a DVD, one for us and one Pippa can watch in the morning...or not." He didn't mean to imply that DVD babysitting was acceptable. Once in a while couldn't hurt, but he couldn't read Anna's reaction.

"Eating in sounds good," she said with a smile.

"Any particular movie you want to see?"

Anna laughed halfheartedly and stopped Pippa's fortieth acorn from rolling off the bench.

"Jack, I haven't seen a movie in six years, if you count how busy the end of vet school was. Take your pick. I don't even know what's been released since then."

Jack mulled that one over. She was right. Busara didn't even have a television. No marketing influence on the kids, no need for parental controls. And considering how difficult their internet connection was, she probably didn't waste time on it for fun. As for a movie, he knew just the one.

"I think I have one in mind," Jack said. "I, um, have to check in at the lab tomorrow, just briefly in the morning. I want to make sure everything is under control. Then I was thinking—do you remember that wildlife park we used to go to as kids?"

Anna's face lit up. "The one with the blind tiger? Yes. What about it?"

"I thought we'd take Pippa there tomorrow. It would feel a little more like 'normal' to her than shopping malls and hospitals."

Maybe help her homesickness. Jack wanted this to feel like home to her.

"That sounds wonderful." Anna's eyes glistened, but she pretended to look at a car backing out of its spot, and dried the corner of her eye with her fingertip. She sighed and rubbed her hands along her thighs. "This has been quite a day."

"We should leave before the squirrels amass an army to chase us off," Jack said.

"We should," Anna agreed. "Ready, Pippa?"

"We need to take these," she answered, hugging her pile of acorns. Several rolled to the ground.

"We can't take them all, honey," Jack said.

"Sweetie, I bet the squirrels who live in this tree are so thankful that you helped them gather nuts. You saved them a lot of trouble and energy," Anna remarked.

"But I want to take some for Haki and Ambosi." Pippa's chin wrinkled and started to shake. *Oh, no.*

"I'll tell you what," Jack said. "Why don't you take those two big ones and we'll plant them. There's a little park where I live, and we can plant them there—one for Ambosi and one for Haki. You could even name the trees they grow into." He didn't know if the seeds would take, but he'd be sure to go buy two seedlings and plant them for her. She'd never know.

"But they won't see dem!"

"I'll take a picture and send it to them. How's that?" He pulled out his cell phone and snapped a picture of her on the verge of crying. That was a keeper. Then he snapped one of her pile of acorns. "See, look at that. Here's your pile, and when the trees grow, we can take a picture of them the same way," he said, showing her the phone screen.

Her chin quivered a little more, followed by a sniff, then a concession. She wrapped her hand around two acorns and pressed her face against Anna. Time to go before she changed her mind.

JACK WAS LEARNING. He ended up ordering Chinese takeout because steamed rice seemed like a safe bet for Pippa. And Anna had approved. Pippa had fallen asleep shortly after they ate.

"We forgot to stop for a movie," Anna said, pouring two mugs of decaf coffee and carrying them to the living room.

"I already have one I thought we could watch." Jack opened the cabinet under the TV and pulled out a DVD case. He handed it to her from his crouched position, figuring she might want something else. "I could run out and grab one of the recent flicks you missed if you'd rather."

Anna took the case from him and her lips parted the second she recognized it. She flipped it over and ran her thumb over the old Scotch tape he'd used when the plastic cover had ripped.

"My copy of *Hatari!*," she said. "I can't believe it. I thought I'd lost it."

"You forgot it at my place the week before graduation. We never got around to watching it that time, so I hung on to it for you." Jack shrugged. "We don't have to watch it again." He'd seen it more than once with her, and was certain she'd seen it more than that.

"Are you kidding me? This is perfect, Jack! Thank you." She handed him the case, then, without warning, bent over and planted a kiss on his cheek.

Heat rose in Jack's face and he touched his cheek in surprise. Anna froze with her mouth open. She might have acted on impulse, but he was not letting her apologize for that.

Jack grinned. "Why thank me?" he drawled, in his best imitation of Sean Mercer's response to Dallas, thanking him for letting her keep the baby elephant.

Anna shoved his shoulder and laughed. He fell onto his rear and stayed there with his elbows hooked around his knees, watching her settle in with her bittersweet coffee.

This was like old times, with the added bonus of Pippa snuggled in pink bliss. But just because something felt right didn't mean it was meant to be forever, and Jack had learned early on never to look back. The only option left was to save their friendship.

And this was a start.

CHAPTER ELEVEN

THE WILDLIFE PARK featured a small, zoolike section near the entrance that included a petting area with goats, sheep and one character of a donkey. Next to the petting area was a small arena where visitors could pay extra for camel and pony rides. Pippa cackled like a monkey and said her pony needed diapers when he stopped to pee while she was still on his back. That kid was a hoot. Older bystanders were commenting on how she reminded them of Shirley Temple.

The rest of the acreage consisted of a stay-in-your-car driving tour of some larger animals in a more natural setting. Overall, the place looked like it needed some upgrades. There were some families around, but nothing like the crowds that Jack and Anna used to dodge as teens.

It was much more tame than Jack recalled. The driving tour was fun, but it was a mere suburban backyard compared to driving around Busara. Funny how perspectives changed. Still, it was fun remembering and recognizing things, and Pippa seemed to be enjoying it. So far, things were looking good and going according to plan.

Jack paid for a bag of popcorn and took it over to Anna and Pippa, who sat on a bench in front of a spider monkey cage. Ambosi would go mad if he was caged like that. Jack didn't know where *that* had come from. Ambosi didn't even like him.

Anna took the bag of popcorn from Jack. "Thanks."

"We should look for the owner and say hi," he suggested. Jack scanned the area. He didn't recognize anyone.

"I guess we could." Anna let Pippa grab a handful of popcorn. "Why don't we go see if he's at the main ticket booth?"

Anna took Pippa by the hand and followed Jack. He doubled back and held Pippa's other hand.

"Ready? One. Two. Three," he said. Anna caught on and they swung Pippa into the air for one giant leap. She cracked up.

"Again," she said.

"One. Two. Three. And up."

"Again!" she demanded.

After three more "agains" they'd reached the kiosk where they'd bought their tickets on arrival. They hadn't seen the owner then, but if anyone knew where he was, they'd be here. It wasn't the biggest deal. Mr. Chase seemed to recall who they were after a few reminders Jack had given over the phone. Anna didn't know they'd spoken and he'd asked Mr. Chase to keep it that way.

"Well, I'll be," a voice said from their right. "I haven't seen you two in ages."

A man who looked to be in his sixties stopped in front of them. Mr. Chase. He'd lost the hair on top of his head but still wore one long braid—now silver—over his shoulder. He'd put on some weight, too.

"Didn't you two used to come around here every other weekend during summers? And you—" He pointed to Anna. "You went to veterinary school, didn't you?"

"Um, yeah," she said, cocking her head. "How'd you know? I can't believe you remembered us."

Jack gave his head a subtle shake and hoped

Mr. Chase would catch on. The man cleared his throat.

"Oh, word gets around. You know how it is. Besides, not many folks came here as routinely as you did. Your faces became a fixture here," he said. "And who is this cutie?"

"This is our daughter, Pippa," Jack said.

"Pippa, did you know your mommy and daddy used to come around here all the time?" Mr. Chase asked.

She shook her head.

"Well, you come by as much as you like, squirt. Bring your mama along. You know, I won't be open much longer," Mr. Chase said.

"You're closing?" Anna asked.

He scratched the back of his head as he looked wistfully at the park's dated attractions. He sighed and returned his attention to Anna, Jack and "squirt."

"I'm losing money. Have been for a while. My staff is getting older and the younger generation has better things to do. They don't unplug long enough to spend time with nature. They watch wildlife shows in HD. Just like the real thing, right? And my parents need someone around full time. Age-related dementia. They live in Seattle. I'll be moving out there. Probably retire in the family home."

"Sorry to hear about your parents and the loss here," Anna said. "This place will be missed. What'll happen to the animals?"

Okay, she was curious. That was promising. She cared. It didn't matter where on the planet she found an animal in need. Anna cared, and she wasn't the type to stand by and watch.

"I honestly don't know. Guess that depends on who buys the place." Chase stated.

"That makes sense," Anna said.

Well, didn't it? Jack stood there in nerve-racked limbo, trying to get a solid read on her. Anna bit the corner of her lip as she looked down and looped her fingers through the curls on Pippa's head. Jack took a slow, deep breath. He was right. They were thinking along the same wavelength.

"I wonder if one of the wildlife organizations or rescue groups could help out? Maybe put you in touch with a facility or person that can place the animals in good care," she said.

So not quite the same wavelength. Jack let out his breath.

"I'm on it," Mr. Chase said.

Anna nodded and gave him a bright smile.

"It was so nice to see you again, Mr. Chase. Jack, it's time to get home. I think Pippa is going to go sloth on us any second. We're way past naptime." Anna shook Mr. Chase's hand and Jack followed suit with a quick nod.

"Good to see you again," he said, then reached down and scooped Pippa up. "No rabid monkeys allowed here, so naptime it is."

Anna beamed at him knowingly. Yes. He remembered every word she'd uttered at Busara, good and bad. Just like he remembered how much she used to love this place.

JACK DROVE DOWN the dirt road from the main entrance of the animal park. Pippa was exhaustingly happy. She'd been far more taken with the little gift shop here than the toy store she'd visited in town. Animal everything, everywhere.

She swung her feet from her car seat as she played with a stuffed lemur plush toy. She'd told the shopkeeper that Ambosi would be jealous of its tail. The clerk had no idea who Ambosi was.

A thud hit Jack through his seat every five seconds. And those little legs held more power than they let on. He flexed his fingers on the steering wheel.

"Hey, monkey, stop kicking, okay?" he said, eyeing her in the rearview mirror.

Anna reached back and held Pippa's ankles. "Stop. Your daddy has to drive," she said.

"Thanks," Jack murmured.

Anna propped her elbow against the door and rested her head against her palm.

"It's sad about Mr. Chase's parents," she said. "I hope he finds a buyer who'll take good care of the place, or at least find new homes for all the animals."

"Maybe zoo breeding programs?" Jack suggested.

"I doubt it," Anna said. "A few of the animals, maybe, but most of them were too old... or not endangered. Breeding programs tend to focus on endangered or at-risk species."

"Well, hopefully he'll find someone interested in the place." Jack glanced at Anna.

"It won't be easy." She sighed.

Another kick bolted him. "Hey, no kicking," he stressed. Pippa stopped.

He glanced in the rearview mirror and saw his daughter's big eyes staring back. Her thumb was nestled in her mouth. His throat clogged up. He was a parent. He hoped Pippa would never feel burdened with taking care of him if his health declined in old age. He never wanted to be anyone's burden again. His biological parents hadn't suffered from dementia, but they'd fried enough brain cells on heroin. They'd stared at him plenty of times when he'd been a little boy, looking as if they had no idea who he was. Pippa would never experience that.

"Hey, Pips. I can't drive with the kicking, but I'm not mad. Okay?"

He got a quick nod in response and felt his chest go limp.

Everyone got sucker punched by life sooner or later. Some more than once. Right now, he had a lot to figure out. Stuff he could handle without burdening Anna. She'd taken on enough…made it this far on her own. It was his turn to step up to the plate.

"Nothing meaningful is ever easy," Jack said.

From the way Anna rested her head back on the seat, reaching behind her to rub Pippa's leg softly, he knew she agreed.

JACK'S PHONE RANG just as he merged onto the main road into town. Zoe's name appeared on the screen. Anna jolted at the sound. She'd dozed off and he'd enjoyed stealing glances at her peaceful face.

"I'm sorry. Could you answer that for me?" he asked. "I've been getting flak for ignoring calls."

Anna pulled her hand back from Pippa, whose head kept nodding, then jerking up. Drool glistened at the corner of her mouth. Anna picked up his cell and answered. Her voice sounded drained and tired. Jack suspected it wasn't all about being jet-lagged. This was probably the first time in years she wasn't surrounded by the responsibilities of camp. Here, she could let go. He could do his part. He liked that.

"Oh, hey, Zoe. He's driving. Hang on." Anna pressed a button and held it up. "Okay, you're on speaker."

"Jack?" His sister's voice came through.

"What's up?"

"Can you guys swing by later? I need your help," Zoe said.

"What kind of help?" he asked. He'd help no matter what, but she was his sister and giving her a hard time was a requirement.

"I'm expecting Ben to Skype this evening,

and I need to get to the boxes at the back wall in the garage. The boxes you stored with us during your apartment move are in the way."

He'd never intended to leave his stuff there that long, but he was always so busy at the lab. Ben had helped him unload some of his stuff in their garage while he was in town during his last leave, a couple months ago. Moving boxes right now... Not the best time.

"Hang on. When I helped carry your crib and boxes of Chad's outgrown clothes down, I thought we stacked them behind my boxes. Wasn't that the point? So they wouldn't be in the way?"

"Yep," Zoe said, her voice exuding energy.

Anna's eyes widened and she straightened in her seat. She splayed her hands out as if to say, "Don't you get it?" Jack squinted at her, then at the road ahead.

No. Way.

"Zoe, are you pregnant again?" he asked.

"Yep!" she squeaked through the speaker. "I need to get the outfit Maddie and Chad came home from the hospital in, so I can put it in the background when I Skype Ben. It's how I told him about Chad. Maddie wants to put it on one of her dolls and carry the doll while she talks to her dad, see if he notices. I think it's a great idea, don't you?"

"Very cute. And congratulations, Zoe," Anna called out.

"Congrats, Fertile Myrtle," Jack said. And here he and Anna were just talking about breeding programs earlier.

"Jack!" Anna said, punching him softly in the arm. She closed her eyes and shook her head.

"What? It was a joke," Jack said.

"Jack, dear. I love ya, but promise me you'll never quit your lab job and go to work in public relations." Zoe chuckled. "You guys stopping by or what? I hate to ask. I know you probably have plans, Anna, and I don't want to—"

"Are you kidding? We're on our way," she said, before Jack could answer.

"Thank you. You guys are the best."

Zoe disconnected the call. Jack put his right hand over Anna's. Anna turned her head in surprise.

"Thank you," he said, then quickly let go, because he realized he didn't want to and the feeling scared him.

She slipped her hand back into her lap and

stared straight ahead. Her cheeks glowed. Because of his touch or because of Zoe's news? He decided it was the latter.

Was that how she'd looked and acted when she'd found out she was pregnant? Or had she been robbed of that joy because she'd been alone? Right now, she'd be experiencing it vicariously through Zoe, but he'd never be able to give her back what she'd missed. Unless she hadn't missed out entirely. Clearly, she hadn't missed or needed his friendship. Sharing the news? Showers and shopping and all the other stuff women bonded over? She had Niara.

Suddenly, Jack felt more appreciation for Niara's role in Anna's life, and in Pippa's, than he had before. She really was like family to Anna, just as the Harpers had become his. But the one person who she should have been able to turn to hadn't been there for her, because he'd somehow hurt her and she'd cut him out of her life.

Anna had always been there for Jack. She'd been there through his toughest years. His awkward, quiet teens, hiding in the chair at the back of their health ed. class because he could hear his name being passed around when drugs were discussed. The kid whose parents were addicts and had died of an over-dose. That's how he was known to every-one—except Anna. She had never walked away from him until the morning after Pippa was conceived. He missed that friendship. Owed it to her. He'd rebuild it, rebuild their connection, but this time he'd stop short of breaking it.

He glanced in the rearview mirror at Pippa again. His parenting instinct had kicked in and he kept automatically checking on her. Her eyes were drooping. What was it with cars, kids and sleepiness? He had a lot to learn.

Ben was about to find out he was a dad again. He had yet to find out he was an uncle. Jack couldn't wait for him to get back in a couple of months. Ben would have plenty of dad advice, for sure.

Jack had friends he hung out with on oc-casion—a group of other doctors and lab techs who'd meet up at a pub on Fridays after work—but not the kind he really connected with. He'd never caught on to the whole hang-out-with-buddies thing. There was Ben...or Kamau, he realized. Talking to Kamau was like talking to a college buddy he'd known for years. Jack liked the guy. Found his advice entertaining, and he'd never admit it to him, but the vet was pretty astute. Observant. Spot on, in fact.

Kamau wasn't here, though. It was good to know, however, that if Jack's idea didn't work out, someone trustworthy would be around for Anna when she returned to Kenya.

Alone.

ONLY FOUR OF Jack's boxes had fit into his car, so he'd left Anna and Pippa at Zoe's while he went to drop them off at his place. The rest had gotten moved aside for the next load. In the meantime, Zoe had found what she needed.

Anna was relieved to get some time away from Jack, but being with his mom after the way he'd touched her hand in the car felt uncomfortable. His mother had softened and had even insisted on being called Nina, but still. Anna wasn't a part of any of this. She couldn't even let her mind go in that direction. She knew life. She knew Jack. She knew impossibilities and disappointment. But the touch of his hand, the sincerity of his thanks, had caught her off guard.

Anna rubbed her upper arms as she took in the framed family photos clustered on the built-in shelves flanking Zoe's fireplace. With everyone connecting with Ben, Anna felt like an intruder. Plus, as confused as she felt, she didn't want to get cornered by Nina, as she had her first night here. Looking at photos— and they were all so beautiful, every face full of joy—gave her some semblance of a reason to be in the room. Family-crashing.

"Anna," Mrs. Harper whispered over her shoulder. "Why don't we take Pippa to the swings out back?"

"Of course," she said. She waited for Pippa to wave bye-bye to her new uncle, then led her out of the room. Anna didn't know why, but she felt a little embarrassed being here.

They followed Mrs. Harper into the kitchen, where she poured some cheese-flavored crackers into a plastic container for Pippa, grabbed a plate of chocolate chip cookies and motioned toward the screen door.

"How about we sit on the deck. Pippa can have fun on the play set," she suggested. They both looked back at the living room, the sound of Ben's voice carrying to them.

Anna opened the screen door and followed

Mrs. Harper outside in order to give Zoe and Ben some alone time. Pippa ignored the crackers and ran straight for the play set near the edge of the fenced yard. The structure was small enough to be safe for little ones, and she had no problem climbing the ladder for the slide. *Little monkey.* Anna hoped it wouldn't give her any stunt ideas back at camp. Pippa would graduate from imitating animal calls, and start climbing trees like Ambosi. And acacia trees had thorns.

It was a little cooler this evening. Anna sat on the top step and wrapped her arms around her knees. She'd forgotten how much she loved having four seasons. Early fall, with its crisp air, warm colors and harvest-themed gatherings, had always been her favorite time of year. It held the promise of Thanksgiving, one of the few meals of the year where both her parents would be present. It was the only time her family appeared to be traditional… together.

The rest of the holidays would inevitably go downhill. Too much of a reminder. Too much of a trigger for her mom. And any other time of year, they ate on their own, whenever it suited their schedules. Sure, Anna shared many meals with her mom, but most of the time she wandered alone into their empty kitchen, grabbed a snack and left. Here at Zoe's, every meal seemed to be a family event. Zoe's kitchen—and even Mrs. Harper's, as Anna recalled from the few times she'd stopped over to study with Jack during their school days—was modest, but always smelled wonderful and was always full of family.

Anna took in a slow, deep breath through her nose and closed her eyes. *You could never be like one of them. You could never make your life like this, because it isn't what you know. It's not you. You would never be able to hold everyone together, and breakups hurt everyone. But what about Pippa? What if this life became her model? Could she grow up normally? Be happy?*

Anna opened her eyes at the sound of Pippa yelling, "Run, run, run!" as she circled the playground over and over. Zoe had found an old sweater of Maddie's in one of the boxes and given it to Pippa. She would have a whole wardrobe of Maddie's hand-me-downs if she lived here. Pippa was definitely starting to act more at home now, especially after visiting the wildlife park. That had been so thoughtful and considerate of Jack. He was paying attention to his daughter.

Mrs. Harper sighed and Anna looked at her.

"I'm sorry. I didn't mean to ignore you. It's just been a long day and this is all so beautiful. The yard, the weather. It's dreamy," Anna said.

"I love it here. There's something about September that makes me want to cook and bake nonstop. And being close to my grandkids is such a joy."

Anna smiled and linked her fingers together. She glanced at Pippa playing. The missing grandchild.

"Oh, I didn't mean that as a jab," Mrs. Harper quickly added. "I mean, it would be so perfect if Pippa were nearby, too, but—"

"Don't worry. I didn't take it the wrong way. I'm sure Maddie and Chad love having their grandparents around. And Zoe...I'm sure it's such a help for her. Especially with Ben gone so much."

"We help when we can. That's what family is for, after all. Good friends are priceless, too."

Anna nodded, grateful for the acknowledgment that her friends in Kenya were indeed invaluable. She wouldn't have survived without them.

"Look, Anna. I promise I won't pry anymore, and I'm sorry about that first night when I came on strong. I let mama bear take over and wasn't thinking about your feelings. That was terrible of me. I'm also sorry about tweeting and telling your mother when she called the other morning," Nina said. "I was so excited that I didn't think, and she never connects with me online or anywhere, so she wasn't on my mind when I sent out the message."

"It's okay. It all turned out for the best. And I completely understand the mama bear thing, although I have to admit I've gotten in the habit of switching the expression to mama elephant. They are highly protective." Anna grinned.

"Still, I'm sorry," Nina said.

"No, you didn't know, and don't be sorry. If anyone owes apologies to everyone, it's me. Especially to Jack."

Seeing Ben talking to his family over a monitor had twisted Anna's heart. He wasn't always around for them, but he was gone because he was trying to follow his calling, do right by all and give his family a better life. He missed out on so much as his kids grew. So many milestones. For all his sacrifices, he deserved more. And Zoe... She was phenomenal, always positive and upbeat. If she ever felt down, she didn't show it—at least not in the time Anna had spent with her. And Anna suspected she held it together for Ben's sake and for their kids.

That was love. Zoe and Ben's love was strong enough to survive his deployment. Marriage needed that. Jack had never loved her that way. Anna had been nothing but a familiar comfort to him. He didn't know the difference.

She did. She'd seen love and the lack of it. It's what had been missing between her parents and why their marriage didn't make it. It's why her mom couldn't let go of the past... and why Anna had needed so badly to protect her from more pain.

Her mom had trusted her to watch over her baby brother. If her mom had found out about Pippa, and grown attached to her, she'd have become paranoid about Anna raising her so far away and under strange circumstances.

Her mom would have lost it. She was fragile as it was. Noncompliant with therapy and
meds, and Anna wouldn't have been around
to make sure she was okay. No one, Jack included, could have comprehended the fear,
guilt and doubt that had plagued Anna when
she found out she was pregnant. Those first
months after Pippa's birth... Bless Niara for
having been there, consoling and reassuring
her that she was a good, caring mother.

Deep down, there was a niggling need
to prove that she could protect a baby, that
she could give life and save a life. She was
so sorry now for Jack having missed out on
so much with his child, but she hadn't had
a choice. He would have taken Pippa. He'd
have gone out of his way to disrupt the family
and the life she'd built—her sanctuary where,
for once, life made sense.

"Life's scary, isn't it? There are never any
guarantees, but there are so many possibilities. Trust me. You don't get to my age without learning a thing or two about life. Have a
cookie," Mrs. Harper said.

A cookie—with a glass of advice. Anna
took a cookie and waited.

"You know, when Jack first came to live

with us, he barely spoke for several months. So glum and withdrawn. He would sit on his bed, reading for hours on end. Loved science and how-to books. I'd been told that he might use fantasy or fiction as an escape, but I think the nonfiction books made him feel in control. Made him feel like he understood or had a grasp of something concrete, since he hadn't had control of his life before.

"Anyway, I digress. My point is that it didn't matter how I decorated his room, how many new clothes he got or how much praise we gave, he'd simply thank us and clam up. I saw so much in that boy's eyes, in his face, that it killed me not to be able to break through, to see him let his guard down and embrace life. It was almost a year before he gave me a sign. It was a Valentine's card made just for me. Not the ones every kid makes at school, but one he'd come up with on his own, in his room. I still have it. You know what it said?"

Anna shook her head in spite of the rhetorical question.

"'You're more important to me than all the genetic material on earth,'" Mrs. Harper quoted.

Anna broke into laughter, the kind that released with an unraveling of nerves, and Mrs. Harper joined her. Pippa looked at them and clapped, thinking all the commotion was for her successful turn at the slide. Anna waved.

Mrs. Harper was right. Jack had always been such a bookworm. Even as a kid, he loved reading. Books had always been a big deal to him, especially science books. In fact, he'd always had a book with him whenever they hung out.

"That's so like him." Anna laughed. "I guarantee, he won't live that down."

"Don't tell him I told you."

"Fine. I won't. But I'm not sure I'll be able to keep a straight face when he gets back," Anna said. They both laughed, and this time Pippa ran up and barreled into Anna's knees.

"What's so funny?" she asked.

"Nothing, sweetie," Anna said. "Go back and slide some more. I'm watching." Pippa ran off to perform.

"I guess I'm trying to say that not everyone shows love the same way," Mrs. Harper said, then softened her voice. "And I don't want to see Jack hurt. Not again."

Anna was saved from commenting. Maddie opened the screen door and helped her little brother crawl backward down the steps into the yard. It would be interesting to see how well Pippa did at taking turns now that she didn't have the play set to herself.

Zoe followed them out and plopped down next to Anna. "He is so-o-o excited," she gushed. "He can't wait to hear if it's a boy or a girl."

"It won't be long," her mom said. "I'll come with you to the appointment if you want."

"Of course I want you to, but I just wish he was going to be here for the ultrasound," Zoe said. She cradled her cheeks in her hands, with her elbows on her thighs.

"But at least he'll be here full-time before the baby turns one," Mrs. Harper pointed out. Well, that was good news Anna hadn't known. All three women looked at the kids.

It was the first time Zoe had sounded sad. Anna thought about her pregnancy in Kenya. Until she'd met Niara, she had no one to share it with. Still, when it came to hearing heartbeats and seeing ultrasounds—and hearing Pippa's first cry—she'd been alone. And scared to death.

Zoe was married and surrounded by family, yet the one person she wanted to share those moments with was on the other side of the world. Anna hadn't expected to feel so connected to Zoe. Their lives were so different, yet their pregnancy experiences were parallel. Zoe didn't have a choice. Anna had, but still, she wished Jack had been there. She wished he'd shared those moments with her. She wished she'd known at the time how much he would have sincerely cared about his baby girl. She didn't doubt that now, but she also didn't doubt that there would have been issues with her working in Kenya and him working here. Same issues as the present.

Chad tripped and fell into the grass.

"I'll get him," Mrs. Harper said, waving at Zoe to stay where she was.

"Thanks, Mom." Zoe leaned back. "I don't know how you do it," Zoe said, once Nina was out of earshot.

"Me?" Anna asked. Zoe was the Wonder Woman.

"Yes, you. Getting through pregnancy and delivery, then raising a baby, all in the wilds of Africa. I don't know what I'd do without the convenience of magic diaper bins or a dishwasher, or anything, for that matter."

"I had a dedicated, giant pot for boiling

cloth diapers, and no, it wasn't a fun task, but it beats elephant funk."

Zoe wrinkled her nose. "Like I said, I'm in awe."

"You're the one who's the perfect mom. You handle everything so well…on your own, too."

"Well, that's something I know you can empathize with," Zoe said. "Even with family or friends around, it's not the same. They're not there at two in the morning and again at four. And heaven forbid one of the other kids wakes up in between or gets sick. I'm convinced I keep the coffee industry alive."

"That makes two of us," Anna said.

"I'm so tired, though. So tired. And here I am complaining when you…you're like Jane Goodall or Dian Fossey."

"Only I work with pachyderms, not primates." Anna grinned and Zoe chuckled.

"Point taken, but still."

"Trust me, Zoe. Life here is more complicated in a lot of ways. You're doing an amazing job."

They watched the kids chasing their grandmother while she pretended she couldn't outrun them.

"I can't do this," Jack's sister suddenly blubbered. She dropped her face into her lap.

"Oh, Zoe. I didn't mean to make you cry."

She shook her head. "No, it isn't you." Zoe's voice came out muffled.

Anna put her hand on her back. She wasn't sure what to say. The last thing she expected was for Zoe to admit she couldn't handle things. She seemed to have a routine down and then some. Maybe this required a mother–daughter moment. Anna glanced at Mrs. Harper, who was oblivious to what was going on, and then back to Zoe. "Are you okay?"

Zoe looked up and wiped her face on the hem of her shirt. "I'll be okay. Let's blame it on hormones. That and seeing Ben. Hearing his voice. It gets me every time."

Anna put her arm around Zoe and gave her a squeeze. She remembered the hormones, all right. She remembered hearing Jack's voice in her head, seeing his face when her eyes closed…and feeling uncertain about everything. She also remembered that sometimes words weren't as necessary as the simple reassurance that someone understood. That someone appreciated what you were going through.

And boy, did she remember the call she'd made to her mom, ready to tell her, needing her to *be* a mom. Instead, Anna had ended up listening to her mother cry, and consoling her worries that something would happen to Anna in Africa, that she'd lose her only other child, and only family since the divorce. The panicked sobs Anna had listened to from her hotel room in Nairobi, right before her first ultrasound appointment, had confirmed that she couldn't tell her. She'd made her mom promise to keep seeing her psychologist.

Anna had been on her own, overwhelmed with what-ifs. What if something happened to her baby? What if she, like her mom, ended up with postpartum depression, or the chronic depression that ensued after the loss of her child? A depression that tore up everyone around her. Anna understood the fears of pregnancy and motherhood as well as what it was like to cope with a parent struggling with anxiety and depression. And Anna had caused enough pain and loss. She so wished she'd been able to have her mom around.

Anna and Zoe sat in silence and watched everyone play. This felt right. It felt like a normal family. Down to earth. Together for one another. Safe. Anna missed that.

But here, she felt like a bird-watcher with foggy lenses. She missed Busara.

ANNA PUT HER HAND against Pippa's head. Burning hot. But just how hot, she didn't know. Jack didn't have a thermometer. Not even the old-fashioned in-the-rump kind. She'd hated going through his bathroom cabinet, but there were priorities at hand. All she found out was that there wasn't any child medicine in there, either.

She brushed her hand across Pippa's cheek. She was fast asleep. Finally. After being rocked for half an hour with a cool washcloth on her brow.

Anna slipped off the edge of the bed and sneaked out of the room. She still needed to get Pippa something for the congestion and fever. The poor thing was miserable.

Jack had gone into work to check on things, and hadn't answered his cell. She'd tried calling it six times, and didn't have the lab's number. *The kitchen.* Anna hurried to the kitchen and started with the cabinet closest to the fridge. No luck in any of them. He didn't keep any medication in the house? In the third drawer from the fridge, she found a box of Band-Aids and a tube of Neosporin, but that was it. She gave up and walked into the living room. This not-answering-his-phone business was seriously annoying. Cells were for emergencies. Who didn't answer their cell?

Anna picked up the house phone and tried to call him again. Still no answer. She was done trying. *Zoe.* Zoe would have sick-kid supplies, or maybe she'd give Anna a ride to the drugstore. She was about to scroll through Jack's contacts for Zoe's number when he walked in.

Anna shoved the phone back in its charger. "Why don't you ever answer your phone?"

Jack stopped midstep, the door still ajar. He gave her a what-got-in-your-socks look.

"I was driving and I hate those earpieces."

"You've been driving for the past four hours?"

"Uh, no. But I had my hands full…at the lab." Jack rubbed his jaw, then scratched his ear. "I forgot to check before leaving the parking lot. I was just checking it on my way up the steps and saw your missed calls, but I'm here now, so what's wrong?"

"Pippa has a really bad cold and fever."

Jack dropped his keys on the counter and went to Pippa's room. He touched her face with both hands and swore.

"She's pretty warm. We should take her to the emergency room," he said.

"I'm sure it's a cold. I'm not taking her to the E.R. for a cold."

"What if it's not a cold? She could be coming down with something she caught in Kenya. What if it's malaria, or something worse?"

"She's been in Kenya all her life, then gets on a crowded plane with recirculated air, spends time with her cousins—who are probably walking petri dishes inoculated with viruses from school—and has had her hands on just about every visible surface in a toy store and animal park, and you think she has some exotic African disease?"

"If you're so sure it's a cold, why are you on edge? You're biting my head off, Anna."

Anna put her hands on her temples and sighed.

"I'm sorry." She slumped down next to Pippa and laid a hand on her tiny shoulder. "I called Mom earlier. I wanted to take Pippa to see her. *I* needed to see her, but she seemed, I don't know, reluctant? It was odd, like she didn't want us dropping by so soon. I thought she'd be happy, but I guess with Pippa sick, it's a moot issue.

"Chad had a runny nose when we were over there. She's not used to being around so many different people, remember? The weather changes. The sleep pattern changes. You know the signs. You can't panic the first time you see your child sick. Trust me on that. It doesn't help." Anna put her hand against Pippa's forehead for the umpteenth time. The fact was, her heart gave out every time Pippa got sick.

Jack nodded. "I still think we should take her to see a doctor."

"I'll tell you what. Just go to the drugstore for me. All I need is a thermometer and some child-strength fever medicine. And get her some nasal saline, too. If her fever gets worse or she's not doing better by tomorrow, we'll take her to a doctor or an urgent-care clinic."

All she needed was for Jack to walk into an E.R. spouting words like *Africa, malaria* or whatever came to mind. They'd end up spending the rest of their short visit in quarantine,

with Pippa being tested for every disease possible when she had no signs of anything but
a cold.

Jack stiffened and held up a hand.

"Um…I've never bought kid medicine. I
wouldn't know which brand—"

"Jack, you work in a lab. You can handle a
drugstore. Just ask the pharmacist for help."

"Or you can come and get whatever works
for her." He gave his collar a tug. He was nervous? Because of medications…*drugs*. Anna
recalled his reaction at the hospital.

"Okay," Anna said. "I guess we'll go together and take her along. You can wait in
the car with her while I run in to get what
we need."

A relieved Jack followed her to the bedroom. He scooped Pippa up gently and pulled
a small pink throw off the bed to cover her
with. Anna grabbed his keys from near the
door and locked it behind them, then opened
the car so he could set her in the car seat.

Pippa woke up while Anna was buckling
her in, and started fussing and crying. It
was going to be a long day and night. Anna
thought of what Zoe had said about not having anyone to help at two in the morning,

and suddenly felt grateful that Jack was here, even if he was jumping to paranoid diagnoses. At least she wasn't alone.

IT WAS LATE, but Anna couldn't fall asleep. She took Jack's cordless house phone and slipped out onto his balcony. He was out cold on the sofa, with Pippa draped across his chest. Bless his heart, he really was a great father. Anna would miss him more than he'd ever know.

How she wished he could let go and love her, but he didn't, not that way. After the way her dad closed himself off to her and her mom, Anna couldn't settle for anything less than soul-penetrating love. Love that would last through sickness and health. Especially the sickness part.

Pippa was snoring. Poor thing was so congested, the beat of Jack's heart and the warmth of his chest were the only things that made her feel better, and had eventually lulled her to sleep. He was a living hot water bottle. A comfort Anna wasn't getting.

She slid the glass door slowly shut, so as not to wake them, and dialed the numbers she'd jotted down on the back of a toy store receipt. Her mom had moved since the divorce and Anna didn't have the new number memorized.

"Hello?" Her mother's voice dragged.

"Sorry, Mom. Did I wake you?"

"Almost, but not quite. I'm in bed reading. I think I started dozing off."

"I can call tomorrow," she said, but she really wanted to talk now.

"Anna, what's up? Is Pippa okay?"

"She's fine," Anna lied. A white lie worth its weight, because she didn't want her mom worrying and getting in a car half asleep and in the dark. "I just wanted to talk. We missed seeing you today and we're not here that long, so I thought maybe we could plan something."

There was a momentary pause where all Anna heard was the hum of cars along the street in front of the complex and the sound of a book slapping shut.

"I'm sorry about earlier. I want to see both of you as much as possible. I, um, the place was a mess and I hadn't showered and all. I knew Jack would be bringing you. I didn't need him seeing me like that."

A car horn honked in the distance and Anna watched the headlights of someone coming home late turning into a parking spot across from Jack's. Anna shivered in the night air. She'd been concerned for nothing. Her mom simply wanted time to clean up. After all, she had been a neat-freak before she started having episodes. Caring was a good sign.

"That's okay. Mom?"

"Yes, Anna."

"Do you still have my old things? My books and the animal figurines I had on the shelf over my bed?"

"Actually, I do." Her mother sounded relieved at the change of topic. "I boxed them carefully and put them in storage when I moved."

"I'd like Pippa to have them. I thought I'd pick them up and leave them here at Jack's, since they'd probably get ruined at Busara."

"Anna, why Jack's place? Why not leave them here at mine? She could stay with me when she visits. Jack would be at work most of the time, anyway."

Anna tapped the phone against her chest and took in a cool breath of night air. She couldn't leave Pippa alone at Sue's. What if her mom had a bad day? Pippa was too young to handle that. Anna had been older and it had been tough enough. And what if there were prescription drugs lying around?

"Mom, she has a bedroom here. You'd see her all the time, and I'm sure Jack will need both you and his parents to help out when she's here. But he's her father."

"Okay. That makes sense, I suppose, but Anna, be careful. Don't let him take her from you."

"We're just talking visits, Mom. We haven't gone beyond that."

"You know I love you and only want you to be happy. I'm simply saying don't let him get more than visits. And for God's sake, Anna, learn from my life. Don't set yourself up for disappointment. Don't marry him. If you can do anything to put my mind at rest, promise me that."

CHAPTER TWELVE

PIPPA WAS DOING much better.

Her fever had broken the following morning and the saline washes were helping tremendously with her stuffy nose. After a day of chicken noodle soup and cartoons, she had slept soundly all night. Anna had given her a morning bath, steaming up the bathroom beforehand with her own shower. That had helped, as well. As did driving around. Pippa loved the feel of gliding on smooth, paved roads. Not a pothole in sight.

Jack had dropped Anna off on campus for her meeting. He said he had errands to run, but assured her that he could handle taking Pippa with him. Anna was positive he and Pippa were having a lot more fun riding around and doing chores than she was having facing Dr. Miller right now.

Miller laced his fingers together and settled them across his paunch. Anna gripped the arms of her chair and tilted her head, as if changing her angle would change what she was hearing.

"It is what it is, Anna," he said. *Unbelievable.* She narrowed her eyes at him, fury drying her mouth.

"How can you sit there and say that?"

"Watch it, Anna. You're sounding ungrateful. I may no longer be able to support your research, but I've given you years of backing. Don't forget who advised you freshman year. Who helped you with your senior project. Who helped establish your career and reputation."

He wanted to play politics, did he? Family, work—she couldn't escape it. Anna hated politics. She let go of the chair and clasped her hands in her lap.

"Dr. Miller, with all due respect, I'm not trying to be unappreciative. I love my work, which is why I've been killing myself to produce data that will not only have my name on it, but this institution's. *Your* name. Your support has always been appreciated, more than you know, but don't you imply it was given for free. I earned it. I'm *still* earning it, but this has become bigger than one study or our reputations. This is about saving a sentient, extraordinary and loving species from inhumane killings and suffering. Those orphaned elephants need us there. It doesn't matter if there are others supporting the cause. It's not enough. If you cared enough to fund research on them, then care enough to continue your support. Please."

Dr. Miller picked up a pen from his desk and studied the engraving on it before pointing it at her.

"You will have earned it when the paper is complete, as is required by your permit to conduct research in Kenya. I won't have my reputation as your sponsor marred. Anna, you've done a fantastic job, but this needs wrapping up. Our efforts to secure funding and grant money need to be concentrated elsewhere."

Elsewhere meant his joint study with Jack. She wasn't getting anywhere with him. Dr. Miller swiveled his ergonomic chair left and right and propped an ankle on his knee.

"Things happen for a reason. I needed to revamp our expenses. My meeting with Jack helped to solidify the board's decision, and it's too late to change it."

Jack hadn't said a word about meeting with Dr. Miller. Of course, she'd known his initial purpose in Busara, but surely after his visit and all that had happened since, he hadn't gone behind her back to undermine her work.

"However, if you want a lab position, I can get you one. In this department or any of your choosing," Miller said, splaying his hands as if all he had to do was wave a wand.

Anna stood. "A lab position? I'm a wild-animal veterinarian. All these years…your advice and mentorship…I thought you respected that." She bent and grabbed her purse. "I'm not working in a lab. In fact, I'll finish things up with the paper. After all, I have my own reputation to uphold. But after that, I'm done, Bob. Consider this my notice. I'll find a way to keep Busara going on my own."

Anna left the room and walked briskly toward the elevator. How it was possible to feel empowered, free, depressed and let down all at once, she hadn't a clue. Nothing made sense. No amount of planning would fix the mess her life was in. Everything had changed, and change was scary. She had no idea what she was going to do to save her sanctuary, but what hurt more was that Jack had sided against her.

His car was parked at the curb in front of their department building. Anna stormed past it and toward the campus exit. She caught him craning his neck and heard him start the engine, but she kept going. She needed to cool off. Pippa didn't need to witness her parents arguing, and Anna didn't trust herself not to blow it.

The situation was sinking deeper by the minute. Of all the things Jack could do... She'd trusted him. Let her guard down. Used the tickets to come see him. The email she'd gotten from Kamau said that everything and everyone was fine and that he hadn't heard anything from Miller. Miller hadn't emailed because he'd planned to meet her face-to-face. And Jack had handed him a way. *I'm so stupid.*

Her eyes stung. Each stride hit the ground like a rhino on the attack, only here there was no soil to absorb the shock. No dust to kick up. Just unrelenting, manmade sidewalk. *Men.*

Jack's car slowed next to her and she heard the whirring sound of the passenger window rolling down. Pippa called to her from the backseat and Anna's steps faltered. She didn't want to ignore her, but sometimes a parent needed a time-out. She longed for her observation platform under her acacia tree.

Anna set her jaw and pushed back the wisp of hair that had escaped her ponytail. She couldn't let Pippa see her so out of control. She glanced sideways, just to be sure her baby seemed all right. Jack looked as white as a lab coat. He grabbed a manila envelope off the front passenger seat and stashed it between his seat and his door.

"Get in the car, Anna," he said, leaning to the side. She heard the click of the door unlocking.

Forget it. She ignored him and kept walking.

"You can't walk all the way back home," he insisted. He didn't even ask what was wrong. *He knew.*

"Ha! First of all, your apartment is not my home. And secondly, I can walk a lot farther than you can imagine," she said. If it sounded like a threat, good. He was playing dumb. He knew exactly why she was so angry.

"Anna, please get in. You'll upset Pippa and she's sick."

"Don't you dare pull a guilt trip on me. You…you *traitor*."

A car switched lanes and passed Jack, honking once. Good thing it wasn't a high-traffic road.

"Drive normally. You're endangering our child," Anna said.

"Then tell me what I've done. And I am driving carefully. You're the danger."

"You stole my funding. He's not sponsoring an extension on my research permit, and you gave him what he needed to do that. Kenya won't let me stay without one. I only have enough funds and permission to stay for two more months, and then it's over. I can't stay unless I can find a job there that needs an expat to fill it. Do you know how long that could take? What happens to Busara in the interim? What happens to our orphans? Seems I've overstayed my welcome everywhere."

"There are other jobs around here, Anna."

"That's what Miller said. Were you banking on that? Did you two have an agreement? Decide that would appease me? Force me back here with Pippa and solve all your problems?"

"I didn't tell him to do that," Jack said. "Get in so we can talk."

"No."

"Fine." Jack stepped on the gas and drove ahead.

Anna stared, wide-mouthed. He had *not* just done that. And now Pippa had heard a fight *and* witnessed her father abandoning her mother.

It was a good twenty minutes before Anna reached the apartment. She knocked, but no one answered. Great. She plopped down on the step to wait. She smiled, muttered a quick hello and agreed to something about enjoying the fresh air when one of his neighbors needed to pass. She scooted over, then resumed her wait. Sitting here was nothing like sitting on her platform at Busara. There she found peace and could think with clarity. Here her senses were overloaded with fumes, traffic noise, other people…and her emotions. Forget her emotions. She was a mess.

Jack pulled into his parking space fifteen minutes later. He grabbed a manila envelope, slammed his car door and climbed the steps two at a time. Alone.

"Where's Pippa?" Anna looked back at the car.

Without a word, he unlocked his apartment and went in, leaving the front door ajar for her.

He was mad at *her?* He had no right to be mad. That was the problem with men. They could flip any situation upside down and make it seem like they were the ones having to tolerate things. If men had to process every practical and emotional detail women micro-managed, they'd go extinct. Anna counted to ten before she got up and followed him in.

He was pulling coffee and a box of filters out of a cabinet. He didn't look up as he filled the coffeepot with tap water.

"*Where's* Pippa?" she asked again.

"What, you don't trust me? Don't worry. I dropped her off at my mom's house. She has plenty of experience with sick kids. She had soup on the stove before I made it out the front door. I figured Pippa could do without hearing her parents argue or make a scene."

Another point against Anna. She'd made a public scene and set a bad example for her daughter. She waited for him to finish with the tap, then washed her hands before grabbing a bottle of springwater from the fridge and taking a long drink.

"I told my mom that Pippa and I would go see her for dinner. I need to give her a bath and change her clothes," Anna said.

"We can go get her before then," he said without looking up.

Fine. Anna folded her arms at her waist and tapped her foot.

"May I borrow your laptop?" she asked. He motioned to where it was on the kitchen table. She took that as a yes and went to boot it up. She needed to send Kamau a warning email. It would still be a few days before she got back to help figure things out. He needed the heads-up. He'd asked for it, warned her, and she'd assured him this would not happen. That she had things under control.

Anna squeezed her temples, then propped her elbow on the table and covered her eyes with one hand, blocking everything out but the electronic chatter of the computer waking up. She jerked up at the thud of ceramic on wood.

Jack had set a mug of coffee next to her and was headed to his armchair. A peace offering? Or an indication of how long the peace talks would take? Well, *she* wasn't at peace and didn't see any in their future. Let him simmer a little. Maybe the caffeine would jog his brain and conscience. If only he could grasp what he'd done and what the consequences would be.

She opened the laptop and used a guest log-in to email Kamau, taking her time to hit Send. She needed to make sure Kam understood what was happening. The walk had certainly cooled her temper, but she was still trying to come to terms with Jack's role in everything. Closing the computer was like closing a chapter in her life. This could not be the beginning of the end of Busara. She cradled the warm mug in her hands and joined him in the living room.

"Thanks for the coffee," she said. Jack didn't look at her.

"I didn't tell him to shut you down," he finally said, after she sat on the end of the sofa closest to his chair. The lines on his forehead had deepened in the last few days. He looked troubled. She had to give him that. Who was she kidding? Jack wasn't a bad person at all, just…misguided, and totally clueless at times. He could handle the most complex scientific questions and calculations, but hand him a basic, simple concept—raw life—and it was like he couldn't whittle his brain down enough to handle it. But that wasn't her problem. Jack was a big boy. He didn't need saving. Busara did.

"If you didn't advise him to shut me down, then who gave him the idea to save on expenses by making arrangements with larger rescue facilities to take my animals?"

Jack wiped his face with both hands.

"I thought so," Anna said.

"He demanded ideas. You'd done everything right with the bookkeeping, but he wanted a way to cut back. He wasn't giving me an option. Don't you see? He'd planned on this all along. He was being manipulative. I warned you."

Anna set down her mug. "If you thought that, then why would you help him do it? Why give him the idea? Why give him freaking options? He ran with it. I mean, why should he bother paying for anything if he figured I'd been there long enough and there were others who could take care of the elephants? It's nothing but paperwork to him. He's never been there. You have."

"Anna, it was the lesser evil. You send those calves to transition at a bigger reserve when they reach a certain age, anyway. I tried talking to him, but he pretty much had his mind made up, if you ask me. The man has weight to throw around. This project I've committed to with him is huge. It's a career catapult. It means I won't *ever* fall short on providing for Pippa. And you have to understand, when I left him my findings, I had just gotten back from Nairobi. None of...*this*...had happened," Jack said.

"This? This what? Friendship? Is this what you do to a friend? No amount of trying to justify what you did will change things. Logic won't work here, Jack. Busara isn't about numbers and test tubes and assays and analyzing. For once—just once—could you think without your head?" Anna folded her own head down onto her knees. She felt sick with frustration, but after what she'd done, keeping his child from him, she had no right to pull that one on him. Betrayal of trust and friendship. Which one of them was guiltier?

"Forget I said that. Forget everything," she said, her head still down.

"I'll figure out a way to fix this," Jack said. "What about asking your dad for help? The man could fund ten Busaras if he wanted to. If anything, he could donate money to whatever reserve your elephants get moved to. They'll be covered and you could have a choice of where to be. I mean, it doesn't really matter where you are, as long as you're saving animals, right? Isn't that all that matters?"

"No," she said softly. "It's not that simple, and I won't ask my dad for help. He didn't even want me going to vet school. Medical school was more prestigious. Gave a better return on the money. He's all about investments, not charities and research, or saving animals' lives."

Her dad invest in saving elephants? He hadn't even cared enough to save her *mom* from suffering. And it would be just like him to demand a say in how Busara was run if he put money into it. She wasn't about to give him that power. Not after she'd spent her life building endurance, proving she could take care of herself and her mother and every living thing that crossed her path since her brother died.

She raised her head and rubbed her palms along her thighs. "I'll figure something out. I still have a few months."

Jack reached out and took her hands in his.

Anna started to pull away, but his hands felt warm, secure, all-encompassing. If only he could see her as more than a friend. More than an option. If only he could have loved her the way Ben loved Zoe. But he didn't. Not then, not now. As with her father and Miller, it was every man for himself.

"Anna, there's always a way. I know I can help, but I need to know if you believe that I didn't mean for any of this to happen," Jack said. Anna looked at their joined hands and didn't answer. Saying yes would be a lie. A second passed, then he let go and she slipped her hands between her knees, but it didn't help. She felt cold, inside and out. More isolated than at Busara.

Jack rose.

"I, um, I'm going to take a quick shower and change before we go get Pippa. That way you can use the bathroom for her," Jack said. Anna frowned. "To give her a bath. You said you needed to do that before going to your mom's."

"Oh, right. But there are two bathrooms."

Jack's nose turned red and his forehead scrunched. He pointed awkwardly toward the hall leading to the bath and bedrooms.

"I'm just gonna save time," he said. Anna nodded and waited until he'd disappeared down the hall, then collapsed back against the sofa. She waited until she heard the water turn on, then pressed her hands against her cheeks and willed herself not to break down. This wasn't happening. Maybe there was a way. Or not. She couldn't think straight.

She got up, grabbed the mug off the table and downed the cooled coffee like water, then went to wash out the mug. A plan. That's all she needed to start with. They had a few months worth of funds at most. They'd contact everyone they knew, for starters. No doubt Kam was already on that. Miller would want his equipment back, or its value. She needed to make a note of that before she forgot. One more thing to consider, but she didn't care how many she got bombarded with. She wasn't going to let everyone at Busara down.

Jack's cell phone started ringing and dancing against the kitchen counter near the fridge. She ignored it. Then it hit her. What if his mom was calling? What if Pippa wasn't doing well? Anna lunged for the phone and looked at the caller. Lake Real Estate? Jack was barely moved in here. The phone went silent and she set it back down, relieved it wasn't about Pippa, but kind of curious. *Kind* of. Jack's life and where he lived was his business, just as hers was hers.

Five seconds hadn't passed before the house line started ringing. Anna could hear the shower still running. She went to the living room, thought twice and picked up the phone.

"Hello?…No. Can I take a message?… One sec." Anna propped the phone against her shoulder. She grabbed the notepad and pen—both imprinted with a lab supply company logo she recognized—that sat perfectly aligned with the phone base. "Okay." She put the pen tip to the pad and listened. Her feet went ice-cold and she set the pen down. "Of course. I'll tell him to call you back right away."

Jack. What have you done?

Anna put a hand to her stomach. She was going to puke. Pretty close to where Pippa had graced the carpet, too. Why that struck her she didn't know. Because it had been the first day she'd woken up here? Because in some ridiculous, subconscious, repressed way, at the time she'd let herself believe in possibilities? *What have you done?*

She closed her eyes, and when she opened them, Jack stood there, hair still wet and disheveled and his shirt unbuttoned and hanging loose over his jeans. The corners of his eyes sank with the tension of his clamped jaw. The only movement was the repeating glide of his neck muscles as he swallowed, and the rapid rise and fall of his chest.

Anna licked her lips and squeezed them together. She hugged herself and shrugged her right shoulder.

"Your Realtor just called. He said it was important and he was afraid you wouldn't check your cell phone messages." She smirked and cocked her head. "You must've been working with him for a while if he knows you that well. He tried to be cryptic, but I don't know, Jack, how many 'sellers' would ask to up a closing date because their parents out West took a turn for the worse? Tell me it's just a coincidence."

Jack scrubbed his jaw and looked toward the patio door.

"Jack!" Anna paced like a caged lioness. "The animal park? What in the world were you thinking?"

"I was thinking it's the perfect chance—

the best way—for both of us to be with Pippa. You could do amazing things to that place. Run an endangered breeding program or something."

"Or something? Are you insane? What in the freaking universe makes you think I'd want to leave Busara?"

"You know you can find care for the elephants, and the animals at this park are the ones who were about to lose their home. A man needed to be with his parents. It all makes sense. This could be your next project. Your research at Busara is essentially over. You don't even know if you'll find funding," he said.

"How perfect for you. Was Miller in on this, too?" Anna rubbed her nose with the back of her hand, then pressed her fist to her chest. "Busara is more than research. It's a rescue. It's my life…and Pippa's. I could never walk away from it. If I had money to invest in a place, I'd be putting it in Busara, fighting poaching and saving those dear, helpless babies. I don't want any animal anywhere to suffer, but those ones are my responsibility, Jack. I don't walk away from those who count on me or need me. I came here. I trusted you. And this is what you go and do? Pretend you're taking Pippa to the park to play?"

"It *was* about taking Pippa to play, and making her happy. This idea came up after I suggested the park, not before. Pippa needs to come first. She's a child, and having her parents spread across the globe isn't fair to her. Not when there's an easy way to have us both nearby. She comes first, Anna. Pippa does." Jack sliced the air between them with his hand, before running it back through his hair.

Anna stopped pacing and stared at him. "Don't you dare make me feel bad for caring, or imply that I don't put her first. Why do you think I came here? Just because my heart is in my work doesn't for one minute mean I don't put Pippa above all. I would give my life for her and I've never put her second. I would have given anything as a child to have the kind of life she has at Busara. If *you* were putting her first, you would've put your savings into her future or into the only home she's known—not that I would ever take a dime from you—instead of squandering it on a place you won't even know what to do with."

"I didn't squander. I invested. In all of us. And I'm not some poor street kid," Jack said, his underlying reference quite clear. "I've been a bachelor—through no fault of my own—with a good income and no real expenses until now. And against my will, Pippa's education has been paid for. So I did put my savings in her future—by trying to make sure she'd have her mother around."

Anna dug her nails into her scalp and let out a frustrated growl that could have challenged Pippa's animal calls.

"Jack! Don't you get it? You bought a park! An entire park without even discussing it with me. How could you do something so stupid?"

"Because you make me stupid!" Jack yelled back, flinging his hands in the air.

"What?"

"No. That's not what I meant. I mean you make me do stupid things."

"That's so much better. Great to know we bring out the best in each other," Anna said. She felt so deflated, disappointed and...dead. Feelings she'd promised herself she'd never experience again when she'd first left for Kenya, in the wake of her parents' divorce and Jack's hollow attempt at proposing.

Anna understood where he was coming from right now—she did. But why couldn't he understand that she wasn't some prop to move around just so he could have Pippa? Had he ever understood her? Had he ever cared?

She didn't have the energy to fight anymore. All she wanted was Pippa in her arms and the warmth of Busara around them.

Pippa.

The little monkey in the middle.

Anna walked over to Jack's man chair and sank into it. "I've killed myself trying to make right choices, and I'm finding out sometimes they don't exist. And you find that out too late," she said.

He didn't answer.

"I'd like to go get Pippa now," she stated.

He didn't speak, but began buttoning his shirt as he turned toward the bedroom.

"There's only one thing I do need from you, Jack."

He scoffed bitterly and stopped in his tracks. "What's that?"

Anna's eyes burned, but she managed to gather herself. In spite of everything, and given that she'd kept Pippa from him all these years, this was the hardest sacrifice to ask for.

Anna could cope with many things, but everyone had a limit. She wiped her face on her sleeve and frowned. Her head was pounding in alternating waves of hot and cold.

"I need you to understand that I can't let Pippa live here. I'd do anything to make up for not telling you, make up for all you missed, but not that. Anything but that. I need her with me. Busara is her home. She's still so young, Jack. She needs her mother."

Jack walked across the room and braced his hands on the edge of the kitchen table, his back to her. He shook his head but didn't say anything.

"Please don't fight me on this," Anna said. She got up and took several steps toward him. "She can come visit you and spend summers here, or maybe stay here during our rainy season. She'd have plenty of time to—"

"No." Jack jerked around and Anna's heartbeat stumbled. "That's not enough. Life here will be better and safer for her. She stays with me. I'll pay you back child support, that's a given, and you can have two weeks to let her say goodbye and get used to the idea of being here. After that, it's up to you. We can settle this between us or bring in the lawyers."

DROPPING ANNA AND PIPPA off at the airport
for their scheduled flight back to Kenya left
Jack feeling messed up. So messed up that the
last set of instructions he'd left at the lab had
his tech calling his cell phone in total confu-
sion. Good thing Jack had answered it. He
cringed at the thought of what would have
been wasted had he not picked up. Lesson
learned.

He really needed to get back on track. He
needed to adjust his schedule for Pippa, but
after that, he needed to put in his hours and
make sure his research stayed on target. He
had a career to maintain. He was a parent. He
had responsibilities. Including a massive real
estate purchase looming. Man, he'd been so
careful about the paperwork in the envelope
that day, yet of all things, she'd answered his
house phone. He scrubbed his jaw. He needed
to stop wasting time thinking about Anna.

*I don't walk away from those who count on
me or need me.*

Who had she really been talking about?
What *was* he trying to do? Guard against
abandonment? Prove life here was good
enough? Prove *he* was good enough? Or care
for his daughter?

They'd barely spoken after the argument. The car ride to his parents' place had been silent, as was the ride to her mother's, except for talking to Pippa. Both had managed to keep up a pleasant front around family. But now, sitting in his parents' kitchen, because trying to get anything done at the lab was futile, he couldn't pretend anymore.

He grabbed another peanut butter fudge brownie off the plate on the kitchen island and shoved it in his mouth in one bite. His mom pulled another tray out of the oven. He sat on the same backed stool he had as a kid. One of two. The other had been Zoe's, but now Maddie and Chad used them. This kitchen held history. Generations of Harpers would build memories here. Good memories. He was going to have to find a matching third stool for Pippa and, come to think of it, one for Zoe's new kid once he or she outgrew the high chair.

He watched his mom put a new tray in. She never stopped at one batch. She always made enough to pack some for Zoe, the kids, him and half the neighbors. When he was a kid, these brownies had appeared every time he came home upset after school, as if she had mood-sensing elves in the oven.

Jack hoped the thought-sensing ones were on leave, because he had no intention of telling her he'd gone under contract on a zoo. A man had his pride.

"I don't get it," he said.

"Get what?" his mom asked. "Love?"

"Yeah," Jack said, stuffing another bite in his mouth. He gulped. "No, what? Who said anything about that?"

His mom smiled as she sliced a grid pattern into the done batch. The aroma escaped along the knife's edge. Man, those brownies smelled good.

"Who indeed. Certainly not you."

"What's that supposed to mean?" Jack asked, stealing the last cooled brownie off the plate before his mother took it for reloading.

"It means it's about time you manned up and said it. For crying out loud, Jack, *love* isn't a four-letter word."

"It was the last time I saw it written," he muttered.

"Wise guy. When are you going to let go and say it?"

"Say what?"

"Love! In all these years, you haven't once said 'I love you' to any of us."

Jack frowned and dropped his last bite on his napkin, suddenly losing his appetite. "Sure I have," he said.

His mom raised her brows. "Have you, now? Sometimes I think you seriously believe you've said it. Up here, perhaps." She pointed to her head. "But the words don't make it out your mouth, Jack. You've shown it. Sweetie, in so many ways, you've shown it. I'm not faulting you that, but you've never brought yourself to say it. Not since your parents died."

Jack narrowed his eyes at the mention of them.

"*You're* my parents."

"Of course we are. I couldn't have been blessed with a more extraordinary son. You know what I mean. I'm sure you love us all. I know you must love your little girl and I'm pretty sure you love Anna and always have, but I'm not certain you know it. I'm not even sure she knows it, or believes it."

"Of course she knows it." *Wait a minute.* Had he just said that? Didn't logic dictate that if he thought she knew it, then he must have been feeling it? His brownie overload threatened a comeback. Everything he'd ever felt for Anna had gone so far beyond friendship, caring, respect and simply knowing he was happiest when she was with him. She made him strong, always had. But he'd tried showing her. Hadn't his friendship and support meant anything to her? Didn't actions speak louder than words?

Jack reached for the plate. This time his mother pulled it back.

"I—I proposed to her. Doesn't that say something?"

"You did?" His mom took her hand off the plate abruptly, sending crumbs scattering across the counter.

"Twice. And she said no. Flat out." He raised himself a few inches off the stool, just enough for his long arm to reach the plate, and stuffed another entire brownie in his mouth all at once. He'd deal with antacids later, and maybe run a few miles.

"Well." His mom wrinkled her forehead and set the empty tray and knife by the sink. The plate of brownies was piled high. Like Mount Kilimanjaro. Where had that image come from? He was losing it. "Let me guess.

You proposed without saying 'I love you.' Mind you, that's just a wild guess."

Jack looked at his mom. Guilty as charged. But it didn't matter, did it? He and Anna were close. It was understood that they were important to each other.

"Jack, what did you expect?"

"I told her we could get married and raise Pippa together. It made perfect sense. What I expected was for her to say yes. She said no."

"Where did I go wrong?" his mom said, rolling her eyes and shaking her head. She took off her apron and hung it on its hook inside the pantry door. She took a brownie for herself and sat on the stool next to Jack. "What about the first time you asked?"

"I asked her after she graduated. After her mom told her the truth and we—you know. She said no because she hasn't believed in marriage since her parents' divorce." Jack covered his face, then raked his hair back. He really was an idiot. Anna's perspective was slowly coming into…perspective.

"That doesn't sound like the Anna I used to hear about," his mom said. "The one I watched the other day with the faraway look on her face. She's hurt. Guarded. Afraid. Like someone else I know. I think she believes in marriage more than either of you care to admit, but you told her you wanted to get married for Pippa, not for her. And to think you earned a PhD."

Jack looked at her in surprise. His sweet mom had taken a stab at him in Anna's defense.

"Jack. Get over it already. You're about to lose what you've always wanted, and it has nothing to do with that lab you hide in. If you can't say it to your father, sister or me, I understand. I know you love me anyway, but you need to tell her. Marriage is sacred. It's about love—not some formula or duty. Prove to her that you believe that. That you *feel* it."

Jack got up and went to the fridge for milk. Why were the words so important? His biological parents had said them. They'd said "Love ya, Jack," every time they wanted him to do something or wanted him out of the way. "Love ya" meant "get your own cereal because Mommy has a hangover." It meant "sorry, but no TV tonight because grown-up friends are coming over." And Jack, as little as he'd been, knew that meant drugs. He'd gladly hidden in his room. In his closet with a book. "Love ya" meant "thanks for not bothering us." Empty words. Because people who loved you didn't leave you. They didn't go kill themselves because you weren't enough to make them happy.

Actions speak louder than words. Was he the only person around who had taken that lesson to heart?

Or maybe his mom was right. He was afraid. Afraid that if he said those words, then the real love, the love he'd been surrounded with since his adoption, the love he had felt from Anna, would disappear, just as his biological parents had. Dead. His life would become empty, as it had been before. It was feeling empty now, with Anna gone. Emptier than ever. And it blew his mind how nothingness could be so painful.

He shut the fridge without taking the milk out. "It doesn't matter anymore. After what I've done, she'll think I'm saying it to convince her to marry me because of Pippa. Again. And she's made it clear that she won't leave her work in Busara. I know nothing I say will change that. And my work is here. For Pippa's sake, I need to make sure I have a steady income and insurance."

"Maybe she'll change her mind."

Jack shook his head as he wrapped four brownies in a napkin. Maybe it was the chocolate or the sugar. Whatever it was, it was hitting him hard.

He wouldn't want her to change her mind. He'd tried so hard to get her to stay, for selfish reasons. If she did, she'd be miserable. She didn't belong here, and if he cared about her, he couldn't expect that of her.

But love could be such a twisted thing, because Pippa mattered, too. He needed her to be here. And he understood Anna belonged there.

He didn't want to deal with lawyers and fights. He didn't want to put Anna through that. He didn't want to hurt her. He wanted to remain friends, if that's all it could be. What he needed was to find a way to convince her that Pippa would be better off with him, without destroying anything left between them.

JACK SLOWED DOWN and looked for the town house complex with three blue spruces flanking each side of the entrance. He was going on recent memory, having dropped Anna and Pippa off at her mother's the night before they left. He spotted the entrance beyond the traffic signal, and waited for the light to change. If anyone could help him reason with Anna, it would be her mother. She didn't like him much, he got that, but he couldn't think of anyone else who came close to caring about Anna and Pippa as much as he did.

"That's not why I'm here," Jack said out loud. "That's *not* why."

He was crazy, talking to himself, but he couldn't shut his mind up the entire way over. That guilty voice accusing him of taking advantage of her mother's emotions, knowing full well how badly she wanted her daughter and granddaughter back in the States. This was wrong. *No.* He was doing what was right. He was preventing a battle that would only trap Pippa in the middle and rip Anna apart. Wasn't he? *No. You're not playing fair. Stop.*

Jack passed the light and turned into the complex. He parked at the unit on the far end, with the plain patch of grass in front and the small, concrete slab patio surrounded by boxwoods and azaleas on the side. This was it.

Jack walked up to the front door and rang the bell. He'd noticed from a distance that the patio door was open, but he wasn't comfortable enough with Susan to go around the side entrance unannounced. He rang again. Still no answer. Two bundles of morning newspapers lay off in the corner by the door. That didn't make sense. She hadn't picked up her paper in two days?

He knew she was home. The open side door, the mug and pulled-out chair at her bistro set. Jack scratched his neck, then slipped a finger behind the collar of his sweatshirt and gave it a stretch. Something indefinable in the pit of his stomach told him to forget formalities.

He walked around to the patio. An album lay open on the table. A baby album opened to an old photograph. Jack angled his head to get a better look. Anna, with her clean, natural beauty, cradling her baby brother. Another photo was of her mom in the same position. They must have taken turns, Jack realized. Had someone else, like her dad, been there to take the picture, all three would have been in it. But he hadn't been there.

Jack remembered how, after the funeral, time with Anna became more and more scarce. She was always busy at home. Always helping her mom out. It wasn't until they'd grown even closer, when she was in vet school, that she'd confided in him about her mom's mental health.

Jack moved the mug that was holding down a loose, overturned photo. Anna and Pippa. It must have been taken the night she came to dinner. A wave of ice went up Jack's back and the hair on his arms prickled.

"Sue?"

He reached the patio door in one long stride and pushed the screen out of the way.

"Sue!"

Jack went cold. He was a boy again. Standing in his bedroom doorway, looking out at the living room. His parents lying on the floor. His mother's eyes half open in an empty stare, the needle still in her arm. His father slumped across the coffee table. There was white powder, vials…

Jack's blood sucked downward to his feet, then surged straight up through him with a riptide of adrenaline.

"Sue, wait. Look at me. It's Jack. I—I came to have some coffee with you. Let's have some coffee." He took a slow step forward.

Anna's mom looked up at him. Her eyes were distant and hollow and her face ashen. She wore pajamas and her hair hung in tangled strands. He'd never seen her unkempt, like his biological mother used to be after waking up with a hangover. Sue had looked happy and put together when he'd picked Anna and Pippa up from dinner. Anna had told him she couldn't leave the States unless she made sure her mom was okay, and Sue had been, from what he'd heard. She'd shown Anna a job application she'd submitted. She hadn't even cried when they left.

Jack stepped over laundry scattered near a basket by the door. Sue shook her head and he stopped. Uncapped prescription pill bottles were piled in front of her on the table. A big bottle of vanilla extract lay on its side. She sat in a chair, a full glass of something dark in one hand and a pile of pills in the other. She'd have them down before he could reach her.

"It doesn't matter, Jack. What's the point of life if you get nothing from it? Nothing but loneliness and pain?" She looked at the empty pill containers. "I didn't really need these, but I'm glad I never threw them out. They're mostly expired, but alcohol is supposed to make drugs stronger. Right? This is all I have." She raised the glass of extract. "I've been so good about not drinking. My psychiatrist warned me not to. Especially because of the pills." Her chin quivered as she stared at the glass. "It'll work, won't it? You should know. You're a scientist, aren't you?"

Jack's brain was firing in all directions. She hadn't thought this through. The extract. The album outside. The photos. How long had she been sitting in here?

"This probably won't work, Sue. It'll just make you throw up." He wasn't totally sure of that, but he was more worried about the number of prescription pills in her hand. "If this is what you want, let's talk about better ways. Why don't you come show me where your coffee is, and we can go sit and talk."

"You're not talking me out of this." Sue's fist closed around the pills. "How stupid do you think I am?"

"You're not. But swallow those pills and I'll have 911 here pumping you out in a flash. It won't work." The truth was, he had no idea what drugs she had and how fast they'd take effect. "Listen to me, Sue. You're a beautiful, smart mother who Anna adores. And you have little Pippa now, too, and she'll want to be able to wake up Christmas morning and find her grandma baking cookies for her. This won't help you. It'll hurt them. You don't want that. I know you don't. That's why I'm here. Because we both care and need to be there for them."

Sue's chest started heaving and her hand shook. Sweat trickled down Jack's sides. He'd said the wrong thing. Panic sent his pulse out of rhythm. What did he need to say? Pressure built in his ears. He'd been too late, helpless to save his parents.

"Christmas morning?" Tears streaked down Sue's face. "You don't care, Jack. You're not my son. My little boy's dead. I don't have him in my life. I don't have my daughter or granddaughter or husband. I don't have anything. And you'll end up hurting my Anna. I know you will."

Oh, God. He'd said the wrong thing. He was losing her.

"No, Sue. Let's talk about how to bring them back. You and me. We're going to get Anna and Pippa back here. We'll all be together."

"I'll just be a burden. I don't want that. I can't take this life anymore."

She raised her hand and Jack lunged. His

fist closed over hers. Her glass cracked against the table, then hit the carpet.

"Let go of the pills." Jack caught his breath and calmed his tone. "Sue. Let go of the pills. Your son would want you to. He's been counting on you to look after his big sister and niece. He needs you to be here for them, because that's the kind of man he would have been, and that's how you can honor him."

Jack heard the pills clatter against the table, and the sound vibrated in his bones. Sue let out a heartbreaking sob and collapsed against him. Jack wrapped his arms around her and helped her stand. "It's going to be okay. Come here." He inched her toward the far side of the room, for his own peace of mind.

"I don't know what to do," she cried against his chest.

He held her frail body tight. "You don't have to. I'm here. I'll make sure you'll be okay."

JACK ROLLED HIS CHAIR back from his desk and looked around his lab. The pile of paperwork on his desk hadn't moved, and he couldn't get himself to focus on it. The lab was being maintained. Everything that needed to be autoclaved had been. The shelves were organized. The lab was perfect and pristine, down to the white walls. His tech stood at the sterile hood, pipetting samples onto an electrophoresis gel. More data would come of it. Data that, not long ago, Jack had immersed himself in and been thrilled by. A sterile buzz. And now none of it mattered. Feeling at home in his lab, feeling accomplished and fulfilled—all of it was gone. None of it mattered, except to serve as a source of income. He could work every day of his life, but it would all be for Pippa.

He thought about Anna's mom, and how she'd been shaken, scared but resolved to make changes. When he'd accompanied her to the in-patient center, she'd listed him as an emergency contact. She didn't want her ex to know, and she had made Jack swear not to tell Anna. She'd tell her when she was ready.

Change was inevitable. Things happened that no one could control. But one thing neither Anna nor he had had before was closure. *Closure.* Putting the past in its place and moving on. That's what they both needed. Jack took off his lab coat, hung it by the door and left.

THE STACKS OF boxes he'd taken from Zoe's garage lined the wall of his bedroom. Five boxes full of old research files later, he found it. It was tucked in a box with other memorabilia—his school diplomas, a few of his favorite childhood books, the ticket to the first ball game the Harpers had taken him to. The only thing he wanted was the silver bag with the jeweler's name inscribed in gold swirls. He pulled it out.

He sat on the edge of his bed, lifted the velvet box out of the bag and opened it. The ring with the tiny diamond, which he'd bought Anna the day before her graduation, sparkled like new. He'd never returned it, because he'd been so sure she'd eventually come back from Africa. He might not have understood it at the time, but returning the ring would have meant giving up hope, losing something that held his feelings for her.

A slip of paper curled at the lip of the bag. He lifted it out. The receipt. He unfolded it. It wouldn't solve all her problems, but as far as he was concerned, it was hers. She could do whatever she wanted with it.

No matter what had happened in the past five years, she had accepted him when he was lost and disillusioned and needed accepting. She'd protected the underdog as only Anna could, and Jack would never forget that.

CHAPTER THIRTEEN

ANNA SAVORED HER last sip of Kenyan roast before swallowing. Bittersweet. She hadn't lost her touch, though, timing her last sip with the rise of blood-orange hues along the left side of Mount Kilimanjaro in the distance. Still the only moment in a given day at camp where she could get anything to happen on time, or go according to plan. The only moment she used to allow herself to imagine what it would be like to have Jack back in her life.

There was nothing left to imagine, though. The ritual that had grounded her every morning, affirming that she'd made good choices, now felt meaningless.

Jack was still the same Jack from years ago. Willing to do what was right. Wanting to do what was right, so long as it didn't involve opening his heart up…especially to her.

And her mom was fine on her own, too. Perhaps Anna had been the one suffering from paranoia and worry. At the dinner she and Pippa had shared with her, her mother had been so together—calm and happier than Anna had ever recalled. Instead of falling apart over them leaving, Sue had spoken of them visiting again.

Anna had been the one who'd fallen apart once she'd gotten Pippa settled in her airplane seat, trying to hold back so hard she'd started hyperventilating. The poor man in the aisle seat, who'd made some comment about her having a fear of flying, had handed her one of those paper sick bags to breathe into. Not her best moment. Had Busara been the only right thing, the only good decision, Anna had made in the past five years?

Kilimanjaro's snowcap crystallized with light, and Anna let herself get drawn into its shimmering, hypnotic powers. No, she'd been right about Jack, and there was no doubt in her mind that he would try to get primary custody of Pippa now, just as she'd feared years ago. He'd have cornered her into choosing custody or marriage then, too.

Anna ran her hand along the rough wood of her observation platform. For all its fading and splinters, it was solid. For all the desiccation and death surrounding Busara, the land was teeming with life and beauty that ran deep, like the nurturing underground streams of snowmelt. Life here made sense. It was her past that didn't.

Perhaps Anna had been wrong, trying to protect her mother from any more pain. Yet she hadn't been wrong about loving Jack. But like with her father, expecting someone to open his heart and love you back, forgive you, when he wasn't capable of it—when the pain of doing so was too great—was selfish of her. She didn't have time for self-pity, however. Niara would have her neck.

Anna was home again.

She needed to ground herself.

Stay strong.

Love enough for everyone.

Ambosi threw a pit at her. Ah, yes. Love. Anna smirked at him and shook her head. She didn't have the heart to scold him. He'd been ornery since her return yesterday, alternating between giving her the cold shoulder for abandoning him, and trying extra hard to get her attention.

Anna braced her hands on the platform's edge and shoved off, another layer of dry dust coating her boots upon landing. Camp was calling.

One day at a time.

She loved life here. She loved the sounds, smells and formidable wildlife. She loved the pace and simplicity…because life was anything but simple.

Anna squatted and ran her fingertips along the ground, then rubbed them together and stood. The lack of any rain in the past few months had been a curse; but on the other hand, the roads were still passable. She and Pippa had made it back without a hitch, except for the extra night layover because of a missed flight, when Pippa had to use the potty.

The more reliable short rains of November were still weeks away. After rounds today, Anna could start writing. Miller was right about that. Research permits were strict and she'd have to complete her data studies and final paper within a year…and provide proof. Red tape was a killer. There'd be more of it involved in keeping Busara running indefinitely.

She trudged straight toward the mess tent. Now more than ever, she needed those reassuring morning kisses from Pippa. The possibility of future mornings without them made her throat tighten and twist. As much as she understood that Jack needed Pippa, too, she wouldn't let him take her without a fight, just as she wouldn't let Busara die without one.

They needed to secure funding about as much as they needed the rains to come. Since she'd sent him that email, Kam had started making contact with everyone he knew. They were working on it, but Anna was worried. She could barely secure funding for Busara, and she knew lawyers didn't come cheap.

She rounded a cluster of buckets that were being filled from the well for the orphans. Low water pressure meant topping them up took longer. Anna helped, doing her share, but it was hard to keep up.

Kam came out of the clinic and waved the satellite phone at her. "I was just coming to find you. Your mother has been trying to call. It didn't go through the first time, but she's on now," he said.

Her mom was calling? She never called, because of the time difference. They'd relied on emails, but maybe she just wanted to be sure Anna and Pippa had made it back all right.

Anna jogged over and took the phone, hoping the line was still connected. "Thanks, Kam. Mom?" No answer. She headed toward the one spot that always worked. The same one she'd directed Jack to when he was here. "Mom?"

"Anna? Hello?"

"I'm here, Mom. Can you hear me? Is everything okay?"

"Yes, everything's fine, now. How's my Pippa?"

"She's great. Talks about you all the time. How are you, Mom? Really?"

Anna could hear her mom exhale. "I'm okay. But I needed you to know something."

Anna's chest sank. Her mom sounded different. More mellow than when they'd last spoken. She hadn't even lasted a few days.

"What's wrong?" Anna asked.

"Nothing. I'm fine now, but you were right about me handling things. You need to know what happened. You need to know what Jack did."

ANNA STOOD SILENTLY, long after she'd hung up with her mother, remembering how Jack had run in circles with Pippa on his shoulders in this very spot. Making Haki laugh, too. Her throat clogged and her eyes stung in the dry air. He'd saved her mother's life.

Anna lowered herself slowly and sat on her heels. How could she not have seen past her mother's act? All these years knowing how fragile she was, being so careful because of it, and yet she'd let Sue convince her that everything was okay. That she was fine.

Anna folded her legs against the dirt and cradled her forehead, running every moment of their dinner together through her mind. Had she ignored any signs because she'd wanted to leave so badly? Had she needed to get away from Jack and be back home so desperately that she'd let herself be convinced that her mom was handling things well? Why hadn't she trusted what her gut had told her all along?

The acidity of her coffee roiled in her stomach and goose bumps prickled her skin despite the heat. Anna covered her mouth with her hand and rocked back and forth. Jack had saved her mother from an overdose. Jack... who'd been too young to save his parents. Finding her mom on the edge must have terrified him to his core.

Anna took a gasp of air, then swiped her

wet cheeks with the back of her hands, thankful that the tarp on the rear of the mess tent was still down. *Mom's okay. Get it together.*

Sue had insisted that Anna not return, and said she was in good hands at the center Jack had accompanied her to. Her doctors had suggested she not have visitors for a while. She had weeks of therapy ahead of her, but said she would listen to the experts this time and get well, because she wanted to be there for her daughter and granddaughter.

Anna wondered if her mom's recovery would be faster if Pippa were around. If Pippa stayed with Jack for her school year, she'd be closer to her grandmother and her cousins. It would kill Anna not to have her here, but maybe it was the right choice for her daughter and everyone she loved.

Anna rose, brushed her pants off. A shadow passed across the ground. She looked up at a transient cloud. Not enough. She took a hard look at her camp. *Jack.* Doing things out of duty or because they made sense didn't necessarily mean your heart wasn't in it.

"*HABARI,*" Niara said, as she set bowls of *ugali* in front of Haki and Pippa.

"Good morning," Anna replied. She walked around the table and gave a kiss to both Haki and Pippa, letting her lips linger a second longer against her daughter's soft cheek, and breathing in her indefinable little-girl scent.

"So, Anna," Niara said. "I need to talk to you about something that happened while you were away. Things were so busy yesterday afternoon when you arrived, and you looked so tired. I thought it should wait."

Anna straightened and her mind started to race. How much more trouble could she have caused? She'd left Niara alone, the only woman at camp. A friend whose past left her vulnerable. Anna's pulse started thudding. "What happened?"

"Nothing bad. Sorry, Anna. I should have said that first."

He chest relaxed.

"Uncle Kamau is going to be my father," Haki announced with a grin. "He's going to teach me how to play chess. He even got me a wooden chess-and-checkers set."

"Haki!" Niara turned beet-red and cocked her head at Anna. "Please don't be mad. That's what I was about to say. I've been dying to tell you, but I wanted to see your face when I did…and you look like a fish in shock. Plus we haven't had a moment alone since you got back."

"Tell me everything," Anna exclaimed.

"Kamau asked me to marry him three days ago. I said yes."

"Niara!" Anna went to her friend and wrapped her arms around her. "Niara. That is the most wonderful thing I've ever heard, and I so needed to hear something good."

"You mean that? You don't think I'm being crazy?"

Anna held her at arm's length. Her friend glowed.

"Do you love him?" Anna asked.

"Yes. I do."

"Did he tell you that he loves you?"

"Yes, he did. He wrote me a poem, too."

Kamau wrote her a *poem?* Who knew her serious, reserved colleague was such a romantic?

"Friends share everything, right?"

"Oh, no, no, no. He would kill me." Niara laughed and slapped Anna playfully away.

"Come on. Tell me!" she teased.

The screen door clacked shut behind Kamau.

"Kam, you big lug. I can't believe you didn't say something yesterday," Anna said, throwing her arms around him, knowing full well public displays embarrassed him. She'd spent several hours after their return helping him go through things in the clinic, and checking on her elephants. If the way they curled their trunks around her was a sign, they'd missed her as much as she'd missed them. The whole time he never let on.

"Ah. Niara told you. Good. I felt it was her place to share," Kamau said.

"See, Niara. He said you should *share*." Anna winked at her friend. Of course, she wouldn't really pressure her, even if Anna was supercurious about the poem. But teasing a girlfriend was part of the fun of celebrating an engagement.

She turned to Kamau. "How many cows?" she asked with a grin, in reference to the traditional dowry.

"She can have all she wants, but there aren't enough on earth. She's priceless. I never knew what my greatest fear was until this threat of losing funds arose. The possibility of us all going separate ways, of me never seeing Niara and Haki every day. That was the last grain of dust. It pushed me to take a chance."

Kamau stepped up to Niara, took her left hand in both of his and kissed it. Niara blushed harder than Anna thought was possible. Seeing her so happy gave Anna a rush. Something good—extraordinarily good—had come out of the mess her life was in.

"That's beautiful, Kamau. We're not going anywhere, but I give you my permission to take my best friend and make her the happiest woman in the world. And Haki, too. He's so much like you," Anna said.

Kamau ruffled the boy's hair. "Eat so you can get big and strong," he said.

"I can get big and stwong, too," Pippa declared.

Haki shoved a huge bite in his mouth. Pippa tried for a bigger one. Anna watched her dear ones interact.

She was so happy for them. Kamau loved Niara and she loved him back. That's all that mattered. The two of them had stood by Anna, their loyalty and friendship unwavering. They deserved this. They deserved every bit of joy they had coming.

Haki looked at Kamau. "Can we play later?

Will you help me build the Lego Auntie Anna
brought me?"

"Sure," Kamau said.

"I can, too," Pippa said.

"Okay, but only the pieces I let you touch,"
Haki told her.

Anna had never seen so much emotion
from Haki as when they'd arrived back from
the States. He had really missed his friend.
Explaining that Pippa would be moving away
would be excruciating in so many ways.

Pippa had gone on and on about her trip…
and her new room. Her anticipation of going
back to her father's place, her pink room, left
a knot in Anna's chest, and she had to keep
silently reassuring herself that she was doing
the right thing. That no matter what, Pippa
loved her and would someday forgive her.

Trust your instincts. Anna thought about
her parents and the choices they'd made. It
wasn't easy, knowing what was best for your
kid or knowing what was right. There were
no concrete answers.

ANNA SCANNED THE EXPANSE before her. She'd
barely seen an elephant in the valley, let alone
other animals, since she'd gotten back four

days ago. The scarcity of herds gave her a nagging feeling she couldn't shake. Kam had taken the Jeep out earlier and would be back soon. Anna walked back to the clinic, stopping to check on Bakhari before resuming paperwork.

"Hey, Bakhari boy. Are you growing?" She ran her hand down his trunk and smiled when he nudged her empty palm. "No treat right now. I'll bring you something later," she said. He tamped the ground and she laughed. "Yes, I promise."

She settled in at the counter in the clinic and pulled up a letter she'd been writing on the computer. The grind of Kam's engine grew louder. She prayed he wouldn't have another injured orphan on board. She had to get this letter sent off in case he needed her.

She gave the draft a quick read through and hit Send. Without Miller as a sponsor, she had to find someone else to back her stay in Kenya. She hoped Dr. Alwanga would be able to help.

Anna stepped outside and took comfort in the familiar scene of Kam's crew unloading gear.

"Anything?" she asked as he approached.

"Good or bad first?"

"Good."

"The closest water hole has dried up. I think the herds moved in search of water."

"That explains why they haven't been around. I was worried about poachers."

Kam rubbed the sweat from his neck. "The bad is that a large poaching ring was intercepted. The group was arrested before dawn. They'd made a kill, but the ivory has been confiscated."

"Oh, no. How many elephants?"

Kamau looked away. Anna could tell by the way his jaw ticked that it was more than he cared to say. She hung her head for a moment.

A faint rumble sounded in the distance. It seemed more like thunder than elephants, but the sky was clear.

"The good is that some of the recent killings will stop," Anna said.

Kam nodded. "Yes. But do you remember the wedding we took Jack to? I had noticed the groom's cousin missing. Turns out he's been helping the poachers. He turned himself in after the last kill and gave the authorities information that tracked them down. I knew there was someone." Kam fisted his hands.

"The arrows at that poaching site Jack helped with… Now we know where they came from."

"That's terrible! The tribe must be devastated. He's Ahron's cousin, too," Anna said.

"Which is why I must leave you," Ahron said from behind them.

"Absolutely not," Anna said. She stepped closer to him. "Listen to me, Ahron. You're indispensable. The elephants need you. We need you here. You and your family have done so much for us. People do desperate things sometimes. Your cousin made a mistake. He realized that and has helped catch some very bad people. There's no reason for you to leave."

"But I should have seen signs. I should have known," Ahron insisted. The poor boy's face was taut and his eyes downturned. He truly loved the animals. He was meant to work with them.

"If that were the case, I would be as much to blame," Kam said. "Let's not waste energy on what-ifs. We all need to take what *is* and move forward."

"We need you, Ahron. Okay?" Anna waited. He finally nodded. Thank goodness. "Bakhari wants a treat from me, so don't let him con you into one, too," she said, in an effort to lighten things.

Ahron offered a small smile and headed to the pens. "Thank you," he said, before disappearing.

Another rumble sounded, this time closer. Anna looked at Kam.

"Tell me that was thunder."

WITHIN MINUTES OF checking the local weather reports, Anna had the camp in motion, lowering tent tarps and covering anything that needed protection. Just in case. Confident that things were under control, she ran to her lookout. Sure enough, dark clouds billowed in the distance and a damp, rusty smell permeated the air. Early storms were sometimes too brief for any benefit, but this one was looking as if it had downpour potential.

She hoped it wouldn't pass them by. At this point, she would be thankful for any drop the skies unleashed. Anything.

She turned, hearing the whirr of Mac's chopper in the opposite direction. He was nearing the landing area. Was he nuts? Mac was a stickler for weather reports. Why would he take off in the direction of a front? Unless there was an emergency.... What if he'd spotted something from the air?

A gust of wind rustled the leaves overhead. Standing on the platform with thunder in the distance wasn't smart. Anna climbed down and took long strides toward camp. Mac had to have a good reason for coming, because he'd be grounded for as long as the weather stayed bad.

And he was in a hurry, because halfway home, Anna could already see one of their Jeeps headed towards camp from the landing. What on earth was going on? She broke into a run, but by the time she reached the copse of fig trees a few yards from the supply tent, he was already coming toward her.

Jack.

Jack.

"What are you doing here?" Every cell in her body thrummed. He looked just as he had the first time he'd come to Busara. There was a difference, though. His eyes on her... his shoulders back... He had a purpose. He wanted his little girl.

Anna swallowed hard and waited for him to get closer, then took one step and threw her arms around him. She buried her face in the crook of his neck, wanting to remember the scent of his soap, the sound of his pulse beating against her face and the comfort of his warmth. She'd need that memory to last, because it's all she would have.

"What's that for?" he asked, wrapping his arms around her. His voice sounded gruff and weary. Anna pulled back slowly and looked at him.

"That was for what you did for my mother... for me." She couldn't help the tears welling up as she spoke. For once she didn't care. They could fall and she could look like a fool, and she didn't care. "No thank-you could ever be enough. She called and told me everything you did. Jack—"

"Anna—"

"No. Don't try to minimize it. And Pippa... I understand now where she really needs to be." Anna's voice cracked. "I want you to be sure she sees my mom a lot, and her cousins, and I want her to be here summers, but I haven't spoken to her yet. I need some time. I didn't expect you to show up and—"

"Anna, stop. Look at me," Jack said, wrapping his hands around her shoulders. "I'm not here for Pippa. I'm here for both of you."

Anna frowned. *What?* She sniffed back tears. "I thought you understood. I—I can't leave. This is my home. It's who I am. I can't abandon Busara and the baby elephants we've taken in."

"I don't want you to. I know this is where you belong. That's what I think is so incredible about you. Your nurturing strength. Your loyalty. It's in everything here. I'm hoping you might find room for one more."

"I don't understand. One more—"

"Rescue. Only this one is two-legged and hasn't been an orphan for a very long time. But he is blind."

She stared at Jack and couldn't speak if she wanted to. He wanted to stay? Here?

He reached into his pocket.

"Jack, we've been through this."

"No, we haven't. What we've been through is you being too scared, too hurt by your parents, to believe two people could be so meant for each other that even oceans couldn't keep them apart. And me assuming you knew how much—" He shook his head and closed his eyes, then opened them again and looked hard at her. "—how much I love you. I always have, Anna. What we had wasn't just friendship. It was so much more. The last time I said 'I love you' was to my parents, the night before they overdosed. I was just a kid. I think subconsciously it was easier to assume you understood how much you meant to me than to put it in words because I was afraid. Afraid that if I said it, I'd lose you and anyone who mattered to me. I'm so sorry if I hurt you."

Anna took a step away. Her pulse raced and she couldn't feel her feet beneath her. He'd said the word. But he never said the word. To *anyone*. His mother had said so.

Jack pulled a box out of his pocket. A ring box. Anna's mouth felt dry. She pushed her hair back and jolted when a sharp crack sounded, followed by a streak of lightning.

"Jack—"

"Wait. Let me explain before you turn me down again. If you really don't love me that way, I'll accept it," he said. "I still want you to have this. It's the ring I bought before your graduation. Before I first proposed..."

It took a minute to register. He'd bought the ring before her graduation date. Before they'd made love—and yes, it had been love. She knew that with every cell in her body, because in spite of what had made her turn to him that day five years ago, she'd never have let it happen if deep down she didn't believe they were made for each other. That they were meant to be together forever.

He'd planned on proposing. Even if he hadn't been able to define his feelings as love, he hadn't proposed out of guilt, or to try to convince her her fairy tale could happen despite her parents' divorce bomb. It hadn't been because of Pippa, although his heart had been in the right place. They loved each other. All three of them. Jack put the ring in her hand, closed her fingers around it, then held her fist against his heart.

"If it's not worth something to you, it'll be worth something to Busara. You can sell it and use the money to help buy you more time. But I'm hoping you'll wear it and let it be a reminder of how much I love you and how much I want to build a life here with you and Pippa. I don't need to hide behind white walls and protocols anymore. That's not the life I want. What I want is here. Will you please marry me, Anna Banana?"

Everything in her contracted in a wave, from her legs up to her chest. She swallowed, but the lump in her chest kept rising, pressing against her throat and neck, and everything she'd ever held back. She gasped for a breath and the dam broke. Release. Relief.

Jack's arms wrapped around her and she let her strength drain into him, her body limp with fatigue she'd never let herself give in to. Emotion she'd longed for and feared. They held each other tight. An embrace that Anna felt at her core was a promise of forever.

"Yes," she said. "I want to be married to you, Jack. You're the only man I ever wanted to spend my life with."

She let go long enough to slip the ring on her finger, then held his face in her hands and kissed him. She felt a drop of rain on her cheek, and the metallic ping of drops against the clinic's aluminum roof told her they were about to get drenched, but she didn't care. Jack was kissing her. He was staying. That's all that mattered.

"There is someone whose approval we should probably get," he said, taking off his hat and putting it on her head.

"I'm sure Pippa will be thrilled."

"I don't mean Pippa. I mean your Doberman," Jack said, pointing to Ambosi, who clung to the clinic's dry windowsill. The monkey cackled and leaped onto the wood fencing of the first elephant pen. Anna's tears turned to laughter.

"Why, Jack Harper. I think that's his way of saying you're a keeper."

EPILOGUE

Three months later...

JACK PACED THE foyer of the tourist lodge, cognizant of the fact that little Pippa was mimicking his every step. He put his hands behind his back. She did the same. He stopped in front of the floor-to-ceiling elephants carved in rich wood along an entire wall, and rubbed his chin like an art savant. She did the same, brow raise and all. Jack chuckled.

"Okay, shadow. That's enough," he said, grabbing her playfully by the waist and hoisting her in the air. She squealed and several heads turned at the front desk. "Sorry, my fault." Jack waved at the manager.

"No problem, Dr. Harper," the man said.

After the several science lectures he'd given, and the conference he'd arranged here with Dr. Alwanga, the staff had gotten to know him. Lectures brought in money for Busara, but working by Anna's side at the camp was where Jack felt whole. Busara was home and he was grateful that life—that Anna—had led him there.

Everything was working out well. Their efforts and networking were keeping Busara alive, and Jack was using his own savings to build them more comfortable, permanent homes on site. Two, so that Kam, Niara and Haki would have a place, as well.

He'd felt awful when his mortgage fell through on the animal park, after a final audit showed that he'd quit his research position back in Pennsylvania. Regardless of the mess he'd gotten himself into, Mr. Chase shouldn't have had to suffer. But as it turned out, Jack didn't have a choice in the matter. Nonetheless, he and Anna contacted everyone they knew at the vet school for help placing the animals. Last he'd heard, they'd all found homes, and Mr. Chase had moved West, though the property was still on the market.

Jack glanced at his watch impatiently and reminded himself that things didn't always run on time here. He missed Anna. Only a few days and he was out of his mind.

The outer doors swung open and she, her

THE PROMISE OF RAIN

mom and Mac came through. Jack put Pippa down and she ran into Anna's arms.

"Oh, my goodness, you've grown," Sue said. "Do you remember me?"

"Yes, Grandma." Pippa reached out and hugged her. "And I won't ask you if you got me a present."

Everyone laughed.

"We also got a new baby elephant. Do you want to help name her?" Pippa asked.

"I'd love to!" Sue said, letting Pippa tug her down to eye level to discuss names.

Stealing a moment while he could, Jack took Anna in his arms and whispered in her ear. "I missed you."

"I missed you, too."

"Jack!" Sue stepped forward, Pippa still grasping her hand. "It's so good to see you again, and I'm sorry I couldn't be here in person for the ceremony. I'm so proud to have you as a son-in-law."

She hugged him, and Jack knew from the softness of her voice and eyes that she was saying more than she cared to express in front of everyone. They had used Skype so that she could "be" at the double wedding ceremony Jack and Anna had shared with Kam and Niara two months ago. They'd wanted her to come for Christmas, but after discussing it with her and her psychologist, they all decided that Sue staying in therapy this holiday and having her professionals teach her how to cope in the future would be best. There would be many more seasons and celebrations to come.

"It's good to have you here. I really hope you'll extend your stay," Jack said.

Sue had been nervous about traveling in a plane, but she was determined to make changes in her life. Anna had flown to the States just so she could see her mom safely over. She was doing well and the doctors gave her the clear, but Anna wanted to be sure.

"Well, like I said…" Mac cocked his head and winked at Mrs. Bekker. "The job is yours if you want it. I could really use the help of a manager with marketing experience, and they do offer permanent rooms here. Think about it."

"I will," Anna's mom said, blushing.

"Mac, thank you so much for getting us here…and for the offer to Mom," Anna said.

"Anything for you, Mama Tembo," Mac answered.

Jack shook his hand, grateful for all the pilot's help in spreading word and keeping Anna's camp on its feet. Mac left with a salute.

"Just looking at him makes a woman feel young again," Sue said, fanning her face.

Anna grinned at Jack. So long as she smiled at him like that, he'd never grow old.

"I think Mom's gonna love it here," Anna said, slipping her hand into Jack's. He gave it a squeeze, then leaned down and kissed her.

"I'm sure she will, but not half as much as I love you. Let's go home."

* * * * *

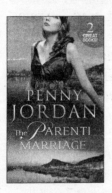

The World of Mills & Boon®

There's a Mills & Boon® series that's perfect for you. We publish ten series and, with new titles every month, you never have to wait long for your favourite to come along.

By Request

Relive the romance with the best of the best
12 stories every month

Cherish™

Experience the ultimate rush of falling in love
12 new stories every month

Desire™

Passionate and dramatic love stories
6 new stories every month

nocturne™

An exhilarating underworld of dark desires
Up to 3 new stories every month

What will you treat yourself to next?

INTRIGUE... *A seductive combination of danger and desire...*
6 new stories every month

Awaken the romance of the past...
6 new stories every month

The ultimate in romantic medical drama
6 new stories every month

MODERN™ *Power, passion and irresistible temptation*
8 new stories every month

True love and temptation!
4 new stories every month

Discover more romance at

www.millsandboon.co.uk

- ❤ WIN great prizes in our exclusive competitions
- ❤ BUY new titles before they hit the shops
- ❤ BROWSE new books and REVIEW your favourites
- ❤ SAVE on new books with the Mills & Boon® Bookclub™
- ❤ DISCOVER new authors

PLUS, to chat about your favourite reads, get the latest news and find special offers:

- 🔲 Find us on facebook.com/millsandboon
- 🐦 Follow us on twitter.com/millsandboonuk
- ❤ Sign up to our newsletter at millsandboon.co.uk